Glacier

VLG – Book Nine

Vampires, Lycans, Gargoyles

By Laurann Dohner

1

Glacier by Laurann Dohner

Since that fateful day she was snatched from her job and turned into a Vampire, Mandy's life has sucked — literally. Forced to become an assassin for the Vampire Council, she finds solace in taking out the scumbag rogues she's often assigned to kill. Things go south when she realizes her next mark is an old coworker from her human days…a seriously hot one, who she had deep feelings for. Worse, the council was wrong. He's not a villain, but a protector. One she refuses to kill, regardless of orders.

Glacier's astonished to come face to face with Mandy in a dark alley. Even more so to learn the sweet one-time human is now an assassin — assigned to kill him, no less. His orders are clear. Eliminate her. But what's a GarLycan to do when duty conflicts with his desire to protect the woman he once had feelings for? He's about to find out.

VLG Series List

Drantos

Kraven

Lorn

Veso

Lavos

Wen

Aveoth

Creed

Glacier

Glacier - VLG – Book Nine

By Laurann Dohner

Prologue

The floor under her feet thumped to the tune of the beat in the club. Massive speakers stood nearby, making her grateful for earplugs. They didn't mute out the music entirely, but they would prevent her ears from ringing long after she went home. Mandy's gaze traveled over the crowd on the dance floor and a smile curved her lips. Working at Bucket had turned out to be the best job ever.

She turned her head, meeting and holding the gaze of the band manager. He inclined his head to assure her that he was happy. The only downside of her job was when the bands Mike hired made her life a living hell. But this one had been cool. None of the members had made her reach for the knife she kept strapped to her thigh. At least so far.

Tommy, one of the bouncers, came up to her but didn't bother speaking over the loud music. He used his hands to let her know Mike wanted her in his office. She motioned back that she understood and for him to take over playing babysitter for the band. The office was to the left of the stage, where she currently stood, so she spun, strode to a heavy door, and shoved it open.

Mandy removed her earplugs once the door closed at her back. She could still hear the song the band played but the volume was a lot lower thanks to thick walls and some attempt to soundproof this part of the

6

club. Some of the band groupies took up space in the hallway beyond. "Excuse me."

She passed the room where the band would take their break and reached the door at the end of the hall. There was no reason to knock. Mike expected her. She twisted the handle and pushed it open. "What do you need, boss?"

Mike sat behind his desk but he wasn't alone.

The sight of the club's head of security always did a number on her. Ice, his nickname, was tall, gorgeous, and the biggest bouncer employed by the club. The silky black work shirt he wore stretched tightly over his bulky arms, wide shoulders, and thick chest. He gave her one quick look and then shifted his stance. That drew her attention to his black slacks. They were molded to narrow hips, muscular thighs and, even though he faced her at that moment, she had already memorized his amazing ass. No flat butt there. She'd checked it out plenty of times, watching him work as he walked the floor in front of the stage to make sure nobody attacked their performers.

"Make the band leave the premises right after they finish their set. No hanging around in the green room area. Lead them from the stage to the back door."

She loved Ice's deep voice. Not only did he look like some kickass bad boy, but he sounded like one too. She'd tried to sneak a peek into his employee file to learn his real name but it hadn't been in Mike's drawer. But it was easy to guess where Ice had earned the nickname. He could be utterly cold, and she'd seen him fight a few times. He didn't lose his temper or show emotion when he dealt with drunks or someone violent from drugs. Ice stayed cool and collected at all times. His eyes fit the name, too, a light blue color that tended to make her compare them to icicles.

"They only had a few drinks last night and I made them put away the drugs. I reminded them we have a zero-tolerance policy about that here because of that bassist a few months ago who overdosed on heroin in the bathroom." She sighed. "And it was only some coke. The lead singer whined a little but their manager took my side."

"It's not that." Mike stood. "You fill her in. I'm going to warn the bar staff." He pointed at her. "You do exactly what Ice says."

She frowned, watching her boss stalk out of the office and close the door behind him. Ice stepped closer and she held his gaze. He towered over her.

"A group of troublemakers came into the club and we're expecting violence."

She felt a little fear. "Why'd you let them in?"

"I didn't. Rod had the door."

She couldn't see the local thugs enjoying the kind of music the club played. They sure weren't there for that. "Shit. Are they armed?"

"Just get the band out of here when they end the set. No encores." He surprised her when he gently gripped her arm. "Transportation for the band has already been called and has arrived. I will have security in the back waiting for you to exit. You will leave too, as soon as you've put them in their van. Get in your car and go. No help with cleanup tonight. Got it?"

8

"Do you think they're planning to rob us?"

"I don't know what they're going to do, but I don't want you here when shit hits the fan."

"Are the cops on the way?"

He arched a black eyebrow at her.

It was a dumb question. While Mike took a hard stance about the staff and bands keeping it clean on the drug front, the club regulars were another story as long as they weren't blatant about it. A group of cops bursting in the doors would cause a panic. At least three hundred people would stampede for the exits.

"Be careful." She had the biggest crush on Ice and couldn't bear the thought of anything happening to him.

"Always." He released her arm. "Go on. I need to get back out there."

She turned away but paused before opening the door. They were never alone. Now might be her only chance. She looked at him over her shoulder. "Would you like to go out on Monday?" The club was closed that one day each week.

Surprise flicked across his face but he locked it down fast. "That wouldn't be a good idea."

She faced him, her heart hammering. It was the first time she'd asked a man out but the attraction she felt toward him had grown to the point that she was willing to risk rejection. He starred in her dreams almost every night, and now she'd begun to fantasize about him while awake.

"I'm flattered, but you're too young for me."

Ouch. "I'm twenty-one." She straightened her shoulders. "I've been living on my own for the past five years. You only look about eight years older than me."

His gaze slowly traveled down her body. She held still and let him look his fill. Men hit on her all the time. Her day job was teaching aerobics at the gym five days a week. It not only kept her in shape but she didn't have to starve in order to stay under a hundred and fifteen pounds. Maybe he preferred tall, more curved women. That wasn't her, at five feet two and with her small-boned frame. Short jokes had always been told at her expense. She would also never call herself beautiful, but as far as looks went, she could hold her own.

His blue gaze lifted until he could study her hair and he cocked his head a little. She had to admit it might be off-putting for some. "I work at a dance club that plays new wave music." She reached up and ran her fingers over the soft fuzz where she'd shaved part of her head, from the hairline at the side of her face to behind her ear. It fell long to her waist everywhere else, but it was dyed jet black with wide, bright blue streaks. "I need to fit in. I promise I don't wear this much makeup when I'm not here. My clothes normally aren't as slutty, either."

"I like the way you dress."

She smiled. "Most men don't complain about bustier tops with peek-a-boo skirts."

"Do you get hit on a lot by the entertainment?"

"More than I'd like to admit but I handle it."

"Debbie quit within three weeks."

She remembered the woman who used to have her job. "She didn't know how to deal with jerks."

"You do?" He straightened his head.

"Ask your security staff."

He didn't seem to like that answer, considering his eyes narrowed. "What does that mean?"

"They hit on me all the time." She reached down and turned her leg, using the side split in her skirt to reveal the knife strapped to her thigh. "I only had to show this to one of your goons. Remember Randy? He was pretty pushy and wouldn't back off when I made it clear I wasn't interested. You fired him about three weeks ago for drinking on the job." She released her skirt and hid the knife. "I'm not into one-night stands, and I'm interested in you. I'd like to get to know you better."

"I don't get involved with women beyond sex, and I never sleep with the same one twice."

It disappointed and gutted her at the same time. Any hopes of a future with him died at his words. Players only meant heartbreak and that's the last thing she needed. Life was tough enough. "Oh. Well, be careful tonight." She turned, trying to play it cool, and gripped the knob to leave the office. The urge to flee was strong.

"Mandy?"

She froze and glanced back at him. "What?"

"It's not you. It's me."

She couldn't help but snort. "Right. I've said that to men, too, but it's really them. I'm just trying not to hurt their feelings. I better go. Just forget I ever said anything." She turned the knob and looked away from him as she cracked open the door.

"Mandy, I'm flattered. I'm just not the kind of man for you. I'm darkness inside, and while you dress as if you know all about sin, you're pretty damn innocent. I don't want to taint you."

She closed the door and turned, frowning at him. "You don't know anything about me."

"I get that you're tough but you're a good girl. I'm trying to protect you from getting hurt, especially from someone like me. I'm not the kind of man you need in your life. Mike might never mention it, but he knows you deal with a lot of self-entitled assholes who think you should come as part of the backstage benefits. You haven't quit though, like the other women have. It makes me worry. I've actually asked him to put you behind the bar."

She smiled, amused. Both bartenders were big enough to be bouncers. "No need. You could say I'm not as defenseless as I look."

"What does that mean?"

She hesitated but then closed the gap between them, staring up into his handsome face. "I usually date guys that are about five feet six at most. Under a hundred and forty pounds. I can take them in a fight. Big men scare me because I know how much damage they can inflict on a woman...but for some crazy reason, I'm drawn to you. You make me feel safe.

"I grew up with a lot of domestic violence, Ice. My father was a mean drunk, and he took his frustrations out on his wife and kids. It was worse if you stayed down once he put you on the floor. That's when the kicking

12

started. We got up or we probably would have been killed. My brothers took after him. I'm one of five kids. The baby and only girl." She sighed. "It's why I left home at sixteen. I got sick of being a punching bag for the men in my family, and I knew I'd end up in prison for murder if I ever really lost my temper."

"It would have been considered self-defense if you'd ever killed one of them." He looked pissed.

She gave him a sad smile. "My family would have testified about how vicious I could be at times. When I was thirteen, my father put my mom in the hospital, then the moron passed out in the living room. She almost died. I kinda lost my shit. I figured he couldn't hurt her for a while If he had two broken arms. And I was right. Baseball bats are very effective for that.

"Then there was the time one of my brothers decided to kill my pet hamster by stabbing it with his pocket knife. He left Buttons on my bed with the knife still in her. He thought it would be funny to see me cry, since I never do that. So, I gave him his knife back. He needed a trip to the emergency room, since my version of returning it was to stab it into his thigh a few times until it stayed put. He learned to fear me.

"I'm not as innocent or as sweet as I look. But it's probably best that we don't date. You sound like a player, and I wouldn't be okay with that. I deserve a good life with someone who can commit to me."

She spun and stalked out of the office, leaving him with his mouth hanging open.

In a bad mood now, she just shoved her way through the groupies instead of waiting for them to step aside. The music blasted loudly as she returned to the stage, putting in her earplugs. The fact that her hands shook made it a little harder to do than normal.

Regret came next. She shouldn't have shared her dirty secrets with Ice, but it upset her that he thought she was too sweet for him. Except now, he had an idea how messed up her life had been.

The band finished out the set and she hustled them offstage. The DJ took over as more music filled the club and she slammed the door, yanking out her earplugs. "Listen up."

The manager turned toward her but his group was too busy messing with the pretty girls making passes at them. "What?"

"The head of security thinks trouble might go down. We need to get your guys out of here."

"What kind of trouble?"

"Gang violence. Let's go."

"What about their equipment?" The manager looked pissed.

"Already taken care of. The stage manager will have everything packed up and sent to your hotel. Right now, the important thing is getting the group out the back. The van will be waiting and security is in place."

"Goddamn it!" He looked furious.

She didn't blame him. "Grab your band and I'll lead the way out."

He cursed more, but did as she said. She got in front of them, shoving groupies aside again. "Coming through!"

They made it out the back door and the hotel van sat waiting. She breathed out a sigh of relief, nodding at the manager's rants as if she gave a damn about how upset he felt. The band got into the van and she saw them off, waving. It was their last show at Bucket anyway. They'd drawn a good crowd during their three-night gig. It meant they'd probably be back. She spun around but Tino gripped her arm.

"You're to leave now."

"I've got to grab my purse."

"Fuck. Ice said you aren't to go back in."

"It's hard to leave without my keys. I'll only be a minute."

"Fine."

She rushed inside to the break room, opened her locker, and grabbed her stuff. She took the time to put on her coat. By the time she reached the back door again, Tino was gone. One glance and she realized the second security guard had returned back inside, too. Ice wouldn't like that they'd abandoned her, but she wasn't a tattletale.

She headed to her car and unlocked it, opening the door.

A slight rustle of clothing made her turn—and stare at the man who towered over her. He wore pale makeup, all black clothing, and showed off a set of sharp fangs when he smiled.

Shit. She put one hand on his chest to keep him from trying to get any closer and slid the other one down her body, going for her knife.

"You need to back off. I'm not into the whole Vampire fetish thing."

"I am."

"I guessed that. Do those fangs pop out or are you one of those people who pay a crazy dentist to glue those babies on like crowns?" She inched her fingers into the slit on her skirt, staying close to him so he wouldn't notice what she was doing. "I have to say, whoever it was did a good job."

His grin widened, showing off how seamlessly the fangs went up to his pale gums. "They aren't fake."

He was one of the fanatical freaks who did more than role-play. She guessed he'd probably bought a coffin to sleep in at home. Some of them hung out at the club and bragged about that kind of crap. They even carried pictures to impress the other fang lovers. She also knew they usually kept razor blades on them, slicing the skin of Vampire groupies, and would lick the blood they drew from the idiots who allowed it. It sounded nasty to her, and a disease waiting to happen.

"I'm still not interested. There's a bunch of girls in the club though who would be all over you, especially if you tell them you're a lost boy. Everyone loved that movie. You should go find them." She eased the knife free of the holster and maneuvered it from her skirt.

"But you're the one I plan to take to my master. He's going to love you."

She clenched her teeth and adjusted her grip on the knife. "Listen up, Vamp Boy. I'm not interested in whatever freaky game you have going on. You touch me and you will regret it. Fair warning. Now turn around and go in the club. I'd hate to hurt someone on drugs. I'd feel even worse if you're crazy but I'd get over it. Back off!"

He grasped the hand on his chest and licked his lips. "I bet you taste as good as you smell. It's a shame my master won't let me fuck you, but I'll be watching while *he* does. You're going to get into your car with me quietly or I'm going to hurt you. Do you understand?"

Fear and adrenaline jolted through her as she swiftly stabbed the knife into his side. She twisted her body at the same time as she shoved at his chest.

Vamp Boy stumbled and almost fell. He reached down, his hand coming away coated in red blood.

She put her left shoulder toward him, turning her body and freeing up her right arm to stab at him again if he came at her. "Get the fuck away from me. That was a warning. Next time I'll go for a fatal spot. You don't want to bleed out in this parking lot."

He lifted his head—and she stared in horror at his eyes.

She'd seen Vamp fetish people wear contacts before, but no way had he put them in that fast, especially while bleeding...and they were actually glowing.

That wasn't right.

"Drop the weapon, you bitch."

Chills ran down her spine at the hissing tone of his voice and, to her shock, her hand opened. The knife clattered to the ground.

He reached out and grabbed her, his wet, bloody hand wrapping around her throat. "You're going to pay for that. Sleep."

She blacked out in the next second.

Chapter One

The present

"Do you ever come to the conclusion that our lives suck ass?" Mandy looked over at Olivia.

Olivia sighed, shifting her body a little on the roof where they lay side by side. "Twelve more years. Then we are done with this shit. It's not so bad."

"Bullshit."

"I see the bright side. We weren't trapped in Cain's harem of horrors until he grew bored enough to kill us. You got lucky when the council came for that prick the night after you were turned. He was waiting for you to completely transform before he introduced himself to you. He had me for almost a week before we were rescued."

The sadness in her friend's voice prompted Mandy to reach out and place her hand on her arm. "I'm sorry. You've told me how bad it was."

"The worst part was coming out of bloodlust and remembering everything he'd done to me. I didn't even try to fight him off because once he drew blood, I lost my mind. My body actually *wanted* that sick son of a bitch to degrade me. The council taught us control and gave us blood without doing that, Mandy. We owe them everything. You just don't realize it since you never woke up naked and covered in blood, then had to live with the things that were done to you while you were feeding."

"I'm sorry," Mandy repeated, averting her gaze but keeping her hand in place. "I just don't like killing on command."

"It's better to be an assassin than some sick bastard's sex toy."

"Give me details on our target. That usually helps."

Olivia sighed. "Those morals of yours aren't your friend. The council doesn't like to be questioned and disobedience means torture before death. Don't forget that."

"Just tell me something about our target that's going to help me day sleep, okay?"

"He's a Were who started eliminating the local nest one by one."

"And?"

Olivia turned her head, peering at her. She arched one eyebrow.

"Oh, come on. Some of these pricks need taken out. I can only tolerate about one out of every ten Vamps I've ever met. The other nine, I wouldn't feel an ounce of pity for if someone shoved them into the sun to fry."

"Vampires have the right to live, Mandy. Duh. *We're* Vampires. This hunter doesn't see it that way. Four Vamps in the local nest have been killed in the past week."

"If the local alpha has one of his enforcers targeting our kind, you know it's got to be for a damn good reason. No alpha would want the council coming down on them otherwise. The pack would take out a rogue on their own."

Olivia hesitated. "I agree, but you know policy. An investigation was done. The local pack is involved. It's not our job to question orders. We just do what we're told. That's to kill this enforcer to send a message to the pack to stop killing our kind."

"I have a brain, and I use it, Olivia. Maybe the investigator was lazy, or an asshole with something against Werewolves. I just can't see them going after a nest without cause. Before we kill this enforcer, let me reach out to the alpha to talk to him."

"No way! For fuck's sake, Mandy. Don't make this another nightmare mission. We're here to take out the target. That's it."

"Hey, that human family was justified in killing that Vamp. He was tormenting them and keeping them prisoner! I would have taken him out too. It's called self-defense. Their only crime was the prick hadn't wiped their minds, so they went to the police when they escaped his lair, rambling about Vampires being real. Yeah, it was a mess to clean up, but the council ordering us to butcher those humans was *wrong*. And yes, *that* would have been murder. I'm willing to take the blame all over again."

"Was it worth the month you spent locked up for allowing the humans to escape?"

"Absolutely. That family is still alive, and now they have a new set of memories that aren't going to draw the council back to them. I removed the problem when I went into their heads, before I convinced that nice FBI agent they needed to be added to the witness relocation program."

"You'd better hope the mind work you did stays in place and they never remember what was done to them by that sicko. They pop up on the council's radar again, ranting about Vamps being real, and you're going to lose your head. The council will have someone digging into their memories to find out what you did. That was a huge risk."

"They were innocents."

"It's not our job to make those decisions. We do what the council orders, damn it! You're like a sister to me. My partner. We have a dozen years to go and then we're out of service. That nest in L.A. we picked out is perfect for us, and Master Michael already said we could join. Don't fuck it up."

"I'm not a monster, Olivia. I couldn't live with myself if I killed someone without a good reason. What if this enforcer we've been sent to take out is protecting his pack from a predator? I couldn't find out shit about this Master Marco who reported the killings. I asked some of the other assassins who've worked this area before. They told me they weren't allowed to speak about him. What does that tell you?"

"He's probably a pure dick protected by someone on the council. Not our problem. We kill the target and get out. I want to go home."

Home. Mandy flinched. She wouldn't exactly call the council house they lived in a friendly, safe place. Or warm. Ten assassins shared it. Olivia was the only one she trusted or liked. The other eight were nutjobs with major hard-ons for killing. Cold, brutal, and about as feeling as a stack of bricks. They loved it so much, all of them had stayed past their obligation time with the council. That proved they were nuts. She couldn't wait to leave her job.

Her friend's arm tensed under her palm and Mandy was jerked from her thoughts, seeing movement on a lower roof across the street. It was a Vampire male. He leapt from one building to the next, easily making the

21

eight- to ten-foot distances. He paused and cocked his head, listening. He crouched down, watching the humans on the street below.

Mandy clenched her teeth. It was obvious he wasn't just patrolling but instead looking for a meal. *Bastard. No wonder someone's been hunting and taking out your nest.*

It wasn't illegal for Vamps to feed from humans but the excited expression on his face may as well have been an admission that he enjoyed it a bit too much. There were smart ways to get blood and stupid ones. This guy seemed to randomly pick his donors. He ran the risk of finding someone immune to mind control. Not many humans had immunity, but he might have to kill if he ran across one.

She glanced over at Olivia, seeing her friend's distaste in the way her lip curled up. She wasn't impressed either with the bastard.

Movement drew her attention and the Vamp froze, his gaze trailing something on the street. He leapt to another building, watching someone below, until Mandy was able to figure out which human he'd chosen.

Fury filled her.

It was a kid. The girl couldn't have been more than fourteen, maybe. The fact that her parents let her wander around alone at nine at night also made her mad. Didn't humans know someone might hurt their child? She lifted up and backed away from the edge.

"Damn it, Mandy." Olivia rolled and sat up. "Don't do it."

"Hey, he's bait, right? Master Marco said he'd send out one of his nest to this location to see if the enforcer came after him. I'm just doing my job."

"You're going to kill that jerk if he touches that little girl."

She didn't bother to deny it. "Stay here. You can't report what you don't witness. Damn, is that Werewolf good—and *fast*. Too bad he killed another Vamp before we could get there. Such a shame."

"Mandy! We're supposed to take out the enforcer. Not set him up for another death!"

She was done listening. That girl would disappear as soon as she could be snatched. Vamps weren't the most patient of hunters.

She walked to the back of the building and dropped twenty feet, landed on a balcony, and then another until she reached the alley below. She rounded the building, hurried down the alley, and stepped out onto the sidewalk. It was just in time to see the girl turn a corner ahead. They'd be having a talk about using common sense once she took care of the asshole. The kid was dumb to go into an alley, and someone needed to give her some survival tips. Mandy appointed herself for that task.

Some human jerk grinned as she walked down the sidewalk, blocking her way. "Hello, gorgeous. Want to go to my place?"

"Screw off." She shoved his body to the side, not willing to spare a moment to deal with him.

He stumbled, tripped, and cursed as she kept going. She ignored him. The long alley the kid had gone into was dark, moving cars from a block down the only light source. Her vision adjusted to help her see better and she paused, listening.

"I'm going to have a lot of fun with you." It was the Vamp, judging from his hissy tone. "I hope you put up a fight."

Mandy rolled her eyes, moving forward silently. She hated the dramatic types. He didn't just want to feed, but intended to terrorize and play with the kid first.

She saw them when she reached a set of dumpsters. The kid had been backed against the wall, trapped between the two large trash containers. The Vamp stood with his arms open to snatch her if she tried to rush past.

"Hey!"

He spun, staring at Mandy. His eyes glowed and his fangs were out. He sniffed but then grimaced. She didn't blame him, since the trash stench in the alley was strong enough to almost taste. No way was she going to breathe through her nose with her hyper sense of smell.

"A kid? Really? What is wrong with you?" She let her own fangs slide out. "I hate perverts. You give us all a bad name. Why can't you find some homeless person to help? Did that ever cross your mind? Give them some money so they can eat hot meals in exchange for a little blood. It's not rocket science. Win for both of you. They get fed. You get fed. But no." She stepped closer. "You went after a kid. Big mistake, asshole."

"Who the fuck are you?"

"You can call me pissed." She gave a little curtsy. "I'll call you Dusty. I'm about to dust your ass. It was so nice to meet you."

She lunged forward.

He tried to rush past her but she grabbed his jacket and threw him at a wall. He hit it hard, grunting in pain, then glanced around for an escape route. She had a runner on her hands.

"Admitting that girls over fourteen scare you is the first step to facing that you have a problem. Are you really going to run? You've got to outweigh me by forty or so pounds. I guess I should call you pussy instead, since you're acting like one." She snorted. "Does your master know you're a coward who runs from grown women? I bet Marco would ash you himself if he saw your reaction to me. Pathetic."

Rage twisted his features when he glared at her. "How dare you!"

She put her hands on her hips, slipping her fingers under the shirt that hung loose past her waist. Her fingers curled around the handle of the blade she kept sheathed tightly across her flat belly, and gripped it firmly.

She lifted her other hand and waved him to come at her. "I have super-low expectations from you but you could at least try to give it your best to kick my ass."

He clawed his hands and stormed at her. She held still until he got three feet away. Then she reached out, grabbed him by the front of his jacket again and braced her arm, withdrawing the blade. The bastard went for her with his fangs.

She tucked her chin to protect her throat, slamming her forehead into the underside of his jaw. He roared in pain and she shoved him hard. He hit the wall again before bouncing off and landing on his stomach. Blood ran down his chin.

"Did you bite your tongue? Ouch." She grabbed him by his hair before he could get up, stood against his spine, and swiftly moved to take his head.

He threw an elbow, catching her in the thigh. Pain shot up her leg but she didn't let him go. He hit her again in the same spot with every ounce of strength he possessed. Agony came next but she didn't release him. She pressed the blade against his throat.

He stopped slamming his elbow into her thigh, put his hands on the ground, and managed to flip onto his back in an attempt to keep his head. It tipped her off balance enough that it might have worked, but she twisted around, threw her leg over his body and just dropped onto his chest to straddle him. Her blade sliced until it hit his neck bone, and she began to saw. Blood sprayed her shirt. It soaked through to her stomach, breasts, and down the front of her pants. He bucked under her, trying to toss her off, but she squeezed her knees tightly along his sides until she managed to cut off his head.

He went still under her.

"Fuck!" She released his hair and got off as the crumbling body turned to ash. One glance down made her thankful she wore all black, but she could see the wet stains as well as feel them. "I've got bad guy grossness all over me. I think it's in my underwear too." Then she remembered she wasn't alone. "Shit." She looked between the dumpsters.

The girl's head jerked up from what remained of the Vamp's ashes and she gaped at Mandy.

Mandy lifted her shirt, sliding the razor-sharp blade back into the sheath. "Easy there, kid. You're safe. We're going to have a little heart to heart though about stupid decisions teenagers make. You should be at home watching something age inappropriate on the internet and texting your friends words your parents would ground you over. I'm going to have to wipe your memories, but be assured that you won't be strolling around at night by your lonesome anymore or taking detours down alleys. That's dangerous and dumb. I want you to grow up and hopefully live a long life. I'm going to implant some basic safety rules to follow while I'm in your head. It won't hurt."

The "kid" started sprouting fur, fangs, and claws.

Mandy's mouth fell open. "Oh."

The girl snarled at her.

"Stay." Mandy opened her hands and backed off a bit. "Don't attack me. I didn't know you were a Werewolf."

There was a soft thud as something dropped from the building behind her. She didn't want to take her gaze off the Were girl. "I got this, Olivia. She's just scared."

She bit her lip and sighed. "Look, kid. You might think you're a badass since that's a Were mentality for the most part, but there's a nest in this town. Vampires are bad. I'm probably the only nice one you'll ever meet. I don't want to bite or hurt you. I just want you to take some advice. Don't leave home at night without pack mates. There's safety in numbers. You can't judge by looking at Vamps how strong we are, or how fast. That jerk I turned into ash was considered a baby in Vamp years. It was pathetic how easily I took him down, but the next Vamp who comes after you could be like me. I'm ten times more dangerous than that pile of ashes was. Do you understand? Never underestimate your enemy and stick with your pack. Two rules to never forget. Now go home." She pointed toward the street. "I'm no threat."

"I am."

The deep male voice had her whirling around.

Astonishment slammed into her hard at the sight of the big man standing so close she could have reached out to touch him. He *definitely* wasn't Olivia. His hair had grown longer but that face was one she had never forgotten.

He lunged at her, and the instinct to protect herself should have kicked in, but it didn't. She remained frozen as he gripped her arms, jerked her off her feet, and the air whooshed from her lungs as he slammed her against the wall a few feet away from where she'd just killed the Vamp.

"What kind of mind game are you trying to play, bloodsucker? Did your fang buddy go after your entertainment for the night, so you killed him? That's fucking cold. Are you trying to give Teenie a nice sense of security, just so you can attack her once she feels safe? Does that flip your on-switch? You are all sick in your heads."

He leaned close, pinning her body aloft with his much bigger one, and let go of her arms. He fisted her hair with one hand to keep her head in place and drew back his other fist, revealing long, lethal-looking claws gleaming in the dim light.

Her voice finally worked, and she managed to get out one word. "Ice?"

He stilled, frowning.

She stared into his eyes, certain it was him. "You're a Werewolf? I thought you were human."

28

"What's going on, Glacier?" The girl came closer, her shoes scuffing on the alley floor.

"Back up, Teenie." Ice's eyes searched Mandy's. "How do you know me?"

"I'm Mandy. From Bucket."

His hold on her hair loosened and the mask of anger faded from his face. He stared hard at her, taking in her features, before leaning in again. His leery expression seemed to imply he didn't believe her.

"The new wave club in the late eighties. We worked together. Remember me? My hair was dyed black with blue stripes. I'm actually a blonde. Also, not wearing layers of makeup anymore. You're a *Werewolf?*" She tried to smell him but the rancid stench of rotten food from the dumpsters had her instantly regretting that idea.

"You quit the club."

"I got snatched by Vampires," she corrected.

"Kill it!" the girl encouraged. "I lured it into the alley just like we planned."

Bloodthirsty little mongrel. Mandy didn't spare the girl a glance though since the threat stood in front of her, nearly crushing her against a wall with his bulky body. It sank in that the Werewolf kid had been the hunter's bait to catch his prey. Only he'd caught *her* instead.

"I wasn't going to hurt the girl, and that Vamp was not my buddy. I killed him because he was a twisted jerk who targeted a kid. Can we talk before you behead me? For old times' sake?"

29

He growled low and didn't ease his hold on her. If anything, he looked even more furious. "You bloodsuckers are done stealing Lycan children and killing them!"

She felt her body go lax, his words making horrible sense. *That* would piss off a pack enough to send their enforcers after Vampires. No wonder the local Vamps were being killed off. "That's what the nest is doing?"

"As if you didn't know."

"I didn't. I'm not a part of the nest. They're murdering the pack kids? Why? Are they trying to make the pack flee the area?"

"Don't act stupid. They're forcing them to fight each other to the death for their bloodthirsty amusement."

It turned her stomach, but she couldn't say it shocked her. "You hate Vampires. I understand. Not a huge fan of them myself, but the council sent us here to take out whoever has been killing off the nest. I get why you're doing it. I take it you're stopping them?"

He didn't answer.

"Well…good. Watch your ass, okay? The council will send more than just two assassins after you. We didn't know about the Werewolf kids. The nest master is named Marco, and he must have a friend or two in high places. Otherwise, we'd have been ordered to take out the nest if that shit is really going down here. We're supposed to police our own. The fact that we were sent after *you* instead, says it all."

He kept his claws up, prepared to rip her head from her shoulders. She glanced at the deadly tips, then back to him. Rage still showed on his features. Any hope of him setting her free because they used to know each other died a quick death. Vamps had attacked his pack by going after their kids. It would mean he would perceive her as the enemy.

"You're warning me?"

"Yes."

"Why? What's your angle?"

"None. If you feel you must kill me, I understand. You look good, Ice. Still the protector you always were. I'm glad that never changed." She offered a small smile and then closed her eyes. "Make it fast, okay? And watch out for my partner. Her name is Olivia. She's not bad, but the council doesn't take no for an answer on following their orders. They *will* kill her if she doesn't bring them your head. Don't take it personal when she attacks."

The strike didn't come.

She waited long seconds. Nothing happened.

She opened her eyes to find him staring at her, claws still raised at the ready to punch through her throat.

"Fuck. You're going to torture me? *Really*? What else do you want to know? There were originally twelve in the nest. You've taken out four and I got the fifth. That means seven more remain. The council just sent Olivia and I to deal with Marco's problem. They train us to kill and take out threats. We're indentured servants. It sucks, but it beats being in the nest that changed me. *That* master was a nightmare who collected pretty women to create his own harem of sex slaves."

"You're an assassin for the council?"

"I thought I made the clear. Yes."

31

"How did you become an assassin for them?"

"They sometimes save newly turned Vamps from psycho masters slated for execution. The council figures we haven't been tainted yet, and they cull us from the nest before destroying it. We're often young enough to have family and friends still alive, too. They use them against us." She shrugged. "I didn't have many friends. You know what I think of my family. Fuck 'em if the council wants to take them out to teach me a lesson. I only regret that I'm not allowed to kill my father and brothers myself.

"I went along with doing the job because I'm a survivor. I didn't want to die. Plus, they said I could take out bad Vamps. I was kind of angry about my life being taken from me. Payback sounded great."

"What about your mom?"

"The council keeps me far from my family, but I keep tabs on her via the Internet. She's living in a nursing home suffering the final stages of dementia. It would probably be a blessing at this point if they did end her life. Mom didn't recognize me, talk, or even seem aware of what was going on around her the one time I got to visit her. I was tempted to end it for her but...she's my mom. I couldn't do it. Olivia covered for me so I could slip away to see her by putting my tracker in a human, then babysitting him. And don't feel bad for the jerk who didn't survive when she put the tracker back into my body. He was a serial rapist we caught in the act."

"Tracker?"

"All council assassins have them. It's how they know we're where we're supposed to be. An alarm goes off if they aren't embedded in a living body, to prevent us from removing them. They go off after a minute if they're not inside living flesh. Olivia figured out a way to transfer it fast into another person if we were both submerged in warm water. They also put them where it's impossible for one of us to get out on our own. Olivia and I are a rare team because we trust each other. She did me a solid by letting me see my mom one final time."

"What happens if the alarm goes off?"

"They call us on our phones, which also have trackers. Both better be in the same location. If we don't answer with a damn good reason why the tracker went off, they assume we've gone rogue. Then we're moved to the top of every council assassin's hit list. They'll contact all nests, packs, and even the VampLycans with a tracking kit. They usually say we're radicals or something, who want to expose our kind to humans, to make certain we're taken out on sight. *Nobody* runs from the council."

"Tracking kit?" He backed off and let her drop to her feet. He kept her trapped against the wall with his body blocking any escape. The claws remained out too, his hand still raised to strike.

"Photos of us, body description, a piece of our clothes for scent, and blood samples. It makes it easier for us to be tracked down and found, even if we're able to change our appearance enough to fool someone on sight."

"Why would they involve others?"

"It gets the results the council wants. Also assures no one will give us sanctuary. Assassins who run don't survive long. They put a large bounty on our heads too, just in case someone doesn't trust what they're told. Double measures."

He took another step back but stayed in front of her. "No one would give a Vamp sanctuary anyway except a nest."

"Wrong. It's rare, but some less-than-stellar pack alphas will protect rogue Vamps for our ability to mind-manage humans. I've had to go after a few hiding with packs before."

"Why aren't you trying to flee, Mandy?"

She stared up at him. He seemed taller than she remembered, with only a few feet of space between them. She wasn't wearing four-inch heels anymore though, either. "I'm dead anyway if I don't kill you. I already used my one fuckup when I helped a human family escape council judgment. There's never a second one given. And I won't fight you. You're protecting kids. That's noble.

"It's okay, Ice. They'd torture me first, probably drawing it out for weeks just to make an example out of me for the others. You're doing me a solid this way, as long as you make it fast. My life has sucked since that night I was kidnapped from the club. Pun intended." She forced a tight smile. "But be careful. Olivia is good. She could show up at any time. Like I said...watch your back." She closed her eyes again. "Just do it."

She tensed when his fingers slid into her hair, holding her head in place. It was going to hurt but she trusted him to be a quick, efficient killer.

She'd always wondered what happened to Ice. Now she knew. He wasn't human after all, but instead an enforcer for a pack. It made sense to her now, looking back. There was always something about him that screamed alpha male.

Pain slammed into her face instead of her throat. It was the last thing she remembered.

Teenie growled. "Why'd you just knock her out, Glacier?"

He ignored the young-looking Lycan and lifted the Vamp, tossing her over his shoulder. Mandy didn't weigh shit. He ran his hands over her body to locate her phone and pocketed it. "Go home and tell Kevin there's one less threat."

"You're supposed to kill all the Vamps. Just because you know that one makes no exception."

"I don't take orders from your alpha *or* you. I want to talk to this one more."

Excitement lit her features. "You're going to find out where they hid the nest by torturing the info out of her? I want to watch."

"I don't need you around anymore." He turned and strode down the alley to almost the end, where he stopped at an abandoned repair shop. He'd picked this location for a reason.

Teenie followed him but he spun on her when he unlocked the door to shoot her a glare. "Goodbye."

"Kevin would want me to stay with you until dawn. More Vamps could be out hunting."

He snorted. "You might look like a child, with your breasts wrapped tight to your chest and your size, but we both know you're not helpless. Your car is on the street fifty feet down. Go."

"I want to watch you torture that bitch."

He didn't have any plans to make Mandy suffer, but he refused to admit that to the pack enforcer. "I'm going in alone, without you. I'll stay here until you make it to your car. *Go.*"

"Goddamn it, Glacier! We're a team."

"I'm only working with you because the nest has been kidnapping your children. There's one less, just the way we planned. Leave now so I can watch you get to your car."

"No. I'm staying."

"You're not. Last chance, or I'm leaving you out here alone." He watched her, but Teenie didn't budge. He sighed. "I'll see you tomorrow night."

He stepped inside, closed and bolted the door. He adjusted Mandy in his arms and laid her on one of the shop counters, thinking about what she'd said to him. The weapons strapped to her body were easy to locate and remove. Not only did she hide a seven-inch blade across the front of her lower stomach, she also had a gun strapped to her rib cage.

He placed both on the floor before rolling her over, and then shoved her shirt up to expose her skin. She'd said the tracker was embedded somewhere difficult for a person to reach. He flexed his fingers and began searching at the back of her head and then downward.

She had very soft skin, and he couldn't find any signs of scars or bumps. Vamps healed better than he could though. He gave up once he explored her from the back of her neck down to her spine.

Next, he slid his hand under her hips, unfastening her pants. It was easy to tug them down to expose the lacy black panties. The fact that she had a nice ass made him growl. He gripped her cheeks with both hands,

36

squeezing. He felt a slight imperfection under the skin in a meaty part near the center of one rounded globe, and released her, reaching for the dagger he kept in his boot.

"Fuck." He hated to cut into her, but the tracker needed to go.

He stared at her creamy white skin and knew she might wake soon. It would be best if he did this while she remained out. He hesitated only a second longer before slicing the skin where he'd felt something. The scent and sight of her blood distracted him but he found the tracker. It was the size of a horse pill, smaller than he suspected it would be. He carefully got it out. The device had a tiny red light in the center; it began to blink as he studied the gadget.

He left her there, marched to the door, and unlocked it.

Mandy's phone in his pocket vibrated just as he stepped outside. Apparently, she hadn't been lying to him.

Teenie and her car were gone. He wiped the blood off the tracker onto his clothing, returned to where the ashed Vamp remains were spread across the alley, and dropped the tracker in the middle of them. The phone he also wiped down before throwing it under the dumpster. It stopped vibrating but then started up again.

He glanced around, his senses on alert, but didn't get the sensation of being watched. Only humans seemed to be walking in the streets at each end of the alley. He hurried back inside the shop and locked the door. Mandy remained unconscious on the counter, her ass exposed.

He sheathed the dagger in his boot and pulled up her pants before hoisting her over his shoulder again. The room he had been sleeping in was above the shop but he carried her down a set of stairs into the

37

basement storage instead. The only window down there had been bricked off at some point in the past, probably to prevent robbers from getting inside. He flipped on the harsh lights and strode over to another counter. This one had a metallic top and legs, covered in old computers that had been abandoned. He used his arm to clear it. They crashed to the floor and he laid her out on her back.

Memories filled his head from the past. Mandy had been human then...and a temptation. He'd resisted fucking her, despite wanting to. She'd made him feel a longing to get to know her a lot better but that couldn't happen. Not in his line of work. He bedded humans often but she'd seemed too fragile with her smaller size, and she hadn't been some club honey.

Those were his type. Easy sex, no strings, and an absolute lack of emotional ties. Bed them once and never think of them twice. That wouldn't have been the case with Mandy. He'd actually wanted to take her to his place and keep her there, where she'd be safe. She'd tugged at his protective instincts. The thought of climbing into bed with her each morning when he got off work had often crossed his mind. She'd just been so goddamn sweet and cuddly.

He growled low. *Now she's a fucking Vamp.*

He ran up to his current sleeping room and returned to the basement quickly to restrain her to the sturdy table. He always carried chains and cuffs in case he needed to torture information from his targets. He thought about gagging her but the damage to her face already made him wince. He'd tagged her hard with his fist to knock her out. A bruise had already formed but it would fade completely once she'd fed. He dragged a rusted chair over and took a seat to watch her.

His phone beeped in his pocket and he withdrew it, glancing at the screen. Surprise hit when he saw the caller, and he answered. "Hey, Kelzeb."

"Do you want to explain what part of 'play nice with the Lycans' you don't understand? I just got a call from the alpha that you refused to allow his enforcer to be a part of information gathering. I hung up on him bitching at me, but if I have to hear that shit, so do you. Two words for you: joint effort."

"I ran into a snag."

"What kind?"

He sighed and rolled his shoulders. "The Vamp Council sent two assassins to come after me for taking out this nest."

"They have assassins?"

"Guess so."

"Since when?"

"No fucking clue."

Kelzeb chuckled. "You grabbed one of the assholes to gain intel? Smart. I'm glad you cut the pack out of this one. We're the ones who deal with their Vamp issues when it's too much for them to handle. Give me updates and I'll share them with Aveoth. He can let the VampLycan clans know what you learn."

"I know this Vamp," Glacier admitted. "Remember that job back in the late eighties? The master's name was Byron? You sent me there after

39

a lot of missing persons reports were filed and we tracked the disappearances to a dance club. He's the one who was trying to start up a cult of human followers and kept them under his mind control."

"It's one of Byron's Vamps? I thought you took them all out."

"I did. She used to be human, worked at the club I was using as a cover, and she mentioned being turned by a master who wanted women for sex slaves. That wasn't Byron. He only went after human men, and all his Vamps were also male."

"The assassin is a *woman*?"

"A tiny one. It's fucking brilliant. Talk about underestimating an opponent and using it as an advantage. She looks about as threatening as a cute fanged garden gnome."

Kelzeb laughed.

"It's not funny, man. I liked her. I *still* do. And I didn't kill the Vampire who went after Teenie. The Vamp I'm watching sleep right *now* took his ass out before I could. Then she warned me about the council and offered up her damn throat without a fight. I just couldn't kill her. She's not coldblooded."

Kelzeb's tone wasn't amused anymore. "Bullshit. Did she recognize you?"

"Yes."

"She's going to try to fuck with your head and then kill you once you let your guard down. It's a game to Vamps."

"That's why she's presently chained down."

"Get information and eliminate her."

40

"Easier said than done, Kelzeb. She was a fucking sweetheart as a human. What if some part of her still exists? It sure seemed that way to me."

"She works for the council. Was she sent to take out the nest killing the pups?"

"No. They sent her after me."

"That says it all. The council is fucked up. They would have destroyed what humanity she had left after the turn. She kills for them, Glacier. For all you know, they sacrificed the Vamp she killed to gain your trust. They're probably wondering why we got involved and how many of our clan are there. Don't fall for that bullshit. I actually like you and want you to keep your head."

"I hear you."

"Should I send one of your brothers as backup?"

"No. I've got this."

"The council will probably send more assholes after you."

"I look forward to it. She's waking up. I need to go."

"Ask her questions and get rid of her, Glacier. That's an order."

He disconnected the call and slid his phone back into his pocket.

Mandy remained still, her chest rising and falling rhythmically. It was possible she'd be out until the next night after she day slept. He just hadn't wanted to listen to Kelzeb anymore. He knew his job but currently didn't like it much. The idea of killing Mandy twisted up his guts.

Chapter Two

Mandy woke to darkness. *Huh.* She should be dead. Ice hadn't removed her head but instead clocked her in the side of the face with his fist. He'd withdrawn the claws first, or she'd still be in a world of pain. The enforcer had an iron punch though, so as it was, her cheek throbbed a little.

She lifted her head and peered around. Her eyesight was pretty good in the dark but no light came into the room at all. She sniffed and regretted it. Death clung to her in the form of dried blood down her body. It had begun to decay. She tried to ignore that though and figure out where she was. The scent of chemicals hung in the air, a lot of dust, and mold. Ice smelled like leather and sandalwood, but it was faint, as if it had been a while since he'd been near her.

She strained to hear anything. Traffic in the distance helped her figure out she remained in the city. Ice wasn't in the room. That was for certain, since she couldn't pick up his heartbeat or the sound of breathing besides her own. She tried to sit up but realized fast that her wrists were restrained above her head and her ankles somehow shackled to keep her legs straight on a flat surface. Her thigh hurt like a son of a bitch too. That stupid Vamp she'd taken out had probably fractured her leg and it would be badly bruised. A quick wiggle of her toes revealed her boots had been removed but she still wore clothing. They were currently stuck to the front of her body where she'd been covered in blood.

"Ice?"

No response. It was daytime though. She could tell by the way her body felt lethargic and heavy. Maybe he thought she'd be out for the day. Most Vampires were unless they were far older than her. Ice wouldn't know that the council had made certain their assassins retained as few weaknesses as possible.

She took deep breaths and tested the restraints. They wouldn't give way. Whatever he'd used were Vamp-strength resistant. She lowered her head, wiggling her body. The surface she lay on felt hard and unforgiving. Cold too.

The question she wanted to ask most was why he hadn't killed her. His alpha would be furious. That was the last thing she wanted.

Hours passed as she napped on and off, trying to ignore how her body ached from being uncomfortable and from her injuries. They weren't healing as fast as normal. She needed to feed.

The floor creaked above her head and she opened her eyes, alert. Every footstep she was able to track by sound. A door to her left squeaked open and the person came closer. She could make out a big form and inhaled. Ice had returned.

The lights he flipped on blinded her for a few seconds. Two large industrial ones were hung above her. She blinked a few times and then openly gawked at Ice. His hair was mussed, as if he'd just woken from bed. Her gaze lowered to his exposed chest. He was perfect, muscular and tan. The dark gray sweats he sported hung low on his hips, revealing those little side muscles just above the waistband. He was all man and incredibly sexy. Her gums throbbed and it embarrassed her when her fangs slid down.

He moved with the full grace of a sleek predator. A sexy one as he approached her. "It's still day. You're awake."

Her nipples beaded and she squirmed a little. His deep, raspy tone turned her on more. Great, he wasn't only eye porn, but his voice got to her too. She broke eye contact, knowing her eyes would respond to him as well by blazing brighter. Full-on bloodlust hit, and she knew he'd smell her arousal soon. He was a Werewolf with a super sniffer.

It sucked waking up starving since she hadn't fed in a few days, but it was made ten times worse by her fantasy dream guy in that state of undress while she was injured. Her response to him would come to his attention and there would be no hiding it. She might as well get ahead of it.

"I'm hungry and hurt," she admitted. "Sorry. My body is going to do some Vampy things until I drink blood. Try to ignore it."

He frowned, staring at her. "How are you awake?"

"We're fed council member blood to make us stronger. Assassins would be too easy to kill if anyone could just break into our hotel rooms during the day and we couldn't defend ourselves." She avoided looking at him at all costs. As a human, she'd been really attracted to him, but as a blood-starved Vamp, it was a hundred times stronger. "You need to know that the council will have activated my tracker and will send Olivia here as soon as the sun goes down."

"I removed it and ditched your phone. I left them with that ashed Vamp, hoping they'll think it's you. You're not going to be found."

That surprised her enough to meet his gaze as he stood next to her. It also made her slightly relieved. He would be safe.

44

"Don't even try to break into my head."

Her eyes still glowed. She turned her head, looking at anything but him. "I told you. I'm hungry and hurt. I'm not attempting to control you. It's also why my fangs are out. You should put on a shirt. You know...show me less skin."

"You're strong enough to resist becoming comatose during the day but you wake starving like a newbie?" He sounded amused and his voice turned huskier. "Interesting."

"Yeah. That's me. Interesting." She swallowed. "Why am I still alive, Ice?"

"My name is Glacier. I just went by Ice as a nickname."

"Did you used to belong to a pack in California? That's weird. Most packs don't move territories."

Unless he's taken a mate.

That was a horrible thought. Had he mated to someone and transferred packs? She sniffed the air but didn't pick up the scent of another woman.

"I'm not mated, if that's what you're checking for, and I don't belong to the local pack. You could say I'm on assignment from somewhere else. I travel around."

She bit her lip, resisting the urge to look at him, not wanting him to see her as a threat.

"But you're a Were. I smell it on you."

"What else do you pick up?"

She stared at the brick walls. "This place is old. Is it abandoned? Nobody has cleaned it for years with this much dust in the air. And there's mold. A lot. Some wood rot, too. I reek of death, since I've got dried blood on me." She lifted her head and saw broken computers on the floor. "That accounts for the plastic and metallic scents I'm picking up." Her gaze scanned the room, seeing old cleaning supplies on a shelf. "And there's the chemicals I smell."

He regarded her with narrowed eyes. "Anything else?"

"Just you. I like sandalwood. You smell nice." She let her head fall back and cringed when she hit it a little too hard. "Not to be a pain, but I need to use the bathroom if there is one, to get clean. A hose would work too. I skipped eating for a few days and the dried blood is making it worse. You know what that means."

"I have no clue what you're talking about. Go ahead and look at me. I'll know if you attempt to trespass into my head."

She really didn't want to stare into his eyes. Or see his handsome face. To be in the room with an attractive man while hunger played hell on her body. The fact that it was the guy she'd thought about, envisioned in her head every time she'd masturbated over the years, wasn't helping. Especially with him half naked. But she turned her head and held his gaze.

"Do you know why I didn't kill you?"

Such enthralling eyes. Holy hotness. I could totally worship him. Way better than I remembered.

"Answer me."

What was the question? Oh yeah. "I assume I'm still alive because you want to know more about the local nest. I don't have a lot of answers

46

but I'll tell you what I can. Either ask fast or let me wash the blood off. My control will slip, and that could become kind of traumatic."

"Traumatic?"

"I'd planned to find a donor last night after hunting my target. I never got a chance to feed. Between the fight I had with that other Vamp—where I think he fractured my leg—the punch to my face, and being sprayed with blood, it's all a bad combo. I'm borderline on losing my shit. I'll start hissing and snapping at you soon. It'll get harder for me to think beyond the hunger. I can buy some time to stay in control if I wash off the dried blood. A shower would give me a few more hours of sanity."

"You're going to try to escape if I unchain you to use the bathroom."

"Where would I go? You removed my tracker. I'm possibly enemy number one to the council right now. They'll think I ran from them if they don't believe the ashes are mine. I'll answer any questions you have, but I'd just like to take a shower first."

He leaned over her and peered into her eyes.

The scent of him hit her and her body went a little crazy. She wanted him so bad it hurt. It was just confusing at that point whether she craved his blood or sex.

"I don't trust you."

"You shouldn't. I'm a Vampire. We're mostly bad guys. I have no plans to attack you or run though. I'll let you know when I hit the danger zone on my bloodlust. It's not here yet. I wasn't lying about everyone coming after me when the tracker alarm went off. I'm already dead, Ice."

"Glacier," he corrected.

47

"Sorry. It's going to take some time getting used to the new name. You never did say why you were working at Bucket."

"I was hunting a crazy master who thought it would be a good idea to have humans treat him as though he were a god. He actually had them believing he *was* one. They're probably still in therapy after how badly he'd fucked with their heads."

She curled her lip in disgust. "Did you find him?"

He nodded. "It wasn't gang members who came into the club that night you went missing. It was him and his four nest members searching for new humans to add to their cult. His name was Byron—and he sobbed while I killed him."

The irony wasn't lost on her. "You asked me to leave that night to keep me safe...but I got grabbed in the back parking lot by one of Cain's harem hunters. It's like I was totally screwed on the staying-human front, wasn't it?"

"Byron wouldn't have targeted you. He was only into men. I didn't want you there in case they felt cornered and used human shields."

"Did they?"

"No. I took them out one by one without them even realizing I was there until I was down to Byron and his bodyguard. They went into the men's room, following a victim they'd chosen. I started a brawl so the humans would flee and then ashed their asses once we were alone."

Her fangs ached and the smell coming off her own body was driving her mad. "I really need to get this blood off me. I'm weaker than normal this morning because it's tough on my body to go this long without blood, especially while I need to heal. You could easily take me down, even if I'm

48

lying about not planning to escape." She stared into his eyes, searching for any signs of the caring person he used to be. "Please? I might not be a Were but I have a sensitive nose. It's probably getting to you too. Wouldn't you like to question me when I don't reek?"

He clenched his teeth. "Fine. The only bathroom is on the third floor. It's still daylight outside though, and I'm not covering all the windows. I'll put a blanket over you and escort you to the bathroom. There's a tiny window in there but it doesn't let in direct sunlight. That room is located against an outside wall. If you try to punch through, all you'll do is burn. The buildings around us are locked up tight. I don't care how fast you can run, you won't find sanctuary from the sun before you're ashed."

"I'm not going to run, Glacier." It was odd saying that name. "Can I ask you something?"

He reached into the sweatpants pocket and withdrew a ring with two small keys. "I'm not telling you who I work for or how many of us there are."

"I just wanted to know what your real name is."

"Why would you think Glacier isn't?"

"Well, cold seems to be a theme you go by. Ice. Glacier. I was thinking on your next job you might be Hail or Sleet." She couldn't help but smile. "Frost sounds pretty cool too."

He moved down to her feet. "You always did have a sense of humor and a quick mind. My mother named me Glacier. I told Mike my name, but he refused to call me that. He dubbed me Ice and it stuck."

She decided to believe him. "Thank you."

"For what?" He removed the chunky cuff-like restraints from her ankles.

"It just matters to me that I know your actual name. It's silly but there it is."

He walked up the side of the table to her head. "I'd hate to have to knock you out again. I don't enjoy hitting women. That doesn't mean I won't if you attack me, Mandy. Understand? Behave and I won't have to hurt you."

She held very still as he released her wrists. "I'm not going to fight you. I get not believing me. I honestly do, and I wouldn't be so trusting in your shoes either. Vampires tend to lie. Thank you. Can I sit up now? I'll move slow."

He backed away and shoved the keys into his pocket. "Do it."

She bit back a groan as she sat upright and stretched a little, the kinks in her body making themselves known. The countertop had felt as hard as marble, despite it being metal. "I don't know how they used to do it when Vampires had to hide out in burial crypts and sleep on stone. I'm such a wimp. I bought a pillow-top mattress for my room that feels like a cloud of softness." She carefully swung her legs over the side and slipped off the edge, standing there in her bare feet. Her leg held her weight but it hurt. She avoided stepping on broken computer pieces as she made her way closer to him. "I appreciate you showing me some mercy." She stared deeply into his eyes.

"Walk in front of me to the stairs."

He didn't want to give her his back. *Smart.* She made no sudden movements and picked her way around the debris to the stairs, only stopping when she reached the bottom. Glacier stepped to her side and reached under the staircase, withdrawing what looked like an old canvas tarp.

"That's not a blanket." She wrinkled her nose. "And it's layered in dust."

"It's all I've got down here. Yes or no? You could return to the workbench."

She closed her eyes, tucked her chin down, and hugged her waist. "Do it. I hope this bathroom has warm water. I can dream, right?"

The sound of him chuckling surprised her. She almost peeked to see his face but then he opened the tarp, wrapping it around her as if she were a person burrito. His shoulder dug into her hips a moment later and he hoisted her off her feet. She gasped, unable to even grab at him. Then she got to hang draped over him when he began to climb the stairs.

"I feel like a sack of potatoes over your shoulder, dirt and all."

He ran his hand over her leg all the way to her feet but she couldn't feel more than the weight of it since the tarp covered her. "Tell me if part of you starts to burn."

"I will. Promise. You'll know when I begin screaming."

He came to an abrupt stop.

"That was a joke. Kind of. It hurts like hell when I'm exposed to sunlight."

He began to walk again and she heard the floor creaking under their combined weight. They were on the first floor now. "Does that happen often?"

"No. I'm smart enough to avoid it but training was a bitch. They threw us outside a few times to show us how it felt to be exposed to the sun, and to make sure we could run back inside fast enough not to die. Burns are the worst to heal from."

"Why in the hell would they do that?"

"To make sure we don't freeze up while terrified and in pain."

"What if you couldn't make it back to cover?"

"Only the fittest survive training. We were considered too weak to live if we failed a test. They'd get new recruits to replace the ones who died."

"Cold." He started up more stairs.

"That's the council for you. They aren't exactly the compassionate types."

"I'm sorry they got their hands on you, Mandy."

"Thank you. Life sometimes sucks, and now so do I. That Vampire joke never gets old."

He paused, brushed her body against a wall, and then she heard the sound of a door opening. "How can you keep your sense of humor about this shit?"

"Laugh or cry. Want to guess which I prefer?"

The door slammed closed and a soft click sounded. He bent, setting her on her feet. She held still as he unwrapped the canvas and then she reached up, brushing her face with both hands in case dust covered her skin. Ice didn't say a word. She opened her eyes, glancing around the room.

The bathroom was outdated, not very big, and the tiny window over the tub and shower combo had layers of dirt blocking out most of the light coming from outside. A thin plastic shower curtain was pushed to the side. The toilet was a foot away, the sink next to it. He'd turned on the only light bulb in the room, which hung above their heads.

She tipped her head back and held his gaze. "I won't try to escape."

He backed up to the door, leaned against it, and crossed his arms. It was clear he had no intention of going anywhere.

Her mouth fell open but she snapped it shut. "You're going to watch me?"

"I'm not letting you out of my sight until you're chained up again."

She turned her head to stare into the dirty mirror. It had come as a shock when she'd discovered it was a bullshit myth that Vamps didn't have a reflection. Part of her regretted that it wasn't true as she took notice of the yellow and purple bruise fading on her cheek. Her hair was shorter than it used to be, just past her shoulders, and she'd stopped dying it. It was a waste of time to mess with her appearance. The last thing she wanted to be to her co-workers was attractive. That lesson had been learned.

"Time is wasting. Take your shower if you want one. I don't have long before the pack sends Teenie back here soon to begin our night."

She sighed and faced the shower. The curtain was nearly transparent. He'd get a good view at least. She gave him her back, turned on the water to see if it would get warm, and then tore her shirt over her head.

He sucked in a sharp breath.

She smiled, refusing to look at him. "Don't act all surprised that I'm removing my clothes. Doesn't everyone do that when they shower?"

He didn't answer.

She dropped her bra. The gun holster remained but the weapon had been removed. The sheath for her blade also sat empty. She unclipped both from her body and unfastened her pants.

"I'm just surprised you're not arguing with me by demanding privacy."

She shoved them down, along with her underwear, giving him a great view of her bare ass and more if he was looking. It felt as if his gaze was on her. "The council stripped me of modesty a long time ago in regards to people seeing my body. I've learned to pick my battles carefully, Ice." She paused. "Sorry. Glacier. I'm just grateful you gave me access to a shower."

She went to step into the tub but gasped when he suddenly gripped her arm. Their gazes locked as she peered at him over her shoulder. He looked furious.

"What the fuck does that mean? I thought you said the council prevented you from being in some asshole's sex harem."

"It could mean death if you're fighting someone, they rip your shirt, and you try to cover your exposed breasts. Putting an arm down could mean the difference between keeping your head or not. They sometimes made us fight naked to make sure we didn't care what parts of our body are exposed."

"Did any of them force you into sexual situations?"

54

That was a polite way to put what he implied. "No. The council doesn't abuse their powers by making us fuck them. We're viewed as tools they use to kill, nothing more. It's actually a rule they follow...never get involved with an assassin. Emotional attachments are forbidden."

"Does that mean you don't have a companion or someone you're in a relationship with?"

"That's also forbidden to us. We're property of the council. It's seen as a weakness to care about someone else. Olivia and I have hidden our close friendship. They just think we work well as a team and tolerate each other, since we come back whole. I haven't always played well with others when they've assigned me to work with someone else."

"Explain."

She hesitated before giving him an example. "My first on-the-job assignment trainer thought he should also teach me the art of seduction. I wasn't interested. So he decided it would be great payback not to give me backup when we were attacked by the nest we were sent to take out. Then the prick had only gotten us one hotel room, assuming we'd share the bed. He made me sleep on the floor since I wouldn't touch him. I got even when he went to sleep. You'll know who he is if you ever run across a Vamp missing the tip of his pinky finger. We don't grow back body parts if they've been severed and turned to ash. There're a few missing some toes too, but let's just say I've gained a reputation of someone to avoid sexually harassing at work."

His expression never changed.

She wondered what he thought about her past stunts, and decided to explain further. She wasn't a horrible person. "I'm not allowed to seriously damage another assassin or disfigure their faces, since they have to walk amongst humans on jobs. Taking an entire finger or something that might make them less effective at their job would get me killed as punishment. But the tip of a pinkie finger or removing a little toe?" She shrugged. "Nobody would notice that. The council didn't care."

His hold on her eased. "Take your shower."

She got into the tub and closed the curtain, standing under the hot water. It felt good, and it came as a surprise to her that the water heater worked in the old building. He also had products. She quickly washed her hair and scrubbed her body clean. The scent of sandalwood filled her lungs to replace dead Vamp. Now she'd smell like Glacier instead.

It was slightly comforting to know something good would be the last thing she inhaled before she took her final breath. Hunger gnawed at her but she pushed it back. She needed blood but he wouldn't feed her. Werewolves tended to detest Vamps for their need to drink blood. Of course, she wasn't going to point out that her meals survived. Unlike those of Werewolves, who tended to eat a lot of meat.

He held a towel over the top of the curtain when she turned off the water. "Thanks." She wrapped it around her middle and got out of the tub. "Do you have another one for my hair?"

He opened a cupboard built into the wall and withdrew a second one. "Turn around."

She tensed but did as he asked. Maybe he'd be kind and kill her without warning. It was her favorite way to eliminate a target. They never saw the blade coming until it was halfway through their throat.

He stepped close, just inches away, and began to rub her hair dry. It was a personal task a person who cared for you would do.

Tears filled her eyes but she blinked them back fast. He'd accused her of planning to play head games but it seemed that was *his* strategy. And it was working.

"What else do you want to know?" She'd tell him anything and then this could end.

"How many assassins work for the council?"

"At least a hundred. There are eight houses in the U.S. and two in Europe. I've never been there but one is in England, the other in Germany. They put ten of us in each home they set up. We're not called nests, since our masters are every member of the council."

"Why Europe?"

"To watch what the Vamps over there are up to. It's all hush-hush, but I met one of them about ten years ago. His name was Andre, and he'd followed a master into New York who didn't have permission to be there. Andre was stationed in Germany but mentioned he had transferred from England. I asked him if there were more houses but he said he'd only heard of the two. I was called in to be his backup because the master traveled with five guards. He'd also hired half a dozen humans to protect him during the day. We went at him at night though."

"Do all masters need permission to enter the U.S. first?"

"There were rumors that this master planned to take over New York. That's where I'm based. One of the council owns that territory, and it would mean a war for him to keep it. He'd warned the master not to come here and had Andre watching him in Germany. As soon as he flew into the U.S., it became a kill order."

"The council makes you do their territory dirty work?"

"Yes."

"Where are the houses in the states?"

"Tampa, Dallas, Chicago, Vegas, Portland, San Francisco, Denver, and New York."

"What about Canada or Mexico?"

"Not that I know of."

"None in Alaska?"

"VampLycans are up there. From what I've heard in passing, the council thinks any nest that settles there are fools. They do it at their own risk."

"In passing?"

"We hear rumors from time to time from the New York council member's nest of Vamps, when he orders us to come to him to get our assignments. There was a nest in Alaska wiped out not too long ago by the VampLycans after they tried to set up there. Corski was pissed about it. I guess he knew the master killed, and he was trying to gain support from the council for retaliation. He was voted down. Joseph Corski is the council member and master in New York City. He's the one who gives my house our orders from the others."

"The council fears the VampLycans?"

She tugged out of his hold and raised both eyebrows when she twisted her head, staring at him. "I think someone would have to be an idiot not to be wary of VampLycans. I know Weres think they're super tough, but I hope you never plan to take them on."

"What have you heard about GarLycans?"

"They keep to themselves. It's the VampLycans who defend packs and hunt nests that create too much attention with humans. There have been recent sightings of them in Los Angeles, Washington, and Colorado."

"Ever been sent to kill a VampLycan?"

She shook her head. "I'm still here, aren't I? They're total bogeymen."

He scowled.

"They are. Way stronger than masters, even old ones, and they have no weaknesses from what I've heard."

"I think GarLycans are more fearsome. They can fly."

She shrugged and turned her entire body around to face him. "They don't leave their nest. I don't worry about them."

"Nest? They're a clan."

"Good to know, but I don't worry about GarLycans hunting me since I never plan to go to Alaska. What else do you want to know? And you don't have to be nice to me. I told you I'd answer your questions. So enough small talk."

He held the towel between them but didn't back away. Inches separated them.

"My control is better now that I'm clean but being close to you is difficult. I can hear your heartbeat." Her gaze ran along his muscular arms and chest. "I can see your veins. Looking at you is akin to waving a big ol' steak in front of a starving dog." She peered into his eyes. "No games, for old times' sake, okay, Glacier? Just ask and I'll answer your questions. Don't drag this out until you see the ugly side of me. And it *will* be. I'd like for you to remember me this way, rather than what I'll become when the bloodlust takes over."

He tossed the towel in the sink. "Are you going to put your clothes back on?"

"No. I'd just reek again since I don't have different ones to wear. The towel is fine." She inched away to put as much space between them as possible, pressing against the wall. "Fast and furious rounds of questions. Hit me with them." She hugged her waist.

"Where's the local nest located right now? They went into hiding after I took out the first Vamp."

"We reported to Marco at a Chinese restaurant after we arrived in town." She gave him the cross streets and name of the place. "I got the impression they were staying in the basement. He mentioned the strong smells of the cooking hiding their scents from Werewolf trackers."

"Where is Olivia staying? With them?"

She inwardly winced. "I hate to give her up...but will you make me a promise?"

"You said you'd answer me."

"She's my best friend, Glacier. My only friend. It's not her fault that she takes orders from the council. But I don't want you or any more Werewolf kids to die. I'm all about priorities. I understand wrong from right. She'll kill you if she's able, regardless of why you're taking out the nest. Just...promise me she won't suffer when you put her down."

60

He frowned, studying her with his mesmerizing blue gaze.

She lowered her head, unable to look at him anymore, and tears filled her eyes. He wanted her to give up Olivia. *Do the right thing.*

Fuck! The council will kill her anyway if she fails to take out Glacier. He's protecting kids.

"Look at me."

His demanding tone wasn't lost on her but she refused to obey. "She's not bad. I swear. In twelve years we were going to join a nice nest with a decent master. They're tough to find. He likes humans, even allows a pack to live in his city without starting shit with them just for the hell of it. He's all about keeping the peace. Olivia hates this job as much as I do but her family members matter to her. She's got two sisters who have kids. Her niece got married last week and she cried seeing the pictures posted on a social site."

"Mandy," he snarled.

She jerked her head up.

"You're crying?" He growled deep in his chest.

"Of course I am. Did you miss the part about her being my best friend? I *hate* this. But she's smart and an excellent fighter. There's a chance she could take you down. That means those kids would be in danger. You think I'm heartless, don't you? Well, big surprise. I'm not. So yeah, I'm finding it difficult you want me to give up her location, as difficult as I find endangering more children. She follows orders to protect her family. Get it?"

"You said you'd answer all my questions."

"All I'm asking is that you take her out fast and painlessly."

His nostrils flared but he finally gave a sharp nod. "Done."

"Thank you." It was the only comfort she had. "The Smith Hotel. Room two-twenty. Tell her Werewolf kids were being killed...and I'm sorry." Hot tears slid down her cheeks.

"Do you know which council member is protecting this pack?"

"The order came from Corski, but he and the council might have been manipulated by another member with a personal agenda. I can't see all of them knowing Marco was killing Were kids and being dumb enough to think the VampLycans wouldn't eventually be called in. It's why we're supposed to police our own. It's motivation to keep them from showing up. The council doesn't want a war. They're aware that some packs contact the VampLycans for help if the Vamp problem is severe enough. I'd say this falls under that category."

He said nothing more. She wiped away her tears and sniffed. "What else?"

"That's it."

She nodded and gave him her back. "The shower would be easier to clean. Want me to step in there? I'll try not to struggle if you have a problem getting through the bone." It wasn't as if he needed to go grab a sharp blade with those claws of his.

He just breathed evenly.

Maybe he found it hard to kill her since they had a past. She took the initiative for him and stepped over the tub rim, removed the towel so her blood wouldn't get on it, and faced the tiled corner. "Have a good life, Glacier. I'm ready."

She closed her eyes and swept her hair aside to expose the back of her neck, making it easier for him to take a swipe. "Do it."

Chapter Three

"You son of a bitch!"

Glacier carried the struggling and canvas-wrapped Mandy down the stairs. "Stop it. You'll get burned if you kick free. The sun is still up."

He eased his crushing hold on her when they reached the basement and there was no longer a danger of her skin being exposed to sunlight. He strode to the bench but hesitated to put her on it. Then again, it was the only way to restrain her.

He dumped her onto her back and climbed up on the bench, straddling her hips to pin her down. The canvas he'd wrapped a few times around her was in the way of him reaching her arms. It meant unleashing his claws as she bucked and thrashed under him.

"Be still." He started slicing at the canvas.

"I told you what you wanted to know!" She stilled under him. "I even made it easy for you. All you had to do was use the showerhead to wash the tiles if blood sprayed on the walls. Ashes go right down a drain. I should know."

"I'm not going to kill you yet."

She tried to buck her hips to unseat him. "When did you become a dick? You want to watch me lose my mind? That's what's going to happen. Is that your version of fun? Seeing a Vamp in full-on bloodlust?"

He cut at the top of the canvas and lifted his body just enough to slide the material between them and slice open another layer. "I'm not going to cut off your head, nor do I plan to watch you suffer starvation.

Now will you behave so I can get you free of this? I snagged a pair of drawstring pajama bottoms and a shirt on the way down here. Would you like to wear them?"

She became very still under him. "What kind of game are you playing?"

"I'm not." He eased off her and the counter, reaching for the canvas again. She worked with him, almost falling off the smooth surface when she was freed, but he caught her before she could. He took the clothes off his shoulder where he'd tossed them and dropped them on her lap before turning away. "Get dressed."

He heard her movements and turned when they stopped. A laugh caught in his throat. His stuff looked huge on her. The legs of the pants were pooled over her feet until he couldn't even see them, and her arms were completely lost in the long sleeves of his shirt.

The humor died fast though. She looked cute as hell and vulnerable at the same time. He might forget she was a bloodsucker if it wasn't for her pale skin and the fangs peeking out from her lips. Her eyes when she looked at him were glowing blue.

"You're going to give me some of your blood?"

"No. I'm off limits."

Her gaze roamed over his chest and she licked her lips. He caught the motion when she seemed to shiver but she turned away and walked around the table, putting it between them. Her chin dropped to her chest and her wet hair fell forward. "Within a matter of hours, I'm going to lose my shit, Glacier. Probably less time. I think I mentioned I didn't feed when

I should have. I don't have to do it every night, but I can't go more than three days without it becoming dangerous. I hit that last night."

"Why did you go so long without blood?"

"I didn't get to feed the night we left home. It was a wake-up-and-here's-your-orders kind of thing. Pack and leave. I would have found someone to bite in the airport but security has cameras everywhere. The bathrooms were packed when I tried to find someone alone in a stall. I hate those fucking pee-a-boo doors. Why do they have a goddamn inch gap?

"Anyway, I figured I'd feed when we arrived in Atlanta. No big deal, missing a meal. But then there was a problem with the engine of the plane we were supposed to board. It meant we had to get a hotel to day sleep, and then catch a flight the next night, so we weren't stuck in the air while the sun was up. It was a hotel by the airport filled with senior citizens. They weren't really a spry group, you know? There was some kind of power outage where two nursing homes were located and they bussed them all to that hotel. The maid had a medical bracelet on, and the only other person working when we checked in was the clerk. He was all beat to hell and on crutches. It seems he'd been in a car accident a few days before. Who the hell feeds off someone with medical conditions? Not me.

"The bathrooms were packed again when we went *back* to the airport, so I figured I'd feed when we landed. Except Marco sent Pedro, his second, to pick us up. The asshole was waiting to take us to the restaurant. We got our orders to get right to work so we just dropped our bags at the hotel and boom—I ran into you."

66

He chuckled, amused as hell.

Her head whipped up. "You think that's *funny*?"

"It kind of is."

"Fuck you. I was going to find someone to bite after work last night."

"You could have tried to go for Teenie's throat."

"I don't bite Were kids. Or any kids, for that matter. Throats aren't my thing, either. I take from the arms of my donors."

Only the sweetheart he'd once known would avoid biting humans because she felt sympathy toward them. Now he was *really* curious. "Why?"

"Because I'm not a sick jerk who's into kids!"

"I meant, why sink your fangs into someone's arm?"

"Some humans get turned on when there's a mouth at their throats. They're in a trance, thinking happy thoughts that turn to sex, and always try to grope me when I bite them there. That doesn't happen if I sink my fangs into their wrists."

"Don't you ever fuck your donors?" That thought didn't amuse him one bit.

She wrinkled her nose at him. "*No.*"

"Why not?"

"Because I believe in free will, and not taking advantage of someone when they're being controlled by me. I go to the homeless. They need the money, and I try to find ones who are already living in an altered reality, since it's a risk that someone may be immune to mind control. I've never wanted to kill someone, Glacier. If I pick someone who thinks aliens or shadow people are after them, it won't matter if they rant about Vampires, too. They aren't seen as a threat."

He arched his eyebrows. "I can't believe you're an assassin for the council."

"Let me rephrase that. I don't want to kill someone *innocent*. I mostly get sent after rogues or bat-shit crazy Vamps who are putting us all at risk of exposure. Those are assholes who deserve to die."

"What if they weren't rogues or crazy? Did you still kill them?"

"I wouldn't do it if I knew it was flat-out wrong. That's only happened twice. The first time with a human family who'd managed to kill a Vamp in self-defense. They went to the police about the attack with their memories intact. They said a Vampire kidnapped them. The council ordered them silenced. The humans weren't at fault, so I messed with their memories then helped convince an FBI agent that their lives were in danger from a serial killer. The agent put the family into that witness relocation program. I figured with new identities, maybe the council wouldn't find them. The second time was last night, with you."

He was stunned. "How in the hell did you survive this long, Mandy? You're too soft-hearted to be a Vampire."

She crossed her arms over her chest. "I took out that asshole last night just fine. I feel no guilt about ashing him. He went after a kid. I've killed plenty of Vamps and even some murderous Weres over the years. Human predators, too. Those weren't even sanctioned by the council, by the way. They *love* it when humans go nuts and it becomes a news story. They can shove the blame on those psychos when a Vamp does bad things. I've run across some terrible humans while on assignment and stopped them from hurting anyone else. I don't hesitate to kill bad guys."

He started to feel anger growing. Not at her, but the situation. It would have been so much easier if she'd become a heartless creature. Instead, he found himself drawn to her even more than he was thirty years ago.

She sighed loudly and placed her hands on the workbench, peering at him. "You took the tracker out of me. I'm a dead Vamp walking. It was really hard to expose my throat to you and face my death, but I did— twice. I'm going out anyway. What are you waiting for, Glacier? You said you don't plan to feed me. Have you ever seen full-on bloodlust? I'll attack you. I could even hurt you. Or worse, if I get away from you, I *will* go after anyone unlucky enough to cross my path. That would be a helpless human, and I'd probably kill them without meaning to. I won't be able to stop myself."

"I'm going to chain you up again."

The sadness he saw flashing in her eyes made him feel like a bastard.

"Fine." She hopped up on the table and stretched her hands over her head. "You better gag me though if any humans are nearby. I've heard Vamps being tortured by starvation. I'll start screaming when the pain becomes too intense. I wouldn't want to live anyway if I ended up killing some good Samaritan who rushes to my rescue. Ignore what happens to my body, too. The hungrier I get, the more I'll confuse the need for blood with wanting sex. It's nature's way of helping women bait men to get within striking distance."

69

He knew that but kept silent, restraining her wrists first, and then her ankles. "I'm sorry I don't have somewhere more comfortable to put you. The frame on the only bed in this place is cheap wood you'd snap with ease. I have to get ready, since Teenie will be here within the hour. I'll see you soon."

He walked out of the basement but left the light on, refusing to leave her in the dark. He closed the door and hurried up the stairs to shower. It was probably the fastest one he'd ever taken and when he turned off the water, he heard pounding coming from somewhere below.

"Give me a few," he yelled, knowing Teenie would hear him.

The pounding stopped as he dried off and entered the small bedroom he'd taken over. He put on a pair of black jeans, a T-shirt, and his boots. One check of his cell phone showed six missed calls from Kevin. He growled low in irritation. Sometimes alphas were the bane of his existence.

It wasn't just Teenie standing at the back door he unlocked and jerked open. Kevin and one of his male enforcers also waited. He stepped outside, not wanting them anywhere near Mandy. He blocked the door and leaned against the frame. "What?"

Kevin stepped close and puffed out his chest. "You haven't been answering my calls."

"I had my cell off while I slept and then showered. Did something happen?"

The alpha clenched his fists hanging at his side, a show of anger. "Yes. I wanted to know what you learned from the Vampire you captured last night. You should have allowed Teenie to help you torture it. I shouldn't have had to wait all day to hear the results."

"I work alone unless I need bait." Glacier hated pissing contests. Some alphas just naturally couldn't help trying to intimidate everyone around them who they viewed as a physical threat, but it didn't work on him.

"Move aside."

Glacier shook his head. "No. This is my private space while I'm in your territory. That was the deal."

Kevin's expression showed he didn't like being refused or challenged on his authority one bit, nor did his two enforcers. All three of them rumbled protests. The big bastard on Kevin's right even sprouted some hair.

Glacier smiled, amused. It would piss them off more, but he was only in their city because they'd needed his help. Otherwise, they wouldn't have reached out to Lord Aveoth. He didn't care if he offended the entire pack.

"What did you learn from the Vampire?"

He held Kevin's glare as if he were bored. "I know where the nest is hiding."

Kevin withdrew his phone. "I'll call in the rest of my enforcers."

"Don't bother."

A snarl came from the alpha and he clenched the phone he'd withdrawn from his front pocket tight enough that a crack could be heard. "What did you say to me?"

"They're in a basement. They wouldn't hole up there unless they had a way to escape. First, you're going to need to reach out to a contact in the city for schematics of all sewer and water runoff drain lines around the building. Then we need to wait until dawn to go in after them."

"We'll just hunt them down if they run."

Glacier snorted. "I'm the expert on extinguishing nests. Do you want to know why? I've done this many times. You can't track them through the sewers if that's their escape route. All you'll be smelling is shit. A seasoned Vamp could hold his breath, slow his heart rate, and stay under water for almost an hour. Your trackers would pass right by them." He shook his head. "We do this my way. That means being smart. We find out what their options are, block them to keep them trapped, and take out the entire nest when they're at their weakest. That's daylight. I'm hoping only the master has the ability to move once the sun comes up, but he's the one we want the most. He survives, and he'll just remake another nest. Hell, he could be so pissed over the loss that he turns humans into dozens of soldiers to unleash on your ass. I've seen it happen before."

"Those bastards murdered some of our kids!"

"I understand, but you have your pack locked down and protected. One night is worth the wait. We can take them all out at once with no mistakes, or deal with the consequences if any get away. Don't you want to make sure every member of that nest pays?"

"We should go after them now," the male enforcer growled.

Kevin raised his hand, motioning for silence. "Fine. We'll do this your way, Glacier."

"Good. I'll turn my cell on. Let me know when you have the information we need, and then we'll form a plan on how to trap them in that basement come morning."

The alpha narrowed his gaze, studying Glacier. "We can go back to the pack house now and start planning. I'll have Ted here go pay a visit to our human friend who works for city sanitation. He'll bring the maps and a blueprint of the building to us."

"I have a phone call to make first. I'll drive to your pack house when I'm done."

Kevin shook his head. "Now."

"Twenty minutes," Glacier stated.

"We'll take my car and you can make your phone call on the way."

"I have shit to do first, and I don't want you listening in on my conversation." Glacier let his irritation sound in his voice. "I don't take my orders from you. I have to check in with Kelzeb and give my report to Lord Aveoth."

"Did you end the Vampire?"

He debated about lying but decided to go with the truth. There wasn't a damn thing the pack could do about it. "Not yet. I still have questions for her."

Kevin snarled, clearly unhappy.

Glacier arched his eyebrows.

The tense standoff lasted for a full minute before Kevin stepped back. "I want that fucking thing dead."

His response pissed Glacier off. "She's a Vampire, not a thing."

Ted smirked, looking at Glacier in a way that he didn't like.

"What?"

"You're one of *those*."

Kevin glanced back at his enforcer. "What are you talking about?"

Glacier wanted an answer, too.

"I heard about a group of enforcers in another pack who caught a female Vamp feeding off their human neighbors. They were ordered to bring her to their alpha so he could take her head himself. The thing was, she put up a hell of a fight and they had to really mess her up. They muzzled her to keep her from biting but while they were driving her in, she went into heat. It seems getting clawed and beaten turns on those fanged bitches like nothing else. Is that why you haven't killed her? You enjoying getting some Vamp pussy? The more you hurt 'em, the hotter they get, wanting to be fucked. I heard it was the wildest piece they ever had."

Glacier felt his skin cool as his rage flared inside. He didn't need to look down at his arm to know his body had turned a bit gray. "It doesn't turn them on. It sends them into bloodlust, you asshole. That captured Vamp probably lost so much blood that her body was starving. Are you accusing me of being the type who'd torture and then rape a woman? Rape is *exactly* what it would be to take advantage of a woman lost to bloodlust. You should answer carefully."

Ted paled and backed up a step.

"You better hope I never find out what pack those enforcers were from, or I might go hunting for what they did to that Vamp before she was killed."

His gaze jerked to Kevin. "Obviously intelligence isn't a requirement to be one of your enforcers. Get him the fuck out of my sight before I hurt him for implying I'm some twisted sicko."

Kevin nodded. "Be at the pack house soon." He shoved Ted ahead of him, and Teenie trailed hot on their asses down the alley.

Glacier spun, entered the shop, and slammed the door. He snarled, wanting to punch something. He looked at his fist, focused on it, until his skin returned to flesh tone.

His temper eventually faded as he took deep breaths. He left the store, locked the door, and made damn sure no Lycans were hanging around to watch his place. He left the alley and walked a block over to where he'd seen drug dealers and hookers hanging out. He approached one of the women and smiled. "How much?"

She smiled back, revealing some missing teeth. Scabs covered her exposed arms and chest. He knew it was a result of doing drugs. She reeked of them, as if she had them coming out of her pores. "What do you want?"

"How would you like to make two hundred bucks?"

Her eyes widened. "That's a lot of money."

"It is. I won't hurt you. I promise. I have a place right around the corner. I've been sleeping in the basement and could really use a blow job. You up for that?"

She got to her feet. "Yes. Can I have the money now?"

He glanced around and withdrew his wallet, taking out a hundred. "This for now. The rest for after." He made sure she could see the thick wad of bills.

"You got it, honey." She smiled and batted her eyelashes.

"Come with me."

She stayed right at his side as he returned to the shop and unlocked the door. The moment she stepped inside, she turned and reached for the front of his jeans.

"The bed is downstairs. I like to lie down. Bad knees."

Nervousness crossed her face as she glanced around at the dilapidated shop.

He withdrew his wallet again and took out another hundred, passing it to her. "I'm not into hurting women. I swear. Ten minutes at most and you'll be returning to your spot where I found you. I won't even last long. It's been a while."

She nodded.

He led the way and she followed. They were halfway down the stairs when he figured she'd finally see Mandy restrained to the counter. He spun, grabbed her, and put his hand over her mouth. She tried to scream as he carried her down the rest of the stairs, careful not to hurt her.

Mandy stared at him in shock as he approached.

"Take over her mind, damn it! She's terrified," he ordered.

Mandy's glowing gaze left his to focus on the woman. "Look at me. It's okay. Relax. You're fine. Everything is good."

76

The woman stopped struggling and he gently put her on her feet next to the counter, easing his hand away from her mouth. "You feed from her and let her think she gave some faceless guy a blow job. Can you do that? Also wipe this location from her mind, along with seeing you. I don't want her coming back here on her own looking to score more money from me."

Mandy glanced at him. "You're lucky she's susceptible to mind control."

"She's a drug addict. I've never met one yet who had the willpower to resist you Vamps. Feed, do your thing, and then I'll escort her out of here."

Mandy nodded and focused on the woman. "I want you to think of your favorite childhood memory. Do you understand? You'll be in that moment again," Mandy told her. "Nod if you're there."

The woman nodded.

"Lift your arm and put it to my mouth."

Glacier backed away, watching. Mandy had the woman adjust her arm until her wrist pressed against her lips, and then licked her skin, sinking her fangs in. The drug addict didn't even flinch. She just stood there grinning as if a Vamp wasn't taking some of her blood.

Mandy stopped and then bit her tongue, licking at the two puncture marks. It fascinated him, watching Mandy implant memories. One of the things she told the woman was to go buy food right away and eat.

She looked at Glacier then. "Now. She'll come out of her trance when you tell her thank you."

Glacier took the woman's hand, leading her upstairs and out of the shop. He left her on the street. "Thank you."

The woman stopped grinning and just walked away as if he wasn't there. He watched her enter a donut shop down the street. She never looked back once. He returned to Mandy. She lay on the bench with her eyes closed.

"Better?"

"Much. Thank you." Her eyes opened and she stared at his face with a frown.

"What?"

"You fed me. Why?"

"I don't want to see you suffer. Was that enough to last you a few days?"

"Yes. I didn't want to take too much though. She was pretty thin."

"Sorry. It was either pick up a hooker or a drug dealer. The latter wouldn't have willingly followed me down here without putting up a hell of a fight, thinking I planned on robbing him."

"I bet you have no trouble sweet-talking women into anything." She blushed. "Sorry. I fed but my body is still a bit, um, off. Thank you, Glacier. I mean it."

"You're welcome."

"I'm glad you're not a twisted sicko."

He let her words sink in. "You heard my talk with the pack and what that asshole said."

"Yes. I have good hearing and the door to the basement doesn't seem thick."

He strolled over to her and leaned down, not close enough for her to bite, but so he could really look into her eyes. The glow had faded to a deep blue. "Is that what you thought? That I'd wait for you to go into bloodlust and then fuck you?"

"No."

He believed her. "Good. Because I wouldn't do that. I have to go. Are you going to behave by staying quiet while I'm gone or should I gag you? Promise me you won't yell out trying to draw the attention of some human to set you free."

"I promise."

She still appeared to be sincere. "Trust is earned, Mandy. Don't fuck with mine. I don't give it easily. This is your chance to show me that some of the girl I used to know still lives."

"Why are you keeping me alive? The alpha wants me dead. I heard him."

He lifted his hand and brushed her hair off her face. It was slowly drying. "I don't answer to him."

"What are you doing, Glacier? I've been thinking, and you said you left my tracker with that Vamp's ashes. Do you think the council believes the remains are mine?"

"Hopefully." He liked how soft her skin felt as he caressed her cheek, his thumb tracing her jaw. "They won't look for you if they think you're

79

already dead. I have to go. Be quiet and try to get some rest. I'll be back after I help the pack take out the nest."

"Are you planning to let me go?" She looked as surprised as she sounded.

"I don't know what the hell I'm going to do yet." He released her and straightened. "Light on or off?"

"On."

He turned and walked toward the stairs.

"Be careful, and don't forget that Olivia is going to be out there hunting you."

He nodded and kept going. He locked the door at the top of the stairs and, for good measure, dragged a heavy counter over to block it. He knew the restrains would hold her in place but he worried about someone breaking in and getting to her. She was helpless. It didn't sit right with him but he couldn't trust her enough not to flee if he unchained her.

He withdrew his phone to call Kelzeb, needing to update him on what was happening with the pack and nest. He just wasn't sure what to tell him about Mandy.

Chapter Four

Mandy lay on the uncomfortable table, trying to figure out what Glacier was up to. He confused her. First, she thought he'd torture her, maybe want to see her suffer and beg for death...but then he'd fed her. He'd risked a lot by bringing a human to her. He had to know what would have happened if she couldn't have taken over the mind of that prostitute. Humans couldn't be allowed to know about Vampires. He'd have had to kill the woman.

"What the hell?" She chewed her bottom lip, closing her eyes. She shifted her body a little, trying to get comfortable. It was impossible.

The way he'd touched her had been nice, though. Caring, even. And who were Kelzeb and Lord Aveoth? She'd wanted to ask Glacier but he seemed a bit paranoid about giving her details of who he really worked for. Did the Werewolves have assassins, too? Some kind of council? They used to have a panel of judges for alphas to go to if packs had disputes they wanted to settle without a flat-out war, but as more packs had formed, intel said the judges had lost their power, with alphas no longer obeying their directives. Maybe the information had been wrong. It was possible they used the term lord instead of judge.

The nest would be extinguished by Glacier and the pack. She wondered what the council would do once they heard the news. Losing her and Olivia to Werewolves would shock them. Two highly trained assassins could handle a pack enforcer. It might make them reconsider sending more. She could hope, anyway. Maybe Glacier could contact the council to let them know what had really happened with that nest to get them targeted. A threat to get the VampLycans involved would definitely work. It was a suggestion she'd make when they talked next.

Her thoughts turned to Olivia, and sadness came with them. Glacier would probably find her soon, or go after her tomorrow while she day slept. Her best friend would wake to attempt to protect herself, but she wouldn't stand a chance against the big guy. He was unbelievably strong for a Were. She'd found that out when she'd struggled to get free of him while he'd carried her to the basement from the bathroom. The canvas had hampered her a lot since he'd wrapped her tight, but he could have broken bones with his strong arms securing her.

He was like some super Were, way stronger than even an alpha. She'd had to fight one once. He'd gone nuts after losing his mate and child in a freak accident. A bond that strong usually killed the surviving mate, but he'd lingered, losing more and more of his sanity instead. His own people had approached a nest for help since he had begun culling his pack. Anyone strong enough to take him on had already challenged him, and died as a result. That nest had sent for an assassin. She'd been the unlucky one who'd drawn the short straw. It had almost cost her left arm. He'd damn near amputated it with his sharp teeth and jaws before she'd been able to take him out.

She didn't hate Werewolves. That pack could have tried to kill her after she'd put down their alpha. He'd hurt her enough that she'd have been easy pickings. Instead, they'd given her their blood, which she'd taken, and offered to protect her while she day slept after the fight. She also respected how they could show emotions. It hadn't been a happy event, having their alpha put down by a Vamp. Most of them had openly cried but it needed to be done when he'd gone insane. It had hurt them to do it but they'd done what was best for the rest of the pack. He hadn't been fit to lead them anymore.

"Damn," she sighed.

A loud noise came from upstairs, and she tensed. The ceiling creaked as someone stomped above her, and then came the sound of something heavy scraping across the floor. The door to the basement shook but held.

Not for long. Wood smashed and she turned her head, watching as a big dark-haired man came down the stairs. She inhaled.

"Hello, Werewolf."

He growled low and walked to the side of the counter, keeping a few feet of distance between them. His gaze left hers to run down her body. "I knew you'd be a nice-looking piece of ass."

She recognized his voice. "You're Ted."

He snarled and took a step back. "How the fuck did you know that?"

"You don't want to do whatever you're thinking about. Glacier didn't let you down here, and I don't think he likes you much either. He'll make you pay for breaking in."

"As if I give a fuck."

Dread hit hard and fast. This wasn't good. It seemed she was about to die unless she could talk her way out of it. "I work for the Vampire Council. Glacier has been getting names and locations of other Vamps from me. I bet your alpha has ordered you to kill me, but I'm more valuable alive than dead until I answer all of Glacier's questions. I had no part of what happened to your pack children. I don't belong to that nest." She tugged on the restraints. "I can't get away. See? I'm no threat."

He lifted his hands and unleashed his claws. "You're a fucking Vamp. I don't care *who* you work for. Your kind needs to die."

Shit. "Glacier's going to be pissed. I would *not* want to get on his bad side. He's under orders to get information from me. You killing me could mean your own death. Think about that."

"Fuck him *and* Lord Aveoth."

He lunged, and Mandy screamed as his claws tore through the thin material covering her, ripping into her thigh and rib cage in the process. The scent of her blood filled the room.

He backed off, grinning. "Hurt? I bet that turns you on, doesn't it, you sick bitch."

"I don't want to fuck you," she gritted out. She'd like to declaw him and maybe shove the talons up his own ass. Blood pooled on the counter, soaking under her. He'd left bloody gouges across her skin. They were deep, too.

He walked around the counter to her other side, smirking. "Bet that stings. This will, too." He lunged at her again, his claws striking. He hit the same spots on her right side, tearing into her rib cage and the side of her thigh.

She screamed at the pain of having her flesh cut open.

He backed off before attacking again. That time he slammed his fist into her face. She turned her head against her bound arm and managed to avoid him breaking her nose, but she couldn't say the same about her cheekbone that took the brunt of the impact. Agony shot through her face. He was strong and vicious. She'd give him that.

Mandy closed her eyes and forced her body to go utterly lax, slowing her heartbeat and breathing. He dug his claws into her already injured ribs, poking at her bones. It hurt like a son of a bitch but she remained still, not making a sound.

"Goddamn it. Weak bitch. That's all it took to put you out?" he snarled.

His claws left her side and he began to slash at her clothes, scratching some of her skin since he didn't seem to care if he cut her up. He tore all of it off until he had every inch of her bared.

"Nice fucking bod." His hand cupped one of her breasts. "I'm going to have a good time with you."

Sick bastard. She remained still, keeping up the pretense of being unconscious. She heard a zipper go down and then he straddled her injured thighs. It was utter torture but she buried the pain.

He cursed when he tried to open her legs. Her ankles were restrained, legs together and arms above her, and Glacier had stretched her tight.

"Goddamn it!" He got off her and one of his hands gripped her ankle. He tugged on the cuff but it didn't come free.

She slit one eye and peeked down. He stared at the floor then backed up, kicking at the legs of the counter. She felt it all the way through her body. It took a few times, but he managed to break whatever held the chain in place that was linked to her ankle cuff. He started in on the other one until it broke, too.

"You know what I love about you bitches? I can do whatever I want and you turn to ash. No evidence left over. Nothing." He freed the chains and then gripped her calves, spreading them as he climbed on the table, straddling the end. "I don't smell Glacier on you. Stupid ass hasn't seen your potential. But I do. I'm going to wake you up and you're going to know what it's like to get fucked by an animal. And you're going to *love* how brutal I get."

When he scooted closer, she knew time was up. The bastard was almost between her thighs. He adjusted her legs until they lay over his, then released her to free his dick. It was the distraction she needed.

Mandy opened her eyes all the way, let her fangs drop, and swiftly jerked one leg to her chest. She kicked out as hard as she could.

Her heel connected with his nose. It hurt, but she knew he'd be in more pain.

He flew backward, landed briefly on his back, then flipped off the end of the workbench from gravity.

She rolled, the chains clanking and tripping her up, but she got to her feet.

He cursed loudly, snarling as she moved to the other end of the table. The chains kept her close to it, her wrists still connected. One glance down assured her the counter was secured to the floor on her end, and the chains were connected to the two legs. He'd kicked and broken two others to get her ankles free, but she wasn't wearing shoes. She'd break bones before she freed herself. Her body would mend but not fast enough, with her bleeding from what he'd done to her so far.

He rose up, hair covering his skin and face in a partial shift.

"I thought you looked bad in human form, but now you're super ugly."

He touched his bloody nose. Red ran down his mouth and chin, dripping onto his shirt. "You broke it!"

"Good."

He leapt up, landed on his feet to stand atop the bench, and glared down at her. "That was me being nice. Now I'm not going to be." He leapt, trying to kick her in the face.

She dropped to her knees, jerking on the chains.

He landed behind her and she hissed, knowing this was going to be bad for her. The damn chains pinned her to that location with only about five inches of room to move. She jumped up just as he hit her back, his claws tearing into her hips, trying to pin her over the bench. He slammed her hips into the unforgiving surface and dropped his weight on her.

"Right position," he snarled.

She threw her head back and made contact with his jaw, since he was a lot taller than her. He stumbled back, his claws tearing from her flesh. She twisted, kicked out, and nailed him where his dick was exposed. He roared, falling on his ass.

"What the *fuck*?"

Glacier's voice startled her, and she turned her head to see him at the bottom of the stairs. Pure rage showed on his face—and then he moved so fast she barely could track him.

He didn't come at her though—but at Ted behind her.

Mandy twisted her head just as he tackled Ted, sending him into the brick wall. She watched as he used his claws to punch the asshole a few times in the stomach. He backed off and Ted just sank to his ass. Blood poured from his wounds.

Glacier turned his head, his gaze raking her up and down. "Did he rape you?"

Her entire body trembled in relief at his arrival. "You got here in time."

Glacier turned away and bent, grabbed the groaning Werewolf from the floor, and hauled him up. He walked a few feet then slammed the Werewolf onto the counter in front of her and dug his claws into the man's scalp. It was Ted's turn to scream. Mandy actually winced at the sight of blood pouring on the counter from the brutal hold.

"Bite him," Glacier ordered. He used his other clawed hand to tear into the man's shirt and skin, exposing his shoulder and part of his back.

She was so stunned, she gaped up at Glacier.

"You're torn up and covered in your own blood. Bite him before he dies, goddamn it. You need to heal."

She hesitated.

"Do it *now*, Mandy. He's dead anyway."

She felt lightheaded and dizzy from blood loss and adrenaline. It might explain why Glacier seemed to have a gray pallor to his skin. She bent forward and sank her fangs into the already bloody flesh. She knew her face would be covered in blood, but she drank. Her injuries tingled as she took more than normal. They were healing.

Ted's heartbeat slowed and he tried to buck away a few times. Glacier held him down in front of her. She took her fill and then jerked away, tried to wipe her face, but her arms wouldn't reach that high. The chains kept them down near her rib cage.

Glacier released the guy's back and scalp, grabbed him by his head and snarled. "You've got no honor, and you're too stupid to live. I judge you rogue—and sentence you to death." He twisted hard, snapping the Were's neck.

Mandy watched as Glacier flipped the body over, bent a bit, and withdrew a dagger from his boot. He plunged the thing into Ted's chest and viciously twisted the handle.

"Don't you think that's overkill?"

Glacier held her gaze. "I've seen some tough fucking Lycans in my time. Breaking the neck doesn't always kill them. He's not coming back now with his heart shredded." He yanked the dagger free, wiped the blood off on Ted's shirt, and then shoved it back into his boot. He threw the body toward the corner and stepped closer to her.

Mandy peered up at him. He avoided her gaze as he walked around her and suddenly crouched. His hands were without claws as he gently touched her hips and then the sides of her thighs. Her body responded to his warm caresses as her nipples beaded in arousal. It made her a little embarrassed, knowing he was just checking to see if she healed.

"They won't scar. Hopefully. It usually only happens if he'd taken chunks out of me. Feeding right after getting hurt also manages to do miracles. I'll be okay, Glacier. I'm healing fast. I drank plenty of blood that time."

Glacier's fingertips grazed her stomach. "He died too fast."

"You're going to be in trouble for killing him. Blame me."

He snorted and straightened to his full height. "Look at me."

She did. He still looked furious but his features softened as she watched. "This building is considered my territory while I'm here. He trespassed. I'm not only going to admit I killed that bastard, but I'm going to hand-deliver his body to his alpha."

"What will they do to you?"

"There's nothing they can do. He earned death. Nobody fucks with me."

"I tried to warn him," she admitted. "That you'd be mad." She tore her gaze from his to glance at the body slumped in the corner.

Keys jingled and she looked back at Glacier. He reached for her wrist and unlocked both restraints, then the cuffs still attached to her ankles. She rubbed her wrists but held still.

"You need another shower. Go take one. I'm going to be late for my meeting with Kevin. Too damn bad for him. The sun is down enough that you won't burn. Two floors up." He jerked his head toward the stairs.

She still hesitated.

"Go. I'll take care of the body."

"You're going to trust me not to run?"

He reached out and cupped her face, his hold almost tender. "I'm a hell of a tracker, baby. You've seen me angry but never really pissed before. You won't run. I just saved your ass, and you know it. It would be a shit way to repay me."

"Why did you come back?"

"I left a second cell phone upstairs and kept the line open to be able to hear what you were doing. I was on my way to meet Kevin when I heard this dickhead break in. I got here as fast as I could. Luckily, I had only made it a few blocks since I had to fill my tank."

"You thought I'd wait for you to leave and then scream to draw a human," she guessed.

"But you only screamed when this prick was hurting you." He released her face. "Take a shower. Stay up there when you're done. I'll bring you something else to wear."

He wasn't lying to her, at least. She inched away from him and walked to the stairs. Part of her expected him to follow but when she glanced back, he was bending over Ted's body. She hurried up the stairs and into a shop. The back door was closed but it showed damage from being kicked in.

Just out that door was freedom. The sun was down enough for her to be able to move in the shadows. Her best guess was within five minutes, it would be completely dark.

Glacier was trusting her. That meant something.

She glanced around and saw another set of stairs leading to a second floor.

Staying was the right thing to do. Glacier hadn't hurt her. He'd protected her.

The bathroom was easy to find. She closed but didn't lock the door and turned on the water, running her hand over her newly healed flesh. It didn't hurt anymore but red streaks remained from the claw marks. They'd fade fast, though.

"You fucking idiot," Glacier muttered, not sure if he spoke to the dead enforcer or himself. He went under the stairs and pulled out another folded canvas tarp, wrapping up the bloodied body. He would need to find the idiot's keys, since he couldn't very well carry the corpse on his bike.

It made him feel sick imagining what could have happened to Mandy if he hadn't arrived so quickly. She was the Vampire who hadn't been able to bite elderly people in a hotel because she felt compassion for humans. He should have trusted her to stay inside the shop and not chained her down, leaving her defenseless against an attack.

Lesson learned. It wouldn't happen again.

He cocked his head, listening. Pipes squeaked. The old building had a lot of issues, including plumbing. She hadn't run but was instead showering. He'd figured it was a fifty-fifty split on what she'd do if given her freedom. Now he knew. Mandy was smart. The council would be after her if they realized she wasn't dead, and the Lycan packs lumped her in with the nest who'd murdered their kids. But she did have her Vamp friend in town to run to.

He carried the body up to the shop and dropped it on a counter. The back door was broken, thanks to the dickhead in the tarp. He lifted his phone, placing a call. Kelzeb answered on the second ring.

"I thought I wouldn't hear from you again until you hit the nest after dawn. Did something go wrong?"

"One of Kevin's enforcers decided to break into the shop I'm staying in and go after my Vamp. He's dead now."

Kelzeb sighed. "*Your* Vamp? I take it she's alive still?"

He gritted his teeth and sucked in a deep breath before blowing it out. "Yes, she is. Mandy isn't like most bloodsuckers. She's good, Kelzeb."

"Shit. What are you doing, Glacier? You killed a Lycan over a Vamp?"

"That bastard broke in here to hurt her. She was helpless, since I had her chained down. What kind of dick does that? He tore off her clothes, used his claws on her, and was about to rape her when I showed up. Don't expect me to apologize for taking out garbage!"

Kelzeb took his time to answer, long seconds passing. "I would have done the same. I take it you have feelings for this Vamp, since you sound so enraged?"

"Her name is Mandy, and I don't know what the hell I'm feeling. I just know she didn't deserve for that dickhead to go after her. I also don't know why the council trained her to do their dirty work. They must be idiots. I've spent time with her, and it's clear that she's too damn sweet to fit in with them."

"Calling a Vampire 'sweet' disconcerts me."

"She is. Wait until you meet her. You'll see what I mean."

"I don't want to meet your Vampire. Hell, I don't even want to know about her. I have to tell this shit to Aveoth. It always falls to me to spin some mess a guardian creates. This could become a shit-storm. The pack asked us to be there the help them, not kill one of their enforcers."

"He deserved it."

"Agreed, but it still won't sit well with the alpha. It never does. They could attack you as soon as they find out. Are you asking permission to fly out of their city and let them deal with the nest on their own?"

"No. I'm going to finish the job. The nest killed Lycan kids."

"And what of Mandy? Do you plan to turn her loose or are you taking her with you when you go on your next assignment?"

Glacier opened his mouth, not sure what to say.

"Let me make it very clear that you're responsible for her actions if you allow her to live. Make damn certain she's worth putting your ass on the line for. You set a killer free and any deaths are on you. You keep her at your side, and she falls under our laws. Including punishments."

"I hear you."

"We also have another problem if you keep her. You can't feed her, Glacier."

"I know."

"I mean it. It's too fucking dangerous."

"I know," he rasped.

"Are you thinking about making her your mate?"

He *didn't* know that one. But the idea of keeping her didn't sound half bad.

His silence must have answered for him.

Kelzeb loudly sighed. "It was stressful enough when Aveoth brought Jill here. She only has partial Vampire bloodlines. He loves her, and she's made him happy. Everyone deserves that. There's no way in hell you can bring a full-blooded Vamp home to the clan, though. We're not miracle

94

workers. You know the damn history we have with Vampires. Some of the clan will full-out rebel."

"I didn't say I wanted to bring Mandy to the cliffs."

"Good. To be clear, I also didn't say you couldn't keep her with you, since you don't live here. Update me if anything else happens."

"I will."

Kelzeb ended the call and Glacier shoved his phone into his pocket. He felt a bit stunned. Kelzeb hadn't ordered him to kill Mandy again, just made him responsible for her actions if he kept her. The threat of refusing a direct kill order from his boss was off the table. The tension eased inside him.

He didn't live at the cliffs, barely visiting the clan home, instead moving from job to job and whatever location he was sent. He could keep her. That was a real option now.

It changed everything.

He respected the hell out of Kelzeb for giving him the green light to proceed as he wished. Lord Aveoth would abide by his best friend and advisor's decision. The two of them were as close as he was to his own brothers.

He jogged upstairs to get Mandy something to wear. The water in the bathroom shut off right as he dug through his bag.

"I'm coming," he called out to her. "Just a minute."

Chapter Five

Mandy wore another baggy long-sleeve shirt and a pair of boxer briefs Glacier had given her. He'd led her into the bedroom. It was small, cracks marred the walls, and the only thing decent as far as furniture went was the queen-size bed. The sheets on it looked new, despite how it was unmade. He pointed at it and she took a seat. He crouched in front of her.

"Here's the deal. I need to get to the pack and plot going after the nest at first light. I'd let them handle this situation on their own but they've proven I can't trust them. Lycan kids are in danger if that nest remains functional. I refuse to let children pay for having a stupid alpha who doesn't vet his enforcers better."

She nodded.

"I'm not going to chain you up again to leave you defenseless. Ted might have equally stupid friends who could show up here."

She was surprised he'd trust her.

"I think you still have a heart in that bosom of yours, Mandy. Whatever you do, from this moment forward, my ass is on the line. I'm accountable. You fuck me over, my ass is going to be handed to me. Do you understand? I'm vouching for you."

Her mouth hung open but she closed it quickly. "Why would you do that?"

"Maybe I'm stupid, too." He glanced away but then back at her. "I'm willing to take the risk. Just be straight with me. Are you going to run? Leave the shop while I'm gone?"

She shook her head. "I'll stay."

"No luring anyone in, either. Fangs to yourself. You just fed."

"I promise. I won't need blood for days."

He put his hands on each side of her but keep inches of space from her hips. "You're allowed to defend yourself. Any Lycans come in, hand them their ass. Try to keep them alive though. Kill only if you must." He hesitated. "Fuck. Don't screw me over, Mandy."

"I won't." She peered into his eyes. "I swear, Glacier. I want you to take out that nest and keep them from hurting other children. Don't worry about me. I'll be right here when you get back."

"Okay. I have to go and find dickhead's SUV to tote his body in. Come downstairs with me and guard the door. I can't lock it since it's broken. Once I take his body out, use something to block it that a human would have a tough time pushing against. I want you to cover the windows up here while I'm gone, too. That will keep you safe at dawn. There's some plywood in a closet on the first floor. The basement is safer but it's too bloody. I know you don't do well scenting that. You'll stay up here tomorrow."

He rose up and held out his hand. She placed her smaller one in his and he pulled her to her feet. He let go and turned, giving her his back. It was a sign of trust.

She followed him down the short hallway and to the first floor, where he jerked open the back door and walked into the alley. The sun had gone down, and she felt at full strength thanks to the darkness and the blood she'd drank. Minutes passed, and then she heard an engine. A big white SUV pulled up in the alley and Glacier got out of the driver's seat. He entered, nodded at her, and then lifted Ted's body.

"Block it after me. I'll return well after the sun is up. Sleep in the bed but leave room for me. I'm going to be tired. Tomorrow night, we'll discuss what we do next."

"Be careful," she whispered.

He met her gaze and grinned. "This is what I do...and I'm damned good at it."

He left and she went to the door, watching as he shoved the body into the backseat, paying more attention to the street at the end of the alley than her. She was ready to take over any human minds if they saw anything. No one came down the alley though.

Glacier got in the driver's seat and drove off. Mandy closed the door and shoved hard to seal it.

She examined the busted doorframe and figured she could do her best to fix it if she could find some tools. It didn't take long to locate the closet with the plywood. A small toolbox rested on a shelf. Memories hit of her childhood but she pushed them back. It wouldn't be the first time she'd patched a door. Her father and brothers had been hell on a house with their short tempers.

An hour later, she entered the basement and began to clean up all the blood. It made her fangs come out but hunger didn't gnaw at her. The worst part about it was the strong chemical smells of bleach in the contained space with no window or fan. It was good to be a Vamp though, as she held her breath for minutes at a time, only taking in small amounts of air when her lungs burned for it.

She finished, then went back upstairs to wait.

* * * * *

Glacier slammed what remained of Ted down on Kevin's war table, scattering papers. The alpha and four of his enforcers appeared shocked at the body-shaped canvas.

"Ted decided to break into my lair to go after my prisoner."

Kevin gawked at him and then snarled.

"Don't." Glacier allowed his skin to partially shell in case the stupid bastard tried to attack him. "That prick tore her up and tortured her. I walked in while he was about to rape her. Do you really want to die for a piece of shit who didn't deserve his title?"

Kevin dropped his gaze to the tarp. "He wouldn't have done that."

"I brought you the body as proof. Unwrap his ass. His dick is still hanging out. I didn't close his pants, and you sure as hell won't find my scent on his crotch. Check his claws, too. You'll smell Vamp blood. I had her strung out flat on a counter with her legs together and her arms above her head. She didn't have a chance of fighting him off."

Glacier tore off his shirt and threw it at the alpha. Kevin caught it.

"Smell the blood on it. That's hers. Compare it to what's on him. My prisoner, in *my* lair, and that's your enforcer who went after her."

Glacier spun away and walked to a marked cabinet in the corner, yanked it open, and found a spare shirt in his size. All Lycans kept clothing in their war rooms since sometimes anger made them shift. He put it on and returned to the table. "Now, are we going to fight over an enforcer you couldn't control, or are we going to take out this nest who murdered some of your children?"

Kevin lifted Ted and carried him to the floor, unwrapped the canvas, and examined the body. He finally got to his feet, strode to the table, and began to sort the papers. He shoved one at Glacier. "You were right. There are some old sewer tunnels under that building. Two ways for them to escape. The water pipes were also upgraded in the seventies but they aren't big enough for anyone to crawl through."

Glacier relaxed and focused on the job at hand. "You're going to need to send two-person Lycan teams into the sewers to block off the openings here and here." He pointed at the blueprints. "I don't see gas lines in these plans. I'd go with automatic weapons. Go for brain shots if they enter the tunnels and take their heads after they're down. We don't know how many can day move. They won't be at full strength, but I'd rather be safe than have your Lycans overpowered."

"Weapons aren't honorable," Kevin rumbled.

"Neither is a nest stealing children and tormenting them to the point of pain-induced insanity to get them to fight each other to the death. They should have stuck to the rules if they expect *us* to. No offense, but the master is going to be coming through those tunnels when we breach the basement door. Shoot first and remove the head when they're down. I'd be the one going into the tunnel if there was only one. But there's two."

"It's only seven Vamps. I'm sure we can handle them without guns."

Glacier stared at Kevin and shook his head. "You're assuming the master hasn't made more, and that he hasn't mind-fucked armed humans

100

into helping defend his nest. *They* will have guns. I can't tell you how many times I've done this shit. I know what I'm doing. Your Lycans will be armed, Kevin. That's not up for debate. I'm sure they're excellent fighters, but they won't be if they're shot to shit by humans before the Vamps rush them."

Kevin paled.

"Been there, seen that happen. This asshole will have day guards, and they'll be armed. We're hitting them while they're trying to sleep. Do you want your Lycans shot full of holes, or able to defend themselves when the Vamps come rushing into those tunnels after sending in humans first?" Glacier arched an eyebrow.

"Fuck." Kevin turned to a blond enforcer. "Arm our men." He faced Glacier. "It will be loud though if there's gunfire. Humans will be drawn."

"That's why we're going to clear out all the humans in the restaurant above and blow the basement when we're done. We go out the sewer tunnels. Have vehicles waiting here." He pointed at the map of the tunnels. "The cops will arrive where the gunfire originates. We'll be long gone."

"Blow? We don't have any explosives."

Glacier grinned. "I do. This is not my first nest, as I've said many times before."

"How do we clear the humans?"

"We're going to dress up before we go into the restaurant as employees of the local gas company. Someone reported a gas leak and they need to exit the building fast. We hit hard at that point. I've already paid someone to steal the uniforms and two vans."

"Who?" Kevin frowned. "You trust a human not to screw us over?"

Glacier smiled again. "It's Graves."

Kevin paled. "*The* Graves?"

"Is there more than one?"

"Who the fuck is Graves?" Teenie had come in.

Kevin shifted his stance but kept quiet.

Glacier didn't hesitate. "He's the one packs normally call in when someone needs to die and for whatever reason, the alpha can't do it. His body count is so high, he's earned the name. He's also a friend. I called in a favor since he's between jobs."

"You brought a killer into my territory without my permission?" Kevin glared.

"You're never happy, are you? You complained because I wasn't a team player. I get in line and use a partner, yet here you are, doing it again."

"I wanted you to work with my pack."

Glacier jerked his head toward the body on the floor. "Yeah. Because you have your enforcers totally under your control." He snorted. "I trusted Ted to be smart enough to stay away from my prisoner. He wasn't. She works for the damn Vampire Council. Do you know much about how the council works, Kevin?"

The alpha shook his head.

"*She* does. Ted tried to kill our best source of information. I told Kelzeb." He glanced around at the other enforcers. "He's going to report what happened to Lord Aveoth."

Kevin looked visibly ill.

"Are we on the same page now? The Vampire prisoner in my lair is off limits to your damn pack. She's not a part of the nest who took your children. Lord Aveoth is very interested in learning about the Vampire Council. Am I clear?"

"Yes." Kevin didn't look happy though.

Glacier didn't give a damn as long as it kept anyone else from going after Mandy. "Make sure your pack is aware of that, Kevin. Your enforcers are supposed to follow your orders. Otherwise they can join Ted there on the floor."

Kevin growled low. "Let's get back to planning the attack."

Glacier was ready to let it go. He checked over the weapons they had, made a call to Graves to verify everything was in order, and then took the time to eat.

His mind kept returning to Mandy. He hoped she wouldn't run. There was no guarantee she wouldn't flee to her friend, since he hadn't taken out the other assassin. The pack was on lockdown, which meant they weren't out there hunting Vamps. Olivia wouldn't have any targets to kill.

What if the other Vampire assassin was like Mandy? He believed they hadn't had a choice to work for the council. It might be a lie, but he had become a good judge of character at his age. He sighed and placed another call when he was alone.

"If it isn't my brother from the same mother."

He chuckled at Pest's version of hello. "I need some advice."

"Shit. What kind of mess are you in now? Did the alpha try to compare dicks with you and you lost? I guess I could show him mine to save our family honor."

"Fuck you." He laughed though. Pest definitely earned his nickname. His humor faded. "I captured myself a Vamp."

"Okay. And that's like saying it's Monday."

"It's one I used to know when she was human, and the thing is..." He peered around to make certain no one was in earshot. "She kept her humanity."

"This isn't sounding good. Were you ordered to kill her? I see the problem already. I'd have a hard time with that too, if it was someone I once knew and they seemed decent. What kind of crime did she commit?"

"It's not like that. I mean, the alpha ordered me to take her out but you know how that goes. He believes all Vamps are better off dead right now."

"Who gives a shit what he wants? He's not our boss. What did Kelzeb say?"

"I can't bring her to the Cliffs and I'm responsible for her actions. He made it clear he wasn't going to order me to put her down."

Pest said nothing.

"You there?"

"Um, yeah. You're banging her, aren't you? What the hell are you thinking? I mean, they aren't fragile like a human but you still have to be damn careful with one in bed. They bite, bro. Huge *no* on that shit. What do you do? Muzzle her? Just take her from behind and watch her fangs?"

"I haven't slept with her."

"I hear a 'yet' in there."

He couldn't deny he wanted Mandy. "You dated a Vamp once."

"For like a week, and she kept trying to bite me. It's why it didn't last. The sex was hot but it's like surfing a landslide. It's just a matter of time before it turns into disaster and you end up burying your own ass. You want my advice? Fuck her until she's out of your system and then run."

He closed his eyes and sighed.

"She needs to feed, and you can't be the meal." Pest's voice dropped low, sympathy coming through. "That's the one law we can't ever break. Too much is at risk."

"I know."

"It's doomed. Think about it. What happens if you get too possessive of her, or worst case, fall in love? How are you going to feel, watching her feed off others? It would drive you insane. It's against the law for us to give blood to Vamps. You'll be signing her death warrant if you ever slip in bed, Glacier. You care about her? Get the hell away."

"It's fucking complicated."

"How do you feel about this Vampire?"

He sighed. "Highly attracted; always was and still am."

"Then run, bro. For her sake as well as your own. Sometimes caring means saying goodbye. This is a prime example."

"The Vampire Council will be after her. Hell, according to her, *everyone* will be. I set her free and she'll be on her own. She won't last long. They'll kill her."

"That *is* complicated." He paused. "I have some days free. I'm coming to you."

"No need."

"I'm your brother. You called me. You wouldn't do that unless you're in over your head and thinking about doing something stupid. We'll sit down together, have some beers, and talk all this out. I'm packing a bag now and will hit the air. I should be there by morning. I know where you are."

"Mandy is at the shop I'm staying in. Don't scare her."

"I won't hurt your Vampire."

"Mandy."

"Damn. You have it bad, don't you?"

"I used to, and she hasn't changed, besides the Vampire thing."

"It's a big fucking *thing*, bro."

"See you in the morning, Pest. I'll be there after the sun is up. Oh, and um, she can move around after dawn. Heads-up. Don't flip out on her."

"How old is she? I didn't know you were into cougars."

He chuckled. "Long story. I'll share it with you tomorrow."

"See you soon."

Glacier ended the call and sighed, getting up and returning to the war room inside the pack house. The Lycans were too hyped up to sleep. He knew they would be.

Chapter Six

Mandy heard a knock on the door at around five in the morning. She frowned, grabbing a hammer.

"Hello? Mandy? Don't attack. I'm coming in."

"I just fixed that door. Don't break it. Who are you?"

"Glacier sent me. I'm his brother."

Curiosity immediately got the best of her and she unlocked the door, opening it up. There was no doubt the big man who stood in the alley was related to Glacier. They had the same handsome facial features, black hair, and sheer body size. She backed up fast, keeping her distance.

He entered, closed the door behind him, and smiled.

"Damn, you're short. No wonder you have my brother in overdrive on the protective instincts." He put a backpack on the floor then crossed his arms over a T-shirt stretched across his wide chest. "I'm Pest."

She gawked at him a bit, perplexed by the name.

"Tempest, but don't call me that. And I wasn't named after a girl. Our mother had a thing for weird-ass names. I was born during a violent windstorm. Glacier got stuck with his name because he was born during a bad winter with big-ass ice chunks as far as the eye could see. My friends call me Tem, but my family calls me Pest. I hate being teased about my name...and we don't want to start off on the wrong foot, do we?"

She shook her head. "Is Glacier okay?"

"He was fine, last I spoke to him."

"Did he send you here to keep me safe from the pack in case another enforcer tries to attack me?"

"Sure. We'll go with that."

She frowned.

"He didn't say much. Fill me in on this enforcer."

She replayed what happened with Ted. Anger grew on Pest's face as she spoke, making him look a lot more like Glacier. He made a low rumble sound when she finished.

"That explains the patchwork on the door. I'm glad my brother killed the bastard. I would have done it too. Point me to the basement and I'll clean up the blood. I hate leaving evidence behind."

"I already did that," she admitted.

"You're handy. So, what's your story? How'd you become a Vamp?"

"I was grabbed in a parking lot. The Vampire Council had already decided to cleanse the nest responsible, and they kept me alive since I was brand new in Vamp land. I had just barely finished transforming when they stormed in. The council figured I hadn't been mentally fucked up yet by the master."

"Cleanse?"

"Let's just say Cain was a shit master who ran a dangerous nest. He liked to send out male Vamps to find women to add to his harem. But he drew too much attention from humans, since he didn't care if we'd be missed or not. His males didn't exactly ask if the women were married, had kids or families. They grabbed anyone they thought Cain would like, regardless of the fallout with their loved ones filing missing persons reports and raising hell on local media outlets for the women to be found. The council wiped out the nest."

"Glacier said something about you working for the council. What do you do?"

She moved over to a counter and hopped up, taking a seat. "I'm an assassin."

He laughed deeply, obviously thinking she was joking.

"I'm serious."

He grinned. "Sure you are, short stack."

"I really am an assassin for the council. At least, I was. Now they hopefully think I'm dead, since your brother removed the tracker from my body and left it with an ashed Vamp that I killed."

He moved over to another counter and leaned against it, crossing his arms again. His blue eyes glinted with some emotion she couldn't identify but he stopped smiling. "You lure men into fucking you and take them out while their guard is down?"

"Never."

He rumbled again, a low growl coming from his chest. "That's the only damn way someone your size would be able to kill, unless they send you after humans only."

"I'm a lot stronger and faster than you can imagine, Pest." She was starting to see why his family called him that.

"How old are you?"

"Just under three decades in Vamp years."

"I call bullshit. My brother said you aren't a full snoozer when the sun comes up. That means you're way older."

"The council feeds us their blood to wean out some weaknesses and to boost our strength. We'd be shitty assassins otherwise. Newbies are too easy to kill and full day sleepers would be at risk on assignment. Any Vamp could hire a human to take us out while we were down."

"Unbelievable."

"It's the truth."

"Why are you lying to me and my brother about your age?"

She shrugged. "I'm not. Glacier knows. He knew me in nineteen eighty-nine before I was turned into a Vamp. We worked together in a dance club."

"Dance club?" He frowned. "The cult leader assignment Glacier had?"

"I guess so."

He paled a little.

"What? Are you okay?"

"I'm fine. You're *that* Mandy? Shit."

"He mentioned me to you?"

"Yeah. We had a job together a week after he took out that cult master, and he got shitfaced drunk. That wasn't like him. I asked what was wrong and he told me about a Mandy. You'd asked him out on a date but he'd had to turn you down, since relationships aren't something we do in our line of work. Then you quit your job. He felt guilty as hell that he'd hurt your feelings that much."

111

"I didn't quit. I was taken by a nest that same night."

"He didn't know. Otherwise, he would have gone hunting. He believed he was the reason you'd quit the club, to avoid him, and not knowing he was leaving town anyway since the job was over."

Questions floated in her head but she didn't dare ask who they worked for. He might have the same reaction Glacier had, suspecting she was some kind of spy or something. "He said it was him, not me."

"That's the truth. We go from one job to the next. Sometimes we're in a place for one night, to…hell. It could be weeks, months, or even years. It depends on our preferences. I like short-term assignments. Glacier is more patient. He's stuck it out for months at times in the same place. Our youngest brother probably won't ever change locations, since he's protecting his mate's pack. Creed is their guardian. We're talking decades in the same job."

"Guardian?"

He cocked his head. "You don't know what a guardian is for a Lycan pack?"

"I'm assuming it's a position like an enforcer. I can't keep up with the Werewolf pack titles or their pecking order. I know they have one alpha, a bunch of elders, and I've met an advisor from a pack once." She shrugged again.

He threw back his head and laughed. "You think Glacier and I are Lycans, don't you?"

She sniffed the air. "You smell like one." She was confused. "Are you half-breeds?"

"Oh yeah." He grinned.

She thought about Glacier's strength. "That's amazing."

"What is?"

"Your brother's very strong for being half human."

Now he roared with laughter. "Fucking priceless!"

Mandy frowned. "What am I missing?"

He pushed away from the counter and winked. "I'm so glad I'm here. I can't wait to watch this go down."

"What are you talking about?"

"Nothing. Is there a spare bedroom?"

"No. There's just one." She pointed up. "It's where your brother told me to stay."

"I'm good with the floor. I'll find a spot when I'm ready to sleep. It wouldn't be the first time. At least this place has a roof. I'm going out to grab some food. I'll be back before the sun rises. You going to be okay on your own for twenty minutes?"

"Yes."

"Lock up after me. You'll hear me when I get back." He left then, just strolling out. She heard him chuckling though, and it made her wonder what he found so funny.

He came back with fast food, grabbed his backpack and went up the stairs. She followed. He stretched out in the hallway to eat his burger and fries.

"The sun's coming. I noticed you boarded up the windows in there. Go ahead and sleep. Nothing will get past me but Glacier when he arrives. You're safe."

"Thank you. I can stay up though. I get a bit weaker after daybreak but it doesn't put me in a coma." She leaned against the wall. "What was so funny before?"

"Ask my brother your questions, little Mandy."

"Are you half human?"

He grinned.

"You're not going to answer me, are you?"

"Nope." He finished his burger and used his pack for a pillow, stretching out flat on the floor. "Go rest. I know Glacier was going to take out a nest this morning." He removed his cell phone, tapping the screen. "I'm going to read until he gets back."

"What are you reading?" She was curious. He didn't appear to be the book type.

"End of the world shit. It always amuses me, reading about zombie apocalypses and how humans think that would go down."

"You're a weird man, Pest."

She walked into the bedroom and lay down on the bed. Glacier's scent filled her nose. The sun began to rise and her body relaxed. She closed her eyes to let sleep come. It was possible that Pest might hurt her but she trusted Glacier. He'd sent for his brother to protect her from the pack. He'd have killed her himself if he wanted her dead. She'd given him plenty of chances.

She dozed—until someone touched her shoulder.

Her body tensed and she came up fast, ready to defend herself. Instinct had her hands fisted, prepared to fight.

Pest leapt back, grinning wide.

"Sorry. Just checking to see if you really could wake up. Go back to sleep."

"Forget Pest...you should be called asshole."

He laughed again, leaving the room. "I've heard that before. Night, short stack."

She lay back down, closed her eyes, and let sleep take her before her worries about Glacier took hold.

* * * * *

Glacier motioned to the Lycans to stay behind him. The gas company uniform Graves had acquired for him and the team didn't fit well. The building had been cleared and the teams covering the escape tunnels hadn't reported any problems. Nor had he heard any guns going off. The basement was hidden but he located it quickly, pulling a handgun as he took the lead down the stairs.

It was a storage room full of things from the restaurant. Another door led to more of the basement. That one was locked. He lifted a leg, kicking it in.

Five Vampires slumbered on the floors. None of them moved. He walked in with Kevin on his heels.

"Shit."

115

"What?" Kevin inched closer. "This has gone down better than we planned."

"The master isn't here."

"How do you know?"

"You see any of these bastards stirring? Attacking us? The fucker left his nest here undefended, too. No human guards. There should be seven of them, not five."

"Let's kill them," one of the enforcers snarled.

"Hang on." Glacier pulled out his cell phone.

Kevin got in his face. "They killed our children!"

"I didn't say you can't kill the bastards. I just want to take photos of them and show their faces to the council Vampire. She's met them. She'll be able to tell me if these are part of the original nest or just newly turned ones the master left here for us to find." Glacier allowed his irritation to show. "This is too damn easy."

He ignored the growls from the pissed-off Lycans and snapped pics of each sleeping face. "Done. Go head. Get your revenge."

He left them in the room, hunting the storage area for any other hidden doors or spaces a Vampire could hide. He even jogged upstairs to check out the restaurant. The master and last remaining nest member were still missing.

Kevin returned to him. "Blow it up."

"There's no need. Have your men sweep up the ash and check for cameras. I was going to blow up the building when I expected a bloodbath. This is an easy cleanup job."

116

"The humans who own this restaurant helped the Vampires. Blow it up!"

Glacier had the urge to deck the demanding prick. "You mean the humans who were probably mind controlled against their damn will? *Those* humans? I'm not blowing it up. Have your enforcers clean up any ash, make sure there're no security cameras, and if there are, take them, along with the recording equipment. I'm out of here."

He walked toward the door.

"I'll burn it down," Keven snarled.

Glacier swung around. "You still have a master and at least one nest member in your town. You do that, and I'm fucking out of here. A fire could spread to other buildings, hurting innocents. Stop being a dick. You've killed five Vamps today. There's no reason to destroy the place where they slept."

He stormed out and climbed into the driver's seat of one of the vans, starting it. The Lycans could pile into the second one. He drove away.

He returned the van to a secluded parking lot and spotted a familiar face. Graves came forward, the Lycan looking grim. "That was fast. Did they move locations?"

"The master wasn't there. He probably took his second-in-command with him since another was missing. I'm just hoping he didn't turn five humans and leave them there in the hopes of fooling the pack that they got the ones responsible for their dead kids. Then again, the alpha is a dick. I doubt he'd give a shit if those were the guilty ones or not." Glacier removed the uniform he wore over his clothes and threw it into the van.

"I've heard that about Kevin. Hotheaded, not too bright, and his control on his pack isn't the best. I've had to come to this area three times before to take down idiots who used to belong to him. He's shit at policing his own."

"Thanks for your help."

Graves nodded. "You need anything else?"

"Get rid of the explosives in the back of the van and wipe it down for me?"

"You got it. I could stick around for a few days if you need help locating this master. I don't usually track neck suckers but it wouldn't be the first time."

"One of my brothers flew in overnight. We've got this handled, but thanks with the van and uniforms. It was a high-traffic part of town. No way were we getting into that restaurant without drawing a hell of a lot of attention. The ruse worked."

"I've had to make a lot of contacts in my line of work." Graves shrugged. "No biggie. I'm always willing to help out the clans. Nobody wants humans to become suspicious. You've helped me out in the past."

"Still, grateful to you." Glacier held out his arm.

Graves gripped it and they nodded at each other. "I think I'll hang out for a day or two, just in case. Call me if you need anything."

"Thanks. I'm going to return to the shop and say hello to my brother."

"Watch out for Kevin. Not kidding about the hothead part. You never struck me as one to get along well with assholes."

Glacier chuckled. "I think we have that in common."

"You know it." Graves released him, striding toward the van.

Glacier went to his motorcycle and climbed on. He hated to wear a helmet but it was a human law in the state. He shoved it on, started the engine, and glanced around. The sensation of being watched struck suddenly, but he brushed it off just as quickly. It was probably Graves. He drove away, heading toward the shop.

Pest opened the door to the alley after Glacier finished parking. He hugged his brother, glad to see him. "You made it. Thanks for coming."

"Is she really an assassin for the Vampire Council? Because I have to tell you, I laughed when she said that."

"It's true."

"Fuck. I guess they get points for surprise, since who'd have thought, huh?"

"Is she sleeping?"

"Yeah. It's why I came down to talk to you. She can actually wake during the day. Are you sure she's as young as she claims?"

"I knew her when she used to be human. Did she tell you there's a second assassin in town, too?"

Pest scowled. "No."

"It's another woman, happens to be Mandy's best friend, and it seems the council doesn't exactly take no for an answer when they give their Vamps an order. I'm the target the council sent them after."

"Do you want me to go hunt the other assassin down and take her out?"

"No. I plan to avoid her at all costs. That way, I don't have to explain to Mandy that I had no choice but to kill her bestie."

Pest cocked his head, narrowing his eyes. "And you care…why?"

"Mandy was always a sweetheart. She still is. The change didn't harden her heart."

"You *hope* it didn't."

"You spent time with her. What do you think? Gut instinct, Pest."

His brother sighed. "I thought her being an assassin was a fucking joke. She seems soft. Like maybe she was just turned and hasn't seen any shit yet."

"She claimed to have grown up with a domestic violence background, but wanted to be a better person back when I knew her. I don't think that's changed. She's just not human anymore."

"What can I do to help while I'm here, bro?"

"I don't trust Kevin. One of his enforcers already came after her. I didn't mention to the pack that you flew in. I can't be in two places at once, and I'm here to wipe out that nest… Mandy isn't included."

"What the hell are you going to do with her when this mission is complete?"

Glacier shook his head. "Fuck if I know."

"You're in dangerous waters."

"No shit. She doesn't deserve to die though. You met her, Pest."

"I also remember you being upset about a human named Mandy on that cult-leader wannabe job a long time ago. Same woman, right?"

"Yes."

"Shit." Pest sighed. "You still have feelings for her. It's never a good thing, and the fact that she's a Vamp? Monumental bad idea to get involved. You know the score. There's no win here."

Glacier didn't need to be told that. "One day at a time right now."

Pest snorted. "I'll keep short stack safe, but you need to figure this mess out and find a solution. Does Kelzeb know you have a past with her?"

"He's got an idea. I've told him enough."

"Did you tell him I flew in?"

"Nobody knows you're here but me, Mandy, and I told Graves."

"He's not one to talk. He's in town?"

"I needed a few favors."

"Get some rest. You look tired. I'm sleeping in the hallway outside the bedroom. Couldn't you have found somewhere to stay with two bedrooms? And for fuck's sake, don't let her bite you if you do the nasty."

Glacier clenched his teeth and entered the shop, his brother behind him. He avoided going upstairs though. It would be a bad thing to climb into bed with Mandy. "I'll sleep on the floor down here."

Chapter Seven

Mandy woke alone but she heard murmured male voices she identified downstairs. The sun hung low in the sky, judging by her instincts. She climbed out of bed, made a stop in the bathroom to freshen up, and walked down the stairs. The voices became silent.

Glacier and his brother were seated on the floor eating sandwiches and bags of chips. Both flashed her smiles but they didn't reach their eyes.

"How did it go with the nest? Are they extinguished?"

"Not all of them. Come here." Glacier patted the floor next to him. "You met the nest, right?"

"Briefly." She carefully sat, tugging at the shirt to keep her modesty since she wasn't wearing pants. It was one of Glacier's though, fitting her more like an oversized dress.

Glacier withdrew his phone and handed it to her. "See if you can identify any of these faces as being nest members."

She stared at the first one. "Yes."

He reached over, their hands touching as he flipped to another pic. She studied it.

"Yeah. Mr. Ugly Shoes. They were orange with green marker on the sides. Not something I'd forget."

"Tell me if any of these are the master." Glacier flipped to another, and then another pic, five in all. She had seen them with Marco the night she'd met him. All of them were slumbering in the pictures.

She turned her head, staring up at him. "Marco isn't one of them. What's going on?"

"I suspected that but wanted confirmation. Marco and one other nest member weren't sleeping under the restaurant this morning, but he'd left *them* behind."

She frowned. "How many day guards?"

"None."

She thought about it. "He sacrificed them to switch up the game. Damn. Call your alpha friend and tell him to expect an attack tonight."

Glacier took his phone back and pocketed it. "You think the hunted will become the hunters?"

"Old tactic, unfortunately, right out of the shitty-master playbook. He left them there to die, probably even put word out on the street where they were located to make sure the Werewolves found them, and now he'll go after the alpha tonight. Cut off the head of a pack and chaos results. Marco knows the enforcers will challenge each other to take leadership. At best, a few will die, or they'll be severely injured if it's not death matches. It will make it easier for him to kill them all."

"Maybe he just ran."

She looked over at Pest, shaking her head. "Marco is a conceited jackass. He'd never live it down if a pack chased him out of his own town. He's also got connections to someone on the council. It would be an unforgivable embarrassment if he fled his territory. Nothing would make him lose face faster than that. It might even earn him a spot on an assassin's hit list. No. He kept Pedro alive, since he's not one of the Vampires in the photos. That's his second. I'd bet money Marco has been feeding him his blood to make him stronger. The two of them will go after the alpha first. Then, while the enforcers are distracted by deciding who leads the pack, he'll attack. Marco and his second won't stop until every Were they consider a threat is dead. I've seen it happen before."

Glacier stood. "Fuck. I better get my ass to pack headquarters."

"You'd better hurry. I can sense that the sun is down enough that I could go outside as long as I stick to the shadows. It's why I'm not worried about the dirty windows down here. Who knows how close Marco and his second got to pack territory, to be able to strike fast? Marco will know the Werewolves will have their guard down, assuming they've been victorious."

Glacier rushed toward the back door. "Stay together."

She jumped up, moving in case some sunlight streamed in. "Be careful!"

He was gone and she heard a motorcycle engine rev, then take off fast. Pest locked the door and retook his seat on the floor. "It almost seems as if you want to help the pack instead of your own kind. Curious."

"Marco targeted pups. He's not worthy of my protection. I hope Glacier kills him."

"Sit down. Are you hungry? I'm not offering my blood, but I could escort you outside to grab a bite. It's a shit neighborhood. You probably wouldn't even have to leave the alley."

"I'm fine. I fed last night when that Werewolf attacked me. I'm good for a few days."

"So not a newbie."

"I keep telling you that. I'm highly trained, and ancient bloodlines have been introduced to my body. I only suffer from hunger after about three days of going without blood."

"How does that work? You having abilities that only older Vampires should have?"

She sat back down on the floor. "You want the official Vamp bullshit, or *my* take on it?"

"Yours."

"I view Vampirism like a virus. I got upgraded to better, stronger strains of it."

He chuckled.

"It's kind of true. Just never repeat that I called it that. Vamps get bent out of shape being called a virus. They like to think it's more of a gift from the gods or some such shit. Only the blessed are turned, according to the council. Yeah, right. I've taken out plenty of jerks who were probably psychopaths as humans and grew ten times worse after being turned. Anyway, the older a Vamp gets, the more strength they acquire. The virus grows stronger. Sharing their blood with weaker Vamps makes the weak ones stronger. But masters won't offer their wrists to just anyone in a nest after they've been turned, unless that master absolutely trusts them. Enough feedings and they'd become equal in strength. Not a good idea, since most masters are dicks who'd end up being killed by their own nests. It's against council laws, but they might get away with it if they all stuck to the same story and blamed someone else. That's what I'd do if I thought I could get away with taking out a few of the council members."

He laughed deeper. "I like you, short stack."

"Mandy."

His humor faded and something weird happened with his eyes. They seemed to darken from blue to near black. "My brother is protective of you. That's a problem."

She eyed him warily. "Are you going to try to kill me? It would be nice to have a warning of your intent."

"No. Glacier wouldn't forgive me for that unless I was given no choice. But I *will* chain your ass to that bench downstairs if you attempt to leave or bite me."

"Fair enough. I gave Glacier my word that I would stay here. I don't make promises unless I plan to keep them. I also don't bite for the hell of it. I told you, I'm not hungry."

"How do you see this ending?"

She shrugged. "I'm not sure what you mean."

"With Glacier. This assignment will end as soon as that master is dealt with. He'll be sent somewhere else. Do you expect him to just let you go? Send you on your way?"

"Truthfully? I don't know why I'm still alive. I've given him opportunities to kill me. I even stepped into the shower to make it easier for him to cut off my head. No mess, no hassle. He didn't do it." She sighed. "As for going free? The council has all their property—that would include me—embedded with trackers. We go off grid and they put death orders out on us. There's no escaping them. Glacier removed my tracker, but that doesn't mean the council necessarily believes I'm the ashes Olivia would have found when she was sent to find out what happened to me. Even if they do, someone will see me at some point if he lets me go.

126

Nowhere would be safe for me to hide. As I've told your brother, I'm already dead, Pest. I figure I'll meet the sun when your brother leaves, if he doesn't have the heart to kill me himself."

He looked a bit stunned.

"Any more questions?"

"You want me to believe you'd ash yourself?"

"It would be better than being captured and taken before the council. Those bastards can think up a thousand ways to make me scream in agony, heal me, and do it all over again before they finally allow me die. I know exactly how vicious Vampires can be. They'd set an example by me and probably force all the other assassins to watch it go down. To see a sunrise one last time doesn't sound so bad in comparison, does it?"

"It would hurt."

"I've been thrown out into the sun more than once during training. Believe me, I know. But it would be quicker than being tortured."

"You could try to kill my brother and take your council his head. They'd forgive you if you admit he captured you and stole your tracker."

She felt sadness at his words. "Wow, either your opinion of women in general sucks or you've met some seriously shitty Vampires in your lifetime. Glacier is a protector. He's a good man. My life already ended when I was turned into this. I've tried to do my best to survive since. Never has that included murdering someone who I knew didn't deserve it. This Vampire has lines she won't cross. I'd never hurt Glacier. *Ever*." She got up. "Enough of this topic. It's depressing. I'm going to go take a shower. Is that alright?"

127

"Are you going to try to run?"

She shook her head. "What part of 'I keep my promises' did you not understand? But go ahead and stay on alert. Just do it from outside the bathroom, please. I wouldn't fit through that tiny window and you'd hear if I tried to break through a wall."

She walked upstairs and entered the bathroom, firmly closing the door behind her. She turned on the water, waiting while it heated before finally stripping off the oversized shirt she wore. Her thoughts were centered on Glacier, worried about him.

* * * * *

Glacier felt utter disgust. Kevin, his enforcers, and a large part of the pack weren't in lockdown anymore. Instead they were outside, most of them drunk, throwing a party. Graves had been right about the pack being led by an idiot.

He approached the alpha. "What the hell?"

Kevin faced him, grinning. "We didn't need you after all. Why are you still here?"

"The master and his second are still on the loose. You know this."

Kevin snorted. "Who cares? He's probably in another state. We scared the shit out of them and they're running for their lives. Have a drink, GarLycan. Chill out. We won!"

"Marco is going to come after you with his second, kill you, and then pick off your pack while they're in turmoil without an alpha."

"Let the fuckers try," Kevin snarled. He took a step toward Glacier and staggered.

Glacier grabbed him by his wrists. "You're drunk and can't even walk straight. Do you honestly think you could fight a master Vamp and win in this condition? Sober up!" He shook him hard and released him.

Kevin began to shift, his claws and fur sprouting.

Glacier wasn't in the damn mood for a pathetic fight.

He decked him in the face, knocking him out cold. The alpha's body hit the ground and everyone at the party became absolutely silent. Shock showed on their features as Glacier glanced around. He shelled his skin until it became a light gray.

"The party is over. Your alpha is too damn drunk to be rational right now. You called me here to deal with this Vamp situation. Everyone seek shelter immediately and return into lockdown mode. Spread the word if anyone left the area. They are in danger. *All* of you are. There's a master Vamp and his second on their way here." He pointed to an enforcer. "Pick Kevin up and carry him to the war room. Take at least six fighters with you to guard his ass. You hear me?"

Teenie rushed forward. "You're taking over the pack?"

"For tonight, yes, I am. Follow my orders." He stripped his upper body and let his wings come out. "I'm going to be patrolling the air. Everyone in lockdown. I'll handle this mess. You just stay alive."

He launched himself into the air. Kelzeb wasn't going to be happy about what he'd done to Kevin or how he'd taken control of the situation, but he'd deal with it later. He'd become a guardian to protect packs from

129

threats, even idiot alphas. He'd be damned before he allowed them to be slaughtered.

He flew high, scanning the woods at the edge of the city. He didn't spot two Vampires but they could already be inside the territory, hiding in one of the Lycan homes abandoned after the pack had gone into lockdown. He turned, flying toward the pack house where the majority of Lycans had been staying. That would be the target.

He landed on the roof of the pack house and crouched, alert. It might be a long night but come morning, he and Kevin would have issues. The alpha would probably want to challenge him. It wasn't as if he'd had a choice to pull rank the way he had. He just didn't plan to become their new alpha.

A short time passed, and finally he spotted movement near the trees.

Four dark-clad figures darted closer, keeping out of the open.

He lifted to his feet, spread his wings, and coasted to the ground. His boots made a thumping sound as he landed. He shelled his skin into battle mode. It would slow him down a little but also deflect bullets if the bastards were armed. He strode forward, right toward them.

"Marco."

All four of them hid behind thick tree trunks. Glacier sighed. "I saw you. Stop dicking around. I am in no mood to play hide-and-seek. I'm Glacier, the GarLycan. You went after Lycan kids. Big fucking no. Step out here and speak to me."

None of them moved. He inhaled. "I smell you, Vamps. See the wings? I fly. You can't outrun me. Talk, or I'm just going to rip you apart. Your call. Make it."

130

One of the men stepped out from behind a tree but stayed next to it. "This is none of your concern, GarLycan."

"Are you Marco?"

The man inclined his head slightly.

"You made two more Vamps? I counted four of you."

"I don't answer to you."

"Wrong. It became my problem when you stole Lycan kids and killed them. I found the warehouse where you held them." It still sickened him. The bodies had been shoved in the basement, dumped in trash bags as if they were garage. "You put them in cages, tortured them, based on the amount of blood I found in that hellish holding place, and then made them fight against each other in your fucked-up fighting ring. Did you really think you could get away with that?"

"Yes." Marco flashed his fangs and his eyes glowed bright.

Glacier felt what the bastard was trying to do. "You're wasting your time, asshole. Gargoyles have thick skulls. You can't fuck with my head."

Marco reached back and withdrew a handgun.

"It tickles a little when you try to control me." Glacier reached up and tapped his temple. "Just a little buzz, like some annoying insect. And you think bullets will take me down? You're as stupid as the alpha of this pack." Glacier hardened his shell a little more and pushed out his chest, keeping his hand up, ready to protect his eyes. They were the only soft spots he had.

Marco began to fire.

Glacier threw his arm over his eyes, feeling bullets slam into his chest, one to his hip, and another grazing the top of his head.

He lunged forward, spread his wings wide and jumped high, spinning in the air as he came down.

A scream pierced the night and the gun stopped firing.

Glacier lowered his arm, staring at the Vampire on the ground. His wing had cut the bastard in half near his rib cage. Horror transfixed the master's features as he realized his entire lower body wasn't attached anymore, and had already begun to ash.

"NO!"

"Yeah. That's some fucked-up shit right there," Glacier admitted. "You bastards are hard to kill without taking your head. You can live like that for a bit. I've seen it before. Your heart is still beating. You won't be able to feed though since you lost your stomach. You'll just linger as you slowly starve to death. It could take weeks. I hear it's really painful." He crouched, ripping the gun from Marco's hand before he stood again. "Why did you think you could murder Lycan kids and get away with it? Who's your contact on the Vampire Council? Tell me and I'll end your suffering."

Marco clawed at the ground, making agonizing sounds, and managed to roll over onto his chest. He used the dirt and grass to inch away.

Glacier watched him, knowing the master wasn't going to get far. He glanced at the other trees.

"Three of you are left. I want an answer, since this one isn't talkative. First one to tell me what I want to know gets a two-hour head start before I begin hunting your ass. It's the best offer you're going to get from me."

132

Ten feet away, a redheaded Vamp male peeked out from behind a tree. He looked about twenty years old. "He didn't tell us. Ronnie and I were made two nights ago. I didn't know about any kids being killed, either."

"Shut the fuck up!" a male snapped to the left.

Glacier turned that way. "You must be Pedro."

The guy stepped out from behind another tree, holding a gun. Glacier lifted his arm to keep it close to his eyes and braced his elbow, as if using it to lean against the nearby tree trunk.

"You fucking monster!" Pedro glared at Glacier before shifting his attention to what was left of Marco, his body shaking.

"I don't kill children, asshole. Look in a mirror if you want to see a villain. Why did Marco think it was okay to kidnap Lycan kids without your own damn council coming after your nest?"

"Tell him nothing!" Marco hissed, now about fifteen feet away, still crawling slowly.

Glacier stared at Pedro. "You see what I did to him. I could cut you in half too. Just to be clear, he's not getting away. I may let him crawl around for an hour or so first. I want the name of the council member who protected your nest."

"Fuck you!" Pedro lifted the gun.

"You know those don't work against me." Glacier tensed though, prepared in case the bastard wanted to waste bullets.

Pedro darted behind the tree and gunshots rang out—only he wasn't aiming at Glacier. He shot Marco in the back of the head at least three times before fleeing.

Glacier walked over to the still Master, knowing his brain would heal. Probably real slow, since he was already so damaged. He bent, pulled his blade from his boot, and removed his head. Problem solved. Marco went out too fast, though.

Glacier turned, listening. "You two, out here now."

The one who'd peeked at him did it again. Glacier saw raw fear in his eyes.

"Your friend, too. I want answers."

"We were just turned," the redhead whispered. "Please don't kill us. We didn't ask for this. Marco grabbed us coming out of a bar. Ronnie and I have been best friends since we were in diapers."

"Step out where I can see you, Ronnie. *Now.*"

A dark-haired guy about twenty years old lifted his head over a bush. He looked ready to faint. It saddened Glacier, reminding him of Mandy. She'd been human, minding her own business, and had been snatched into a nest.

"I'm not going to kill you. I'm going to ask you questions. You're going to answer them. Then I'm going to send you to somewhere safe."

Both men seemed leery as hell, not that Glacier blamed them, but they came out of hiding. Both also appeared scared shitless. He focused on the redhead, since he knew he could talk.

"What's your name?"

"I'm Richie. This is Ronnie."

"You two a couple?"

They both shook their heads.

"Too bad. That would have been cute on your wedding invitations." Glacier wanted them to relax but neither broke a smile. Apparently, humor was off the table. "What did Marco tell you about the pack you were going to attack?"

"He said they were rabid animal people who could shift into wolves and had been attacking people in the city. Pedro taught us how to fight a little. Mostly we were here to watch and learn."

"That was all a lie. Sorry to break it to you both, but I think you were bait. Marco would have let the pack tear you to shreds as a distraction while he went after their alpha. Be happy that didn't happen. Lycans aren't rabid, but they *are* vicious to Vamps. Did Marco talk to any other Vampires around you besides Pedro?"

"He made a phone call." Ronnie had a voice after all. "I never heard him say a name. Something about how he'd take care of the situation and send more videos as soon as he could make more. I got the impression it was a man, though. He said it gave him wood too, like he was agreeing with the person, and girls don't get that."

Glacier let that information stew in his head. *Videos?* He came up with nothing. "Where did you come from?"

"We both live at home with our parents," Richie admitted.

"I meant, where were you staying with Marco and Pedro?"

135

"The basement of a tire store. It closed down a few years ago. The one on Mitch Street right outside the city." Richie hugged his waist. "You're really going to let us go?"

"What are you?" Ronnie gawked at him.

"Return there. I'm sending a friend your way. Don't fucking attack him, got it? His name is Graves. He kills bad guys for a living, so I wouldn't think of trying something. He's a Lycan, but he knows some decent Vampires to pass you over to. Oh, and no killing anyone or you die. Clear? No biting kids, old people, and you don't let humans know what you are. Have you fed tonight?"

Both nodded.

"Excellent. No biting anyone then until Graves comes to you as soon as he can. Run back there now." He waved a hand at them. "Fast as you can!"

Both fled into the woods.

Glacier reached back, grabbed his cell, and called Graves. The Lycan answered on the first ring. "I need another favor. You still in the area?"

"Yeah. I am. What do you need?"

"I've got two newbie Vamps who need a home. Total pity case. Marco made them to use as bait. Both look right out of high school and are two days old. See if they're salvageable." He gave him the location. "You got any ideas on any Vamps who'd take them?"

"Yeah. We're on good terms with a master near our territory. He's pretty decent, follows the rules, and he'll take them in if they aren't crazy.

I'll pick up the newbies and call Parker to let him know I'm driving them to him."

"Thanks. I have one last asshole to chase after."

Glacier hung up, returning his phone to his pocket. He walked out of the thick trees and took to the sky, heading in the direction of the abandoned tire store. It was probably where Pedro would go. He flew over the two newbie Vamps he'd just sent fleeing, glad to see they were following his orders.

He blamed Mandy for his decision to give Richie and Ronnie a shot at life. Usually he'd have just ended theirs. Vamps without masters never lasted long on their own without becoming rogue.

Chapter Eight

It took him over two hours to find Pedro. The bastard had come across a cave to crawl into, probably thinking he'd be safe there. Glacier had gone to ground, tracking him once he realized the Vamp wasn't on his way to the tire shop. Pedro had refused to give him answers, instead shooting his weapon. A large human community was located a block away, and sirens had begun to sound, so Glacier hadn't messed around. He'd ashed the bastard and flew out of there before the cops arrived.

He returned to the Lycan pack safe house and knocked on the door. "It's Glacier."

Teenie unlocked the thick door and shoved it open.

"The threat is over. Marco and his second are toast. There won't be any more Lycan kids taken by that nest. It's destroyed."

Teenie stepped outside and closed the door. "There's a debate going on inside."

"About what?"

"How easily you took down Kevin, and how much safer we'd all be if you become our alpha."

He snorted. "That's never going to happen. Discussion over. I'm not saying I think Kevin is the best choice to lead your pack, but it sure as hell won't be me. I'm leaving. You're all safe to come out of lockdown now."

"We need you."

"*Lots* of Lycan packs need me. I'm a guardian, Teenie. Not an alpha."

"You're half Werewolf. You belong here."

He'd tucked his wings before knocking, but he spread them out to make a point. "This is my version of shifting." He hardened his skin to a dull gray and then unshelled. "I'm mostly Gargoyle. I don't grow fur or a tail. No four legs. Just two. Forget it. I'm leaving now. Tell everyone the danger has passed. I know Kevin will have issues with me when he wakes in the morning. Tell him it's best if he doesn't."

He spun, walked to where he'd dropped his shirt, and put it on after he retracted his wings. The motorcycle engine purred under him as he started it. He felt more than ready to get back to Mandy and Pest. He also planned to call Graves before dawn for an update to see how things had gone with the newbie Vamps.

He stopped for fast food on the way and finally pulled into the alley. Pest came out to greet him. "Handled?"

"Yeah. Hungry?"

"Sure am. I didn't want to leave short stack alone."

"Don't call her that. Her name is Mandy."

Pest chuckled. "She keeps telling me that, too." Pest blocked his way to the door, his expression turning serious as he lowered his voice. "What are you going to do now? The mission is over, right?"

"I'll ask Kelzeb where he wants me to go next, same as always."

Pest stepped closer, locking gazes with him.

"I'm going to take her with me. I don't want to leave her alone, Pest. Kelzeb didn't order me to kill her. Just said not to bring her to the cliffs. It's not as if we go home often. The last time was when Creed had to take out our shithead father. Now Creed is back with Angel's pack, being their guardian. We can visit him and his mate there."

"What about biting? She's a Vamp. Do I need to have the sex talk with you?"

"Fuck you. I'm older than you are. I gave *you* the talk about girls, if I remember right."

"Vamps like to use fangs during sex. I'm not even sure if you could get her off without some blood involved."

"Guess I'll find out if we ever have sex. We haven't."

"Then what's the point of keeping her with you? Are you into torturing yourself these days? I couldn't live with a woman without nailing her every chance I got."

"Stop being a dick. Just let it go. I'm grateful that you came but I'll handle this shit."

"I'm worried."

Glacier nodded. "Me too," he admitted. "I don't know what I'm doing, but I know I want to keep her with me. Mandy and I will have to figure it out."

"The nest is completely wiped out?"

Glacier filled him in on the details.

Pest shook his head. "Fuck. You sent Graves to pick up two new Vamps and asked him to rehome them? They aren't kittens, for fuck's sake."

140

"I know, but they weren't exactly dangerous, either. They lived with their parents until they were grabbed. It *would* have been like killing kittens."

"Maybe you should take some time off, bro. Like, seriously. Deal with this shit with short stack, figure out how you feel and why you're so protective of her before you take on another job. I get why you knocked out Kevin. He sounds like a dumbass, but his pack is probably going to challenge him now. You took him down in front of them. Then let two Vamps live. I bet you didn't share *that* tidbit with the pack."

"Richie and Ronnie didn't hurt those Lycan kids. They were only made to be bait. I asked Graves to pick them up to avoid them being shredded by the pack. Kevin never needs to know about them. He's such an asshole he'd hunt them just because Marco made them, despite their innocence."

"True." Pest sighed. "You'll all fucked up."

"Thanks." He stepped around his brother. "I'm going in. Let's eat."

Mandy waited inside, her gaze going down the length of him. He smiled. She looked worried about him.

"I'm fine."

She rushed at him and dropped to her knees, touching his hip through the material. "Then why is there a hole here?"

Pest came in and closed the door. "Um, should I go back out? I admit I think it's dangerous to get a blow job from a Vamp. I'm giving you points for bravery, bro."

Glacier turned his head and shot him a dirty look. He reached down, grabbed Mandy by her upper arms, and hauled her to her feet. "I'm fine. You don't smell blood, do you?"

She sniffed. "No."

"Unhurt, just like I said."

"Why do you have a hole in your jeans then?" She frowned at him.

"She has no fucking clue, does she?" Pest took a seat on the counter. "You have to tell her."

Glacier released Mandy. "I'm going to eat, and then I have to call my boss to fill him in on what happened." He backed away from her to pass out the burgers and fries he'd picked up. Bottled water had been stacked near the door. He took one, drinking deep.

"Is the nest taken care of?" Mandy walked over to the stairs and took a seat.

"Marco and Pedro have been ashed. They won't be going after more Lycan kids."

"The council won't be happy. At least, one member won't be, if I'm right and Marco has a friend."

"Speaking of, a conversation was overheard. Marco talked to someone about videos and getting aroused over them. What do you make of that, Mandy?" Glacier sat on the floor, unwrapping one of the cheeseburgers. He ate it with gusto.

Mandy jumped to her feet, pacing. He watched her, thinking she was cute as her expressions changed, obviously considering what he had said.

She finally stopped, holding his gaze. Her pale skin appeared whiter than normal.

Mandy wanted to curse and punch something. "Only one thing comes to mind. About five years ago, a master reported to the council that he'd gotten an invitation to a website. It was from another master in Arizona. Kind of a pay-for-membership thing but very hush-hush. Log-in and fees required to access the content. It was rumored to be a way for Vampires to form alliances without the council being informed. The council keeps track of connections between nests to avoid an uprising. Zander was too terrified to get involved with any kind of potential plot against our council."

"Great. Vamps have a rebel website now?" Pest grunted.

Mandy nodded. "They did. Olivia and I were sent out with Danti. He's an assassin we live with. We—"

"You have a companion?" Pest growled. "My brother is putting his ass on the line for you and you're fucking someone?"

She stared at him. "No. I live with nine other assassins. I'm not having sex with any of them. Can I finish now?"

Pest nodded, looking chagrined as he shoved fries into his mouth.

"Danti pretended to be Zander, the master who'd been invited to the website. We were under orders to find out if they were plotting against the council and how many nests were involved. As soon as Danti paid the money and got the password, we logged on. They had some videos of illegal activities on the site. Mild propaganda. Kind of like, 'we could do this to anyone we wanted if the council wasn't around anymore; watch and get motivated' type of crap. It was sick."

Glacier stopped eating and got up, approaching her. "What kinds of videos? Lycan kids fighting?"

She shook her head. "Not kids, but there were a few videos of adult Werewolves fighting each other. They were collared and looked abused, half starved, as if they'd been in captivity for a while. Werewolves go into heat. And the prize to the winning male was a human female." She hesitated. "For sex. They had videos of that on there, too. They threw those women in with the mindless men after they'd fought. The council wanted to shut that shit down *fast*. I told you they don't want to draw the attention of the VampLycans. That would have done it. Missing Werewolves and human women combined? Big red flag."

"Fuck." Pest stopped eating, too.

"Mostly though, it was abuse of other Vampires."

"I didn't think the council would give a shit about that."

Mandy stared into Glacier's eyes. "They do when masters are creating new Vamps at an alarming rate just so they can pit them against soldiers they've made for the sole purpose of fighting, and making bets on how long the Vamps survive. The answer, from what I saw, is less than five minutes, by the way. Lots of videos of that shit going down were loaded. There are laws about soldiers. Strict ones."

"Like what?" Glacier took her hand and led her to the closest counter, lifted her, and sat her on it. He took a seat next to her.

"Have you ever seen a soldier? Know what one is?"

144

"Unfortunately, yes."

She hated them; a shiver ran down her spine. "They're very unstable, and the longer they're alive, the more dangerous they become. Especially if they're hurt. They don't heal the way I do. They become more unbalanced every time they're injured. The council demands any master seek permission to create soldiers first. I've been sent to monitor those situations twice. The first time, it was a master of a large nest who'd survived an uprising by his own. It's against the law for a nest to kill its master. The master didn't just want his Vamps exterminated, but to go out in a grisly way. The council agreed. Five soldiers were made. Myself and six other assassins were sent to make sure none of the soldiers survived after their task had been completed. We also trapped the nest inside the building where they slept to avoid any escaping."

"Why not just have other Vamps kill them and be vicious about it?"

She looked down at Pest. "Soldiers are more brutal than your average Vampire. As in, they literally bite into you and take out chunks. Think gory, blood-spraying kind of nightmare shit where they're soaked in blood. They don't remove the heads of their Vampire targets. They just keep biting, tearing their prey apart, until not enough is left to survive. They are *insane*. It's like the vilest way possible for our kind to die. It's a form of punishment for the worst crimes. The master destroyed the soldiers after they killed everyone in his nest."

"You said there were two situations." Glacier reached out and took her hand, as if he knew remembering wasn't easy on her.

She gripped his hand back, holding on. "The second time, a master had created three of them without permission. He was just a shithead

145

who was curious to see if he could make them and what they could do. Problem was, he left them alive for too long after running his tests. They degraded enough to stop taking orders, attacked all four members of his nest and killed them. The master fought them off but he got trapped when part of his basement hideout collapsed, pinning him under a beam. Fortunately, he had his cell phone and got a signal. He had to call for help. We came. But seven humans died as a result before we were able to kill the soldiers. It was hell..."

Glacier slid closer, released her hand, and put his arm around her shoulders. She liked that he tried to comfort her. "You don't have to say anything else."

"No. It's fine... It was the smell of death that drew us. Their soldier bodies had rotted that much, plus the sickos had dragged their victims into the storm drain, where they were hiding. I'd been trained how to deal with soldiers and warned about what they were like to battle. Nothing prepared me for the real thing, though. They just don't go down, or react to pain the way someone else would. It just drives them into more of a frenzy. I never want to have to take them on again. I had nightmares for months after that."

"Were you hurt?"

"I wore protective gear that kept them from biting me but I suffered broken bones. Those fuckers are strong."

"You have protective gear against biters? Damn. That's kind of cool."

She smiled at Pest. "Yes. We do. Vampires love to swarm. Being repeatedly bitten and bleeding from multiple wounds will weaken anyone. Think metal mesh sewn between the soft inner material and the

146

tougher exterior of a uniform. We just have to watch our joints, where there's no mesh." She raised one arm and bent her elbow. "Plus, a throat plate around our necks and a helmet that locks to it. It protects my throat from bites and my head from being removed. Part of an assassin's job at times is extinguishing a nest."

"I don't want to hear how dangerous your job was." Glacier released her shoulder and slid off the counter before he turned, holding her gaze. "Why did you bring up that website? Is that the only video connection you could think of? Do you think Marco had opened something like that?"

"Here's the thing. We investigated for weeks. Danti had to make friends since the other online members had bogus names. He used Olivia and I as bait to get other Vampires to meet with him."

Glacier looked wary. "What the hell does that mean?"

"Danti said he owned two well-trained lovers he had grown tired of after twenty years. Whatever fetishes they had, he swore we were into. We needed face-to-face meetings to identify who the players were."

Pest whistled. "You had to fuck masters?"

"No." She sighed. "Danti introduced us to the men though, and made promises to gift us to each new friend soon. After we had identified ten of them, the council had all of them arrested for questioning. They gave up Barkley Brimstone. He was arrested and imprisoned, since he refused to give up the true names of other masters who had joined his website. Rumor had it that he admitted to making alliances with over fifty masters in the U.S., and even more in other countries."

Glacier leaned against the counter. "So?"

"Yeah, so?" Pest started eating again.

"Danti had to pay half a million dollars to join that website. Think about the kind of money Barkley made on membership fees. He also bragged about how close he'd been to locating all the council members."

"Don't all Vamps know who they are?"

She met Glacier's eyes. "Definitely not. It's to protect them from the Vampires they piss off. *I* don't even know all their real names or locations. I'm guessing they're like Corski, and must be masters in the cities of assassin houses, but it's just an assumption."

"Who the fuck is Corski?"

Glacier answered Pest. "He's the master of New York City, where Mandy is stationed, and also the council member in charge of her team."

"I'm thinking someone on the council might have seen what Barkley accomplished and stolen the idea. Perhaps not to destroy the council, but the money that website made? It was like sick Vampire porn. Maybe the price of membership includes some council favors, like avoiding being arrested if they load videos. It would make sense why Marco almost got away with the shit he did. Standard procedure is to send an investigator in, who checks out the details, and then findings are presented to the council. Olivia and I were sent to kill a Werewolf allegedly taking out that nest. But I honestly don't believe the council voted to send us based on real facts. My guess? Someone fudged that report and lied to them."

"Who's in charge of sending out investigators and presenting the gathered facts to the council?"

"I don't know. It's not like we're invited to council meetings. Corski hands us our orders after they've decided we need to be sent somewhere."

"Maybe they don't really give a shit *what* Marco was doing and just wanted to kill Lycans," Pest stated.

Glacier explained, "But they fear VampLycans. It motivates the council to police their own, to keep VampLycans from being called in. They don't want to start a war." Glacier glanced at his brother and smiled. "Did you know Vampires believe GarLycans never leave Alaska?"

Pest's eyebrows rose. "I see."

Glacier nodded.

Mandy saw the amusement on both brothers' faces. "What am I missing? What's the undercurrent here?"

Glacier turned to her, grinning. "My brother and I have discussed it at length all our lives. We think GarLycans are way scarier than VampLycans. We just find it amusing that Vamps see it differently. Maybe it's because VampLycans are half Vampire? What do you think, Pest?"

"Not to mention, GarLycans *do* leave Alaska sometimes." Pest chuckled. "I've met a few. Scary fuckers. I ran into one in Texas just a few weeks ago. I watched him take out four rogue Lycans in under a minute flat. They were slaughtering cows, and humans were becoming alarmed. It made the news. I was sent to investigate what was going on. He got there right as I did."

Her eyes widened. "What does one look like?"

"Big. Formidable. They have wings. He flew in from the sky while the Lycans were fleeing after attacking the herd, and did this spinning thing like a fucking blender as he landed in front of them. His wings were stone-hard, and they just sliced through the bodies like butter. Lycan parts were flung everywhere. The bastard made me help him clean up his mess."

149

Glacier chuckled. "He kind of sounds amazing."

Pest rolled his eyes. "Whatever. I'm going to go take a shower now that you're back." He threw his trash in the fast food bag and hurried up the stairs.

Mandy bit her lip. "Have you ever met a GarLycan or a VampLycan?"

He nodded. "I'm sent on a lot of jobs to investigate anything humans report that might be attributed to Lycans or Vampires. They have the same job as I do. Take care of it and clean up the mess to keep humans from discovering what they're really dealing with. I will say one thing I do like better about VampLycans, though. They have the ability to slip into human minds and erase memories. I'd love to be able to do that. It would be damn useful."

She understood. She had the same ability to implant and remove memories from humans, as long as they weren't immune. She nodded, her mind already elsewhere.

Glacier's job was over, now that Marco wasn't alive anymore. What did that mean for her? She wanted to ask but was afraid to. Would he kill her? Let her go? What would she do if he *did* give her freedom? Nowhere would be safe. It would only be a matter of time before the council found out she remained alive, if they had even fallen for the ruse of her tracker being found with Dusty's ashes. For all she knew, a bounty had already been placed on her head.

First thing, she'd have to let Olivia know she was alive. She trusted her. Then again, she was getting ahead of herself by implying Glacier would let her live. *Shit.*

"Mandy? Are you okay?"

150

She lifted her head and met his gaze. *Suck it up, buttercup. Be brave.* "You took out the nest. What now? I mean, what's going to happen to me?"

His mouth parted, something flickered in his eyes, but he didn't say anything.

"I could help you. You know, with the mind stuff. I could go on your next job. I'm not high maintenance. I mean, find me a dark closet to sleep in during the day and, um, lead me down an alley to find a blood donor every few nights. I don't kill innocent people. I wasn't lying about that. You can watch me to make sure. Any humans you need help with, I can slip into their heads for you. If you'd just give me a chance to—"

He suddenly invaded her personal space and put his hand over her mouth. "Shush."

Her hope died. He didn't even want to listen to what she had to offer.

He lowered his hand and sighed. "I already decided to take you with me. I'm not going to abandon you for the council to kill."

Tears filled her eyes. "Thank you!" She didn't think, just flung her arms around his waist, hugging him.

He wrapped his arms around her and drew her in tight, holding her. He spread his legs a little, lowering his height enough to rest his jaw on the top of her head. "We have things to discuss, though."

She closed her eyes, listening to his heartbeat. Her fangs throbbed a little but she had control. "No biting. I won't ever ask you for blood. I know how you feel about that."

"Yeah. No biting ever. I'm in charge. You follow my orders. I guess you could say, I'll be considered your new master now. I'm the boss. Is that agreeable to you?"

She nodded against him. "Yes. You already have my loyalty."

"Um." He cleared his throat. "You might want to let me go."

She released him quickly and backed off. "Sorry. I'm just happy. I'm grateful you don't plan to kill me, aren't just going to walk out the door and leave me here. I don't know where to go that I'd be safe. I mean, Olivia and I planned to move to Los Angeles in twelve years when our service time was up, but the master there won't take me if I'm wanted by the council. It would bring down hell on his nest."

He stared into her eyes. "We need to sit down and have a serious talk. I have to call Kelzeb though first and give him my report. Why don't you go upstairs to the bedroom and close the door? I'll be up in a few minutes."

She bet he would make a list of rules for her to follow. That was okay. Glacier was a protector. He went after bad guys. She would love working with him. It would change her life in wonderful ways. No more council bullshit. She looked forward to it.

"Okay." She turned, rushing up the stairs. A smile curved her lips. The happiness faded slightly, though, as she entered the bedroom and closed the door.

She had feelings for him. Always had, since she'd met him. He wasn't the settling-down kind. Would staying with him mean watching him go off with other women for his one-night stands?

She sat on the bed and closed her eyes. That would be rough on her. Painful too. It would break her heart.

What if staying with him turned into a hellish nightmare of her falling in love with him, but Glacier still refusing to be with her? He'd said to leave room in the bed for him when he came back from taking out the nest. But it would have woken her up if he'd lain with her. He'd avoided it.

She closed her eyes. *Shit.*

Chapter Nine

"Two words for you, Glacier. Two fucking words. Joint effort. How many times are you going to make me say it? That means working *with* the pack, not pissing them off."

Glacier closed his eyes, listening to Kelzeb rant. He deserved it. His boss finally stopped talking.

"In my defense, Kevin is an asshole."

"He said you sucker punched him while shelled."

"He's lying. I didn't shell until after I decked him in the face, and I only knocked him out because he was drunk as shit, trying to fight me. He couldn't even walk straight. I told you the facts. Should I have allowed his drunken ass to attack me and just...what? Bowed down to take it until he wore himself out? The pack could have been attacked while they watched that bullshit. I needed to act fast. Was I wrong?"

Kelzeb growled. "No. But he says his pack has lost all respect for him and he's received two official challenge requests from his enforcers because of your actions. He's pissed, and has threatened to reach out to other packs to let them know you tried to overtake his."

"He *needs* to be challenged. Those Lycans deserve a better alpha. That's utter bullshit about me trying to steal his job, though. You know I don't want to lead a pack. Besides, we both know if I wanted his job, he'd be dead instead of bitching at you on the phone. What else do you want me to say? I'm not sorry. I handled the Vamp situation. This was about saving Lycan kids to me, not soothing that asshole's pride. End of threat. Job done."

Kelzeb sighed. "Understood. God knows I've wanted to punch a few alphas. Aveoth has sent me to visit packs to cement the agreements when they request a guardian. I have to represent him a few times a year, and I fucking hate it. He says I need to leave the cliffs occasionally. Bullshit. But I get why you didn't want to dick around with Kevin. I'm not fond of him after listening to him repeatedly whine. You should leave the territory though."

"I'll leave first thing tonight. It's sunrise in less than an hour."

"Right. Because you have a Vampire to think about. Traveling during the day is too risky. Fuck. I can just imagine getting pulled over by human authorities and them checking your trunk, where you'd have to stash her to keep her alive."

"I drive a motorcycle."

Kelzeb chuckled.

Glacier relaxed. He couldn't be in too much trouble for the stunt he'd pulled with drunk Kevin if his boss had retained his sense of humor.

"You're sure about taking her on your next mission then? You think she'll follow the rules you set?"

"Yes." He waited to see what response he'd get.

Kelzeb sighed again. "Fine. You're responsible though. You're also going to need to keep her away from other Vampires, from what you've told me. That's going to limit where I can send you." He hesitated. "Are you willing to do that for her? I'm talking wilderness shit. Maybe even

155

assigning you to be a guardian to a Lycan pack. You'd have to keep her in their territory and out of cities."

His chest tightened. "I know."

"Damn, Glacier. Are you thinking about mating her?"

"It's too soon. I don't know yet."

"Alright. I know you hate snow and request places to avoid it, but you're shit out of luck. We have a family-association pack in Wyoming. Hawk's brother-in-law is alpha there. Chaz and Fray visit their uncle whenever they have some down time. The pack hasn't asked for a guardian, but they might accept you into their territory with Mandy. There's also Colorado. One of the VampLycans clan leaders, Trayis, has a half-brother alpha there. They would probably be open to having a Vampire in their territory, since I'll make it clear you're responsible for her. I'll reach out to both alphas today. Hopefully one of them agrees. They're two packs we can trust not to betray that she's there."

"Thank you."

"The down side is, they'll expect guardian duties provided. That means you'll be scouting at night. I guess you could have her fly patrols with you. Otherwise, you'll be working while she's awake. You're also going to have to find a way to feed her."

"She can control human minds. That's going to be a bonus when I must deal with poachers. Frankly, I hope they have a bunch of them. She'll have a source of food."

"True." Kelzeb hesitated. "I know you hate being stuck in one location for more than a few months. As long as you're with this Mandy..."

156

"I know. My wandering days are over."

"You thought this out?"

"I have. I'm prepared to stay in one location for as long as needed to keep Mandy safe."

"Okay. I'll call you later today. It would be rude to wake up alphas this early to ask a favor." He chuckled. "You'll hear from me around noon your time. I'll find you a place to live."

"Thanks."

"Good luck."

Glacier hung up and entered the shop from the alley he'd used for privacy. Pest waited inside. "What's the verdict?"

"Kelzeb is cool. He's going to find me a Lycan pack to become guardian to. That way, I can keep Mandy off council radar. No Vamps can report her if they don't see her. I'll just keep her deep in Lycan territory. I should know where we're going around noon today."

"I'll get you a cargo van as soon as the rental places open. I figure that will be good to transport her and your motorcycle in." He lifted his phone, tapping at it.

"I'll just wait until tonight and drive my motorcycle with her. She's going to need clothes though, and I don't have a second helmet. I'll go shopping today while you watch over her."

"I'd rather shop, bro. No offense, but do you even know what size she wears?"

"No, but I'll just ask her."

Pest snorted. "I've got this. Unlike you, I have girlfriends from time to time. Not just one-night stands. I don't have to risk my balls by asking a woman her sizes. Some get weird about it or embarrassed. Save yourself the headache. I've learned to size them up accurately. Have you ever bought a woman clothes before?"

Glacier shook his head.

"Yeah. I didn't think so. I'll go. I didn't get a good look at her breasts though, since she's been wearing your shirts. Then again, I'd be doing you a favor if she didn't wear bras."

"Hers is upstairs. I'll take a peek."

Pest snickered. "Don't get caught, pervert."

Glacier flipped him off. "Then I'll just ask her."

"Don't." Pest turned toward the stairs and raised his voice. "Hey, short stack? Can you come down here for a minute?"

Mandy joined them right away. She'd showered recently, and sported another borrowed shirt and a pair of boxers. Her gaze went to Glacier. "You want to talk down here?"

"I actually had a few questions for you about this council." Pest motioned to Glacier. "You go up and wait for her. Text me what I wanted to know.

Glacier nodded. "Remember the helmet. I want something with tinting to keep anyone from seeing her face tonight while we're traveling. Hair dye, too. One of those quick spray-in deals. The reek from that will help mask her scent too, and we'll only need her hair color changed while traveling. Those wash right out. Black. I want to change her appearance.

Maybe some makeup to hide how pale she is, since we'll be making stops for gas. Can you handle all that?"

"Easy. I'll leave soon. There's one of those twenty-four-hour superstores not too far from here. I won't have to wait for anything to open by shopping there."

"I'll see you in a few minutes," he said to Mandy, rushing up the stairs to dig up her bra size. He found it quickly and texted it to his brother, then took a seat on the bed.

"Do you have a phone number for the council?"

Mandy shook her head at Pest. "I had Corski's number on my cell phone and an emergency contact number in case I couldn't reach him, but your brother tossed my phone. It had a tracker in it."

"Understood. My brother said there's a second assassin in town. Would she have those same numbers?"

Mandy's heart raced. The question implied that Olivia still lived. She had been too afraid to ask Glacier if her friend had found him yet, or if he'd gone after her. Part of her didn't want to know the answer. "Yes."

"Do you know what full name Corski is going by?"

"Joseph Corski." She spelled it. "New York City. I doubt he'd be listed in a phone directory, though."

"Probably not."

"Can I ask why you want phone numbers? Are you planning to let the council know what went down here? It's a good idea, but I can't tell you with certainty that Corski can be trusted. He might be the one who covered for Marco. Corski is the one who gives us our orders."

"Fair enough." His phone beeped. He smiled. "That was it. Go talk to my brother."

Mandy found Glacier sitting on the bed. He'd removed his boots. She closed the door to give them some privacy and leaned against it. He looked sexy but then, he always did. The bed seemed small with his big body sitting on the side of it. The hole in his jeans by his hip bothered her. She couldn't pick up any blood but something had happened. It hadn't been there when he'd left.

His pale blue eyes were beautiful as they locked with hers. "My boss is going to assign me to watch over a Lycan pack on my next assignment. I'll find out where we're going later today. The pack will keep Vampires out of their territory. You'll be stuck inside their perimeter, but no one will be able to see you to tell the council you're alive. I asked Pest to buy stuff to help change your appearance while we ride my bike tonight."

"I heard that part. Black hair like you, huh?"

He smiled. "You look good as a blonde, but I liked the black hair with blue streaks you used to sport, too. We're going to either Colorado or Wyoming. It means we might be on the road for a few nights."

"Day travel is out. I'm sorry about that. You're probably not used to having your movements restricted."

He shrugged. "No biggie. The nice thing is, I might need your mental abilities. Packs deal with poachers more than you'd think. You can make them forget our encounters and embed them with the urge to never return to the area."

"We're going to be work partners then?"

He sucked in a deep breath and blew it out. His gaze slowly lowered down her body before he stared into her eyes again. "I'm attracted to you, Mandy."

She hadn't expected him to admit that, but still she tensed. "But?"

"No but. I just want to be clear. I'm not saying you have to become my lover, but it's on the table." His voice turned husky. "I want you, baby. You can't imagine how much."

She was glad to be leaning against the door. "You don't do the same woman twice. I remember. And I wouldn't be okay with you bed hopping."

He stood and walked closer, stopping inches away from her. "I couldn't allow you to get close to me when we worked together at Bucket. You know what it's like to pretend to be human. Always having to watch your every word and action, to not give something away that could make them suspicious. I knew there was no damn way I could hide my true nature from you if we dated, or hell, moved in together. But I definitely had the urge to take you home with me. There was just something about you that drew me, Mandy. And you know what happens to humans who learn the truth. They are seen as dangerous. I couldn't risk your life."

She resisted the urge to touch him. "I understand that. I felt the same way toward you. Still do."

"I'd like to be more than work partners. Lovers…" He reached out and rested his open palms on the door inches from her arms. "I don't want you to feel forced into it though. I'd take you with me and keep you safe even if you don't want to see where a relationship goes with us. No pressure."

"Would this be a monogamous relationship?"

"Yes."

"I'm in." She reached up and touched his shirt, loving the heat coming off his skin through the thin material. He had such a hard body, and she wanted to explore all of it. Her gums began to ache. "We're going to have a few problems to deal with though."

"You can't bite me."

"That." She nodded. "My fangs already want to drop because you're so close."

"Do you need blood to be able to climax?"

She felt embarrassed to answer. "No. I mean, I masturbate often. I sure don't bite *myself*. I've only had sex a few times as a Vampire..." She paused. "No. We should be completely honest with each other. I want that kind of relationship with you." She inhaled deeply. "I've only had sex once since I was turned."

Surprise registered on his face.

"It didn't go well. That's why it only happened the one time. I've had a ton of male Vamps hit on me but I wasn't attracted to them. I *live* with a group of males. You'd understand if you knew them. They tend to brag about their conquests. It was a huge turn off. It's the ultra-superiority complexes most of them display. I'm a god, worship me. Blah, blah, blah."

He grinned.

"It's true. Some of them brought women home. I've got excellent hearing. It took every ounce of control not to break into their rooms at times to castrate them. It was like some game to do things to women they didn't enjoy but force them to think they did. I wasn't allowed to interfere though, as long as they didn't kill or do something to leave lasting damage on the women. They came willingly. They left with altered memories."

His amusement died and anger glinted in his eyes. "Like?"

"They tend to use mind control and push into any woman's head they're with. It's a dominance thing that I'm not into. They like sex the way *they* like it. There's no give and take. Olivia has done a few Vamps over the years. Let's just say they aren't much different in bed with Vampire women. She swore them off."

"Is that what happened to the Vampire you were with? Did he try to break into your mind? Force you to do things you weren't comfortable with?"

She shook her head. "He was human. It was after I'd finished my training by the council and assigned to the assassin house. I was lonely and sad. I thought I'd take myself shopping to cheer up, you know? The mall was open. I had bought myself a few outfits and then hit the food court just to watch people. To feel a part of being alive."

Glacier pulled her away from the door and led her to the bed, sat her on it, and took a seat next to her. "Go on."

"This guy came up to ask if he could sit with me. Said I looked sad. He was funny, nice, and cute. I'd never had a one-night stand before but there it is. I thought I had my urges mastered, but I was still worried I might take too much blood or mess up taking over his mind in bed. I took

163

him home with me. Olivia promised that she'd make sure I didn't hurt him, and she had more experience with altering memories. Our rooms are next to each other." Tears filled her eyes. "It turned out he was immune."

"Shit."

"He flipped out after we had sex. I didn't bite him until the end. Olivia rushed in and tried to get control of him. She couldn't. By then, two other Vamps in the house had heard the commotion. They rushed into my room...one of them killed him. It happened faster than I could stop it. Not that I would have been allowed to just let him go free. He realized I was a Vampire and he knew where we lived."

"He posed too much of a danger."

She nodded. "Olivia said the same to comfort me. It didn't work. I never tried again. He died because he had sex with me. Out of all the men I finally chose to bring home, it had to be someone immune."

"Oh, baby." Glacier reached out and took her hand.

She pulled herself together. "I didn't want to be with a Vampire for the reasons I mentioned. Werewolves tend to hate us. I couldn't trust that one wouldn't kill me after. I wasn't risking a human a second time." She held his gaze. "I'm glad you can overlook that I'm a Vamp. I *will* want to bite you, but I'll resist. I just might get the urge to feed after. Worst case, to be honest."

He nodded. "We'll have to figure it out together. First thing, though...I am not half human."

"But your brother said you're a half-breed. Was he messing with me? You're all Werewolf?"

He tightened his hold on her hand. "I'm a GarLycan."

She heard his words. They sank in slowly. Then shock hit—*hard*.

He smiled. "We *do* leave Alaska."

Her mouth parted but she couldn't speak; she was too stunned.

"My father was a Gargoyle who mated my Lycan mother. They had four sons together. We took after our father on traits. I use body wash to mask the Gargoyle scent. Mine's faint enough to do that. I don't shift into a Wolf. I grow wings and can shell my body."

GarLycan. He can fly. Shit.

She hadn't seen that coming.

"It's why you can't bite me. You're going to have to trust me on this. Really bad shit would happen if you took my blood because I'm mostly Gargoyle. I belong to Lord Aveoth's clan in Alaska. My job is often as a troubleshooter, dealing with idiots who risk exposing humans to the truth that our races exist. Kelzeb is my boss. He's second-in-command to Lord Aveoth and assigns my missions.

"Sometimes Lycan packs ask for our help, and if Lord Aveoth agrees, he sends someone like me. There are also situations where we form long-term alliances with an alpha and his pack is given a guardian. They watch over the pack, literally. My youngest brother is a pack guardian. Creed scouts their territory at night by flying over it to keep Vampires and poachers from preying on them. He lives with that pack year-round with his mate. That's what I'm going to do next. We'll live with the pack I'm assigned to protect. Any questions?"

She still reeled from his news. "So many."

He smiled. "Go ahead."

"You really fly? That's true?"

He released her hand. "I can. Do you want to see me in Gargoyle form?"

"I'm not sure," she admitted, wondering how frightening he would be. "Yes." She couldn't resist the curiosity. "Please."

He removed his shirt, baring his muscled upper body. Seconds ticked by...and then she heard soft pops. Black wing tips began to peek out from behind his torso and they grew larger, until they filled the space from one wall to the other. She had to close her mouth again. His coloring changed from tan to light gray, then even darker. The texture of his skin also transformed.

She managed to stand, getting closer to him. Her hand trembled as she reached out, brushing her fingertips along his stomach.

"Holy crap." He felt like a statue. She snapped her head up, staring into his eyes. They looked alert but his features had been frozen with the stiffening of his now dark gray skin.

The color began to lighten until his lips curved. By the time he grinned at her enough to flash teeth, she got a glimpse of his fangs. They weren't quite Vampire style, but close. His were wider with a slight curve at the end. They weren't made to siphon blood...but instead to tear something apart.

He reached up and gently cupped her upper arms. "Are you okay? I'm putting away the wings."

She watched them shrink, heard the slight sounds as they shifted back inside his body. It was tempting to jerk free of his hold and walk around him to see where they disappeared into. She could guess it had to be somewhere near his shoulder blades. "Wow."

"You're paler than usual, Mandy. Maybe you should sit."

"I'm good. It's just so surprised. I heard repeatedly that GarLycans never leave Alaska. The council...well, Corski...said we didn't have to worry about your kind."

"They are idiots. We leave Alaska frequently. VampLycans have had more skirmishes with Vampires though. It might be why your council is more familiar with them than us. That nest in Alaska that was taken out? They breached VampLycan territory to kidnap one of their men. Veso got away, and our clans went after the nest in a joint effort. That master was bat-shit crazy. He wanted to breed a VampLycan with a human relative he'd kidnapped in hopes they'd have a daughter, who he could crown as his queen or some such shit. Then one of his Vamps fled and made a soldier, who he left behind. It attacked a small town, wiping out every human it came into contact with. Hell, it even made a few other soldiers before they were stopped."

"That's not possible. Soldiers can't create others."

"Nobody told the *soldier* that. Hate to break it to you, but they can. He *did*. Those are facts."

"Shit!"

"Let's sit."

Good idea. She turned the second he released her and sat heavily on the bed.

Glacier crouched in front of her. "What other questions do you have?"

"My mind is in a spin."

"It's a lot of information to dump on you. I want you to know what you're getting into before you say yes to sharing a bed with me."

"It doesn't change how I feel, Glacier. I still want to be with you."

"Good. We'll live with the Lycan pack, being their guardian. You can help me do that. We'll work nights. How does that sound?"

"Good. I mean, if they don't attack me. Some Werewolves hate Vampires."

"They wouldn't dare hurt you. You'll be there with me." He stood. "We should get some sleep. Tonight, we'll be heading to wherever Kelzeb sends us."

Her gaze snagged on the hole in his jeans and she reached out, fingering it. "What really happened?"

"One of the Vamps shot me but I'd shelled. Bullets bounce off."

She lifted her head, peering up at him. "Show me."

"You want me to take off my pants?"

"Yes."

He crouched again, gripping the mattress on either side of her hip. "I'll do more than show you where the bullet hit, if I strip. My brother is gone right now, but the sun is going to come up at any minute. I want to take my time with you when we have sex."

"I don't drift off, remember? I'll be slightly weaker but that's it. It might even help with my urge to bite. Dull it a bit."

168

"Mandy, I want you... But are you sure?"

"Yes."

Chapter Ten

Glacier wanted Mandy so much it hurt. "We have to be smart about this."

She nodded. "The biting. Right. Avoiding that. You could take me from behind."

He grinned. "I like the way you think. Take off your clothes." He backed off and reached for the front of his jeans, tearing them down his body. He removed his boxers next, avoiding looking at her until he straightened, nude.

Mandy had stripped quickly, since she'd only worn one of his shirts and the baggy boxers. The sight of her on her hands and knees on the bed, her curvy ass bared, and the way she tossed her hair to peer at him over her shoulder, had his hard-on at full mast.

Mandy smiled, showing off those cute little fangs of hers as she spread her legs. He lowered his gaze. A growl rumbled from him. The hint of her arousal taunted him but she wasn't ready for him. He approached her and gripped her hips, flipping her over onto her back.

She gasped, looking surprised. He grinned, dropped to his knees, and grabbed her ankles. He tore her down to the end of the bed. "Spread them for me. I want a taste of you first."

"You don't have to do that."

He arched an eyebrow.

"I don't want to lie to you or fake anything. Total honestly. To get it, you have to give it."

"I'm trying but you haven't spread your legs for me yet."

She actually blushed. "I'm talking about the truth, not oral sex. But you know that. I've had this done a few times by a guy. It didn't really do much for me. I'd like it better if you used your fingers down there to play with me while using your mouth on my breasts. That gets me really turned on."

"I'm not him. Spread your thighs." He licked his lips.

She hesitated.

"You want the truth?"

"Always from you."

"I'm going to make damn sure I can get you off before I'm inside you. I don't think I'll last long enough to make it good for you the first time otherwise. You don't want me to feel guilty, do you?"

She shook her head. "No. Most men don't care though."

"I will. Now open for me and give me access."

She spread her legs wide and broke eye contact with him. He grinned. She looked uncomfortable, baring her pussy to him. A faint tinge of red showed on her pale skin. "Oh baby. I'm going to break you of being shy." He released her ankles, gripped her inner thighs, and pulled her closer. He applied enough strength to keep her pinned down and open but was careful not to hurt her. He lowered his gaze, studying her hairless pussy. He'd never done a Vamp. "You found a razor here?"

"Um, no. Once I was turned, um... Can we just *not* discuss this?"

She was so fucking cute. "I'll get an answer later on that."

"Great."

He noticed another difference. She was pale everywhere, including her pussy. He dipped his head, loving her scent. He took it as a challenge that she hadn't enjoyed oral sex before. He planned to change her mind. He focused on the little nub of her clit, giving it a few soft licks to test her sensitivity. Her muscles under his hands tensed and she sucked in a sharp breath.

This was going to be fun.

He grew aggressive, applying more pressure. He gently sucked and that earned him a throaty moan. He kept at it. She tried to squirm, moaning louder. One of her hands slid into his hair. He lifted up a little and grinned. She was pink now where his mouth had been. The bud had swollen too. He lowered his mouth, licking and sucking harder. Her other hand slid into his hair and she held him in place.

He knew when she got close. Her fingernails dug into his scalp, but it didn't hurt. She tried to wiggle out from under him. He held her more firmly until she cried out his name and her clit began to soften. Her grip on him eased slowly.

He lifted up a little. She was soaked now, the scent of her making him want to snarl and fuck her hard. Her pussy had become all pink and ready for him. He straightened on his knees at the end of the bed, grabbed her, and flipped her back onto her stomach. He backed off just enough to drag her off the bed and bend her over the mattress in front of him.

She was short. Her knees didn't touch the floor. It made him smile as he gripped his stiff cock, adjusted the tip of it, and inched closer to line them up. He began to push into her, and groaned. She was wet and tight.

"Fuck, baby."

"Oh God, Glacier!"

"I'm trying to go slow." He came down over her to pin her in place, braced one hand on the bed, the other on her hip as he pushed into her deep. She felt like heaven and hell combined when he paused there.

"You don't have to hold back."

She was much smaller than him. A buck twenty at most. Probably less. She'd always been petite. He closed his eyes and began to withdraw. He paused, thrusting forward until he was all in again. He tightened his hold and began to rock his hips.

Pleasure and need overtook his ability to think as he fucked her harder, faster. She moaned loudly, encouraging him.

Her hand wrapped around his wrist that he'd planted near her head and her nails sank into his skin. He lost what little control he had left and hammered into her until he came, hard. He groaned her name.

He buried his face into her hair. "Did I hurt you?"

"No," she panted back.

"You didn't come a second time."

She hesitated.

He chuckled. "Don't lie to me."

"I was close."

He released her hip and wiggled his hand between her and the mattress, until he pressed his finger against her clit. She jerked under him as he began to rub. His dick remained hard, not softening yet. He slowly fucked her. She moaned and he felt her vaginal muscles tighten around his shaft until it damn near hurt. She came quickly.

173

He stilled, smiling. "Now we know you can get off without biting."

She chuckled.

"Do you need to feed?"

"I'm good. I *am* tired though. Is it bad that I want to just sleep?"

"No. It's daylight."

She yawned. "I'm like a guy. You got me off and now I'm going to snooze."

He laughed and slowly withdrew from her. He adjusted his hold and helped her climb onto the bed. She crawled up the mattress and he loved watching her move that way. She had the grace of a cat, only a sexy naked one. His dick perked up with interest but he ignored the urge. He followed her, shoving down the covers.

"I need to ask you something."

"What?"

"Is there a chance you'll bite me while you're asleep?"

She turned and faced him. Her eyes widened. "I don't know. I've never slept with someone before."

"Fair enough." He lay down and pulled her closer. "Roll over. I want to spoon you. It'll also help keep your mouth away from my throat, facing away from me. I do want you close, though."

She rolled over and wiggled backward, snuggling her backside to his front. He only had one pillow, so he used it and gave her his arm. He liked it when she placed her head on him. He curled around her, getting comfortable.

"You fit nice here."

"I like being held by you. I feel safe."

"You are. Sleep, baby."

"Glacier?"

"Yes?" He rested his chin on the top of her head.

"Never mind."

"Don't do that. You can say anything to me."

She kept her head turned away but she placed her hand on his arm, caressing his skin. "I was really lonely until you came along. Please don't be too good to be true."

"I have way too many flaws for that."

"You know what I mean. I could get used to this. To you. *Too* used to it, you know?"

He understood what she meant. "I'll make a deal with you. I won't leave you if you don't leave me."

"You might be stuck with me forever then."

He held her a little tighter. "I'm willing to chance it. What's the longest relationship you've ever been in?"

"Seven months, but then I found out he cheated on me."

"I'm not going to do that. I've never committed before, but I am now. We'll make this work. We both want it to. We'll take one day at a time."

"Okay."

"Sleep. We've got a lot of road to cover tonight."

He knew when she drifted off less than a minute later. Her breathing slowed to a pace that would have alarmed him if he wasn't aware that was normal for her kind. It's why most people thought Vampires were dead during the day. She probably took a breath about every minute and her heart only beat four times between breaths.

Glacier napped until he heard the door downstairs close. He carefully got out of bed without waking Mandy, put on his boxers, and went to talk to his brother.

Pest placed bags on the counter and inhaled. He cocked his head, watching him.

"She didn't bite me."

"Good. I grabbed some food. You should eat."

"I'm fine."

"Let me rephrase that. I'm not getting laid, and I love pussy. Eat something so that when you talk, I'm smelling food instead of short stack on your breath. It's just mean."

"Asshole." Glacier sniffed, dug into the bag that smelled like food, and found where his brother had shoved another bag full of breakfast sandwiches inside. He unwrapped one and began to eat.

"I take it you worked out kissing without her nailing your tongue with her fangs?"

"We haven't kissed."

"Shit. That's rough. Then again, you're the one-night-stand king. You probably don't do that. Relationships are different."

"I don't need advice. Mandy and I will figure it out. Did you get her some clothes and a helmet?"

"Yeah." Pest pointed to one of the bags. "Tinted face shields. I bought two with headsets. I figured you'd like to be able to talk to each other without yelling. I tried one on to be sure it fit you, and guessed hers would be smaller. I hope they're comfortable."

"Thanks."

"No problem. Any word yet from Kelzeb on where he's sending you?"

"No. It's just after nine. I figure it will be a few hours."

"I'll stick around to make sure the Lycans don't try to keep you here tonight when you head out. I rented a motorcycle. It's not nearly as nice as yours, but it will do until we blow this city and we're far from their territory. I'll return it when we part ways, before I fly to my next gig. I did get orders this morning."

"What's the mission?"

"I'm on my way to Miami. There's been some bodies found. It might be a serial killer, but I need to make sure it's a human doing the killing and not something else."

"Blood drained? Torn up?"

"Cut up, but not all the pieces have been found. Four dead in the past eight days. I'll hit the scenes where body parts were discovered and sniff around. Some of them were inside buildings. It might mean scents have lingered that I can pick up."

"Good luck. Check in."

"I always do."

"I'm going back to bed to get some sleep. See you around five. We'll hit the road as soon as the sun is down."

Glacier headed upstairs and entered the bedroom, prepared to climb back in, when his cell dinged. He bent, retrieved it from his jeans, and turned it on. He had two missed calls and half a dozen texts. The number all of them had come from had him curling his lip and heading back out of the bedroom. He returned downstairs to find his brother still eating.

"What's up?"

"Fucking Kevin. I'm going to call him back. He sent me a couple of messages." He didn't bother to read the texts but instead just called the alpha. Kevin answered on the first ring.

"I want you to come to me right now to fight. I've assembled the entire pack to witness it."

"Fuck you. I'm not challenging you, Kevin. You were drunk last night and being stupid. I refuse to apologize because you're an idiot."

Pest snorted a laugh.

"How dare you!"

"I saved your life. You're welcome. I don't want your pack. I just wanted to save Lycan kids. And I did. Marco and his second are dead. Your problem is solved. I'm out of here tonight and you'll never see me again."

"I've been challenged twice this morning. I had to kill two members of my pack because of you! I'm not letting this go. Stop being a coward. Get your ass in front of the pack house. I'm going to fucking kill you to show my people that I deserve to be their alpha."

"I'm a GarLycan, Kevin. Not an alpha. You get that I can turn to stone and just stand there until you've worn yourself out from doing me absolutely no harm, don't you? What's the point of that? I don't want to kill you, either. Do you know why? Because I *don't want to lead your pack*. I punched you because you were drunk as shit and not listening to me. Marco and his second were in your territory, on their way to distract your pack. They would have taken you down faster than you could have said 'fucked'. Understand?"

Kevin snarled. "You didn't even give me the chance to kill the Vamps. You humiliated me!"

"You did that to yourself by getting drunk when your pack was still in danger. You had them out of lockdown. How many of them would have been killed wandering around the woods thinking they were safe? Especially since they were drunk."

"You won't come fight me?"

"No. I won't. There's no point. Kick some ass if you're challenged and handle it. It's not my problem."

Kevin snarled.

Glacier met his brother's stare and rolled his eyes.

"I want you to leave my territory within the hour, you coward."

"Kevin, that's not going to happen. I have a Vampire with me that Lord Aveoth wants to keep alive to learn more about their council. She's been cooperative."

"That makes it even better. You embarrass me in front of my pack? Now you'll fail your mission to turn over the Vampire to your lord. I hope he kills you for failing him. You're going to get out of my territory within the hour and leave the Vampire in the building for us to collect. You try to leave with it and we'll attack until it's dead. Either way, you lose, asshole."

179

"This guy is a fucking idiot," Pest whispered.

Glacier held his brother's gaze. Pest could easily hear the conversation in the quiet room, with them standing so close together. He gave a grim nod.

"Don't make threats, Kevin. You don't want to fuck with me *or* Lord Aveoth," Glacier warned.

"Step outside, asshole."

Glacier walked to the door and unlocked it. He peered out into the alley. The scent of trash hung in the air, but sudden movement above drew his eye. He looked up to see six Lycans standing on the roof of the next building, watching him back. He turned his head, spotting more on other roofs. He backed inside.

"What are you doing, Kevin?"

"You're not going to embarrass me without paying for it. I gave you the chance to face me with honor. You refuse to fight? You're not leaving with the Vampire. I'm taking it from you. I don't want to start a war with the GarLycans, but I will. You've got one hour to leave. You try to take the Vamp, my men will open fire. I mean, you *did* encourage us to use guns. We'll shoot the fuck out of the Vampire if you carry it out. Enough holes and it'll ash. And it's daylight, anyway. What are you going to do, asshole? Carry it down the street in a body bag in front of humans?" Kevin laughed.

"Or just stay in there. My men followed Graves after you dropped off that borrowed van. You know those explosives you wouldn't let me use at the restaurant? We have them, asshole. They've been planted around the exterior of your building. So stay there. *Please*. You might survive if Gargoyles are as tough as you claim, but the Vamp won't. It'll be blown to

180

bits. And don't think I didn't learn from you, either. There's one sewer tunnel under that place. It's rigged to blow if you try to access it."

Pest motioned to the door and made a few hand signals. Glacier nodded. "Do any of your Lycans out there have cell phones, Kevin?"

"Of course."

He nodded at Pest. His brother yanked open the door and stepped out, glaring up at the pack.

"You should call them. I'm not the only GarLycan here, dick. Your pack is getting a visual on another one now. You *don't* want to do this."

"Fuck you! I don't care if there are a dozen of you assholes! You're going to pay for embarrassing me."

Glacier grit his teeth. "Fine. You want a fight? I'm on my way."

"That option is off the table now." Kevin snickered. "You leave that building to come after me—hell, *anyone* does—and my enforcers blow it. You might come kill me but your Vamp will be chunks." He laughed. "I *always* get my revenge." He disconnected.

"Fuck!"

Pest backed inside the building, locking the door. "I missed the last part."

"We leave to go after him and he blows the building to kill Mandy. We stay after one hour, he's going to blow it anyway."

"Fuck. How are we going to get her out of here? They're sporting guns. A few of them flashed 'em at me just now. That prick is right about what's going to happen if we wrap short stack in a tarp and carry her out.

I saw humans down on both streets. Gunfire will draw them, the cops will come, and it will turn into a fucking media mess."

"There's only one thing to do then. We all need to walk out of here."

Pest stared at him, precious long seconds passing. "Fuck. You can't do it, bro."

"What choice do I have? Leave Mandy to die? I won't. Stay here and have us both shell around her, hoping our bodies protect her? We'd be buried under rubble and the humans would eventually start digging. They'd find us."

"You can't just make that decision without permission first. This is Lord-Aveoth big."

Glacier closed his eyes. "Yeah. I know."

"He's never going to agree to it. It's law, bro."

Glacier took some deep breaths. "I have to ask."

He called Kelzeb.

"I've called both alphas. They are discussing it. Neither has gotten back to me yet," his boss stated after answering the phone.

"I need to speak to Lord Aveoth."

Kelzeb didn't answer.

Glacier filled him in quickly. "I *need* to talk to him."

"Fuck. I'll call you back in five minutes. He's in his quarters with his mate. I need to give him an update and then you'll get his answer."

"Don't be long. I don't trust that crazy Lycan to not just blow the building."

"I'm leaving my office now." He hung up.

182

Pest began to pack things up. "No means no. If Aveoth denies your request, you can't just do it anyway. It's Gargoyle law. He'll have no choice but to order you punished, and her put to death. He's pretty cool but he can't let something like that slide. It would make him look weak to the entire clan. Shit's already tense, thanks to our departed dickhead of a father. Aveoth has a mate to consider, too."

"I know." Glacier sighed. "I'm going to get dressed."

He rushed upstairs, put on clothes, his boots, and packed his shit. He woke Mandy. She startled and sat up.

"I don't have time to explain. Run downstairs, get what Pest bought for you and blacken your hair right now."

She looked confused.

"Do it fast."

She got out of bed, put on one his shirts, and stumbled past him out of the bedroom. Pest met her in the hallway.

"Here, short stack. Spray-on hair color, clothes, and some makeup are in these bags. Need help with covering your hair in the back since Glacier is busy?"

"I got it, Pest. Thanks. What's going on?"

"You heard my bro. No time to explain. Just hustle your ass. Faster is better. We might be attacked at any moment."

Glacier met her frightened gaze and nodded. "Hurry." He began to shove all his things inside his bag. Minutes later, his phone buzzed. He answered it.

"What a fucking mess," a deep voice rumbled. "Kelzeb told me everything."

"Thank you for calling me, my lord. I can't let her die. You know what I'm asking. But I've been loyal to you. I just need to feed her once. Just for today."

"It's a huge fucking risk."

"I know. We're changing her appearance. No one will recognize her for what she really is."

Lord Aveoth grumbled. "I have Jill. I get it. I'd level this entire fucking place to keep her safe. I have a condition, though. Are you prepared to do whatever it takes to save this Vampire of yours? This is a big fucking rule to break. I need to cover my ass because at some point, someone is going to find out. I can handle the GarLycans, but the full-bloods here might raise hell. This law is thousands of years old. In Europe, it's an instant death sentence for you both. Every fucking clan would hunt you down to end your lives. Thankfully, I'm the biggest power in the United States as far as Gargoyles go."

"What terms? Tell me."

"You mate her, Glacier. I can sell that shit to our clan when they find out. We all respect mates. It also means keeping her away from any Lycan packs. If they find out, we're all in danger because that information is valuable. I'll figure something out though, since you can't bring her here. You have my permission to feed her if you mate her. One other thing."

"What?" Glacier's heart pounded. He was willing to mate Mandy to keep her safe.

"If you ever part ways, it's by death. If she ever betrays us, you put her down yourself. Swear to it. She can't ever share this knowledge. She'll be your mate, or she'll be ash after you feed her. The fucking clans in Europe might come after us if you let her go and word spreads. I won't risk the lives of our people or our VampLycan neighbors, who would find themselves in the middle of a war zone."

He closed his eyes. "I swear on my honor."

"Do it. Feed her. And once she's your mate, your body belongs to her. That includes your blood. I won't have you weakened by your mate in the future. Do you understand me?

He opened his eyes, stunned. Lord Aveoth was giving him permission to allow his mate to feed from him whenever she needed to. "I do. Thank you."

"You're welcome. Get the fuck out of there and call Kelzeb when you're safely out of their territory. *No one* threatens one of mine this way. I'm sending your brothers to deal with the alpha."

"Tempest is already here. Once the enforcer attacked Mandy, I asked him to be with her when I had to leave her alone. He said he had some down time."

"Nebulas is two states over from you. Kelzeb is sending him orders now. I don't expect you to lie to your brothers. Kelzeb will also inform Creed what's going on. Now get the hell out of there as soon as you mate her. You can romance her later."

Lord Aveoth hung up and Glacier shoved his phone into his pocket. "I love that guy."

Pest grinned from the doorway. "I heard what he said. Give me your bag. I'll have us ready to roll by the time you come downstairs. You know that talk Neb had with us about taking our time screwing women? Forget it. Ultimate quickie, bro. I want out of here in ten minutes."

Glacier watched him leave and sighed. Ten minutes to talk to Mandy, get her to agree to become his mate, and seal the deal. "Shit."

Chapter Eleven

Mandy finished her hair, staring in the dingy mirror and tilting her head from side to side, hoping she'd covered every inch of blonde with black. The smell of the spray had her wrinkling her nose. It wasn't the greatest odor. It worked though.

She put the bottle down and ripped open the makeup. They were the wrong colors for her very pale skin but it didn't matter. Any color would be good. She worked fast, spreading the foundation from the roots at her forehead, all the way down her neck, including any spots that wouldn't be covered by a shirt. She even used some on her hands and arms up to her shoulders. Lastly, she used a towel to gently pat and remove any excess, to keep it from staining her clothes when she got dressed.

It was a shit makeup job, she thought, as she dabbed on mascara, a little blush, and an ugly shade of pink lipstick. It didn't matter. She wasn't planning on getting close to anyone once Glacier was able to free her from whatever he wrapped her inside to protect her from the sun. Being transported during the day would be dangerous, but she had faith in Glacier to keep her safe.

The bathroom door opened and Glacier slid in. He closed the door behind him. She turned, staring into his eyes.

"We don't have a lot of time."

"What's going on? Fast version."

"Kevin had his pack plant bombs on the outside of this building. He gave me one hour to leave. He blows us up if I don't. I'm also supposed to

187

leave you behind. He threatened to have his enforcers shoot big holes in whatever I carry you out in, to expose you to sun. He won't let any large vehicles get near the building, either. Pest and I have our motorcycles parked outside the back door. It means we have to drive out on them."

Her heart sank. "Shit. Why are you having me change how I look, then? You need to leave me behind."

"That's never going to happen." He stepped forward and gripped her hips, his thumbs brushing her bare skin since she hadn't gotten dressed yet or even looked in the bag of clothes Pest had shoved at her.

"I spoke to Lord Aveoth. He gave me permission to save you. There are conditions...we have to mate."

She reached out and gripped his arms. "Mate?"

"And we don't have much time. Mate. It's forever. You and me. I can't force you, but please say yes. We can make it work."

Tears filled her eyes. She would love to spend the rest of her life with Glacier. To never be alone, to have him at her side, and to experience what she had earlier, sleeping curled in front of him every time they rested. He felt like home, something she hadn't had since her human life had been taken from her.

"Answer me, Mandy. Yes? Will you be my mate?"

"They're going to kill you if you try to take me out of here. There's no way to do it. We're in a city. It's daylight. Humans can't see you go gray, Glacier. Every race would put a price on your head. I care too much about you to allow you to do that for me."

"Do you trust me, baby?"

She didn't have to think about it. "Yes."

"Good enough. Once a Gargoyle mates, within hours, his woman experiences the calling. It's complicated, but we can't risk that. I don't think Lord Aveoth considered that when he ordered me to mate you first. I trust you too. Say yes to mating me, and then we're going to walk the fuck out of here—together. Tonight though, I'm sealing the bond between us."

"What are you talking about? I can't *walk* out of here. It's broad daylight."

He pulled her closer. "Say yes, you'll mate me. Do it. Promise to be mine. Trust me."

She swallowed. "I promise to be yours. Yes, I'll be your mate."

He lowered his head and put his lips next to her ear. "The reason Vampires and Gargoyles have battled for thousands of years...is because really old masters knew that drinking our blood allows them to walk in the sun without burning."

Her knees almost gave out on her and she clutched him tighter. It shocked the hell out of her. Could that be true?

"It's why it's against the law to feed you. I got permission from Lord Aveoth, but only if you're my mate. Get your fangs out, baby. Bite and drink as much from me as you can. You need to do it now." He cocked his head and bent his knees a little. "Bite. Now. Drink."

She was too stunned.

He gently shook her. "Do it."

"How? I mean..."

"The sun won't burn you if you drink my blood. No more time to discuss it. Bite me, baby. Drink as much as you can hold."

"I'll weaken you."

He snorted. "I'm twice your size and I've lost more blood in a training fight with one of my brothers than you could take from me, even if you're starved. *Do it*. We don't have time to waste."

She had to concentrate to get her fangs to come down. He slid his hands to her ass, massaging her. It helped a lot, her body responding. Everything about Glacier turned her on. She licked her lips, staring at his throat, which he kept exposed. She leaned in and went to her tiptoes. She ran the tip of her tongue over his skin—and sank her fangs in.

He stiffened against her and tightened his hold. "*Damn*. I'm so hard. I wish I could fuck you right now."

She did too. He tasted incredible.

Her body ached as she drank from him, sexual need and bloodlust rising. She caressed his arms, trying to keep her sanity. She couldn't get lost or they'd end up on the floor. The building was rigged to blow; no way did she want to lose the chance at a future with Glacier.

She drank until she couldn't anymore before gently easing her fangs from him, licking at his skin.

His grip on her ass would leave bruises and his hard-on pressed firmly against her pelvis. His cock felt rock hard. She could relate, since she was so wet it dampened her inner thighs. He backed off and leaned against the door. His eyes blazed with arousal and his own fangs were out as they stared at each other.

190

"Do some jumping jacks and get dressed. Use that Vamp speed of yours."

"Jumping jacks?"

"To circulate my blood through your system. I promise, it'll keep you from burning when you walk out of here at my side." He slid away from the door, opened it, and stepped out. Before closing the door, leaving her alone, he looked back. "Hurry."

She was so aroused it literally hurt. It wasn't the best time for it. Glacier's life was on the line. Yes, he was a GarLycan, and she'd seen what his body could do when he turned all gray. The thing she wasn't sure of was whether he'd survive a bomb going off.

She threw up her arms and did what he said, feeling ridiculous while she flapped around. But it did get her heart beating fast.

She was out of breath by the time she'd finished and quickly dressed. Pest had bought her the right size bra. It wasn't one she'd have chosen but it didn't matter. The underwear were thongs. She rolled her eyes, putting them on. The shirt was a bit tight but fell long, almost like a mini dress. Black stretch jeans came next. Again, something she wouldn't have picked but they fit well, hugging her body. They'd be comfortable on a motorcycle. He'd bought her slip-on canvas shoes she found at the bottom of the bag. They were a tiny bit large but she could walk in them.

One glance around the bathroom, then she grabbed the makeup and dye spray, shoving it back in the bag. She didn't want to leave it behind in case the Werewolves came in, searching for her.

She left the bathroom and rushed downstairs. Pest and Glacier waited, holding their backpacks. Both looked grim. Pest sniffed.

"You don't smell like Vamp right now. New clothes and that damn hair stuff is all I'm picking up." He glanced at his brother. "You?"

"Same." Glacier held out his hand and she passed him the bag. He shoved it into his backpack, zipping it up and handing it to her. "Sorry, but you need to wear this. We're walking out, putting on our helmets, and you climb on behind me. Hold on tight."

Terror hit as she shouldered his pack. "Are you sure about this?" It hurt to burn. There were some things so horrible a person never forgot. The sensation of sunlight touching her skin could be compared to being doused in gasoline and set on fire. It had left her screaming in agony. Healing from it, even given blood right after, hurt almost as much while her skin regrew.

Glacier nodded. "Trust me."

"I do."

"Act like it's nighttime," Pest added softly. "Don't move fast to reveal what you are. Blurring your speed is a sure giveaway, short stack. Or looking panicked as shit. Own that sunlight like it's your bitch. It is, with my bro's blood inside you. You won't burn."

She nodded. "How long does it last?"

Pest reached inside his backpack and withdrew sunglasses. "You'll be fine. You drank a lot?"

She nodded. "About two pints. I didn't want to take more than that."

"I'm fine." Glacier smiled. "I feel great. Not lightheaded at all. I told you that you wouldn't hurt me. I'm not human."

192

Pest passed her the sunglasses. They were ugly, the kind that looked more like tinted goggles with curved earpieces to hook around the back of the ears. "The sun might hurt your eyes. Wear these. The face shield on the helmet is tinted but double protection is best. It's possible that you might be temporarily blinded otherwise. Your eyes won't be used to that kind of light, and I read some ancient texts that mentioned it can happen the first time a Vampire feeds from a Gargoyle. Just be cool. Your eyes won't be damaged but it may feel that way at first."

"I'm scared." She stared up at Glacier.

"I'd never let anything happen to you."

She believed him. "Okay."

"Let's leave this dump." Pest unlocked the door. "Glasses on, short stack. Move slow and act normal. Think back to when you were human. Pretend you are. This pack was made aware that Glacier isn't here alone. They might believe you're another GarLycan."

She put on the glasses, her hands shaking. Glacier came to her, gripping her bare arm in a good hold. Probably in case she freaked or chickened out.

Pest swung the door open and the bright light *did* blind her. She blinked a few times. She could see, but everything was blurry and hazy. Pest strode out first, putting on his backpack. He lifted his head.

"We're leaving. What you demanded is in the basement. You guys *are* going to pay for this bullshit. Oh, and she's not restrained. I hope she eats some of you fuckers when you go in there after her. She's strong enough to be awake right now."

"I'm with you, baby," Glacier whispered. He walked forward, pulling her along.

She stepped willingly into direct sunlight for the first time in almost thirty years, more than aware that her arms were bare from the elbows down, her face and neck too.

Her skin tingled…but there was no pain. After a few steps, she also realized she had been holding her breathe. She breathed in and relaxed.

Glacier released her arm, seeming to understand that she was okay.

She couldn't see well so she focused on him, following as he walked to one of the motorcycles. He removed two helmets, passing her one. She shoved it over her head. He put his own on, straddled the bike, and started it. He jerked his covered head and she took the hint, climbing on behind him.

"Don't ever return to our territory!" some guy shouted.

"Fuck you," Glacier yelled back. He lowered his voice. "Hold on tight to me."

She wrapped her arms around his waist and found the pegs for her feet. His bike didn't have a bar at her back. Pest started his own bike and that's when Glacier took off. Pest drove behind them down the alley.

Warm sun caressed her skin. It still tingled a little but there was no pain. The sheer shock of being out in daylight made the experience feel surreal. It was something she never would have expected to happen again in her life after being turned into a Vampire. They stopped for traffic and merged when they could leave the alley. She squinted a little, but her eyesight improved after they'd made it a few blocks. Humans were out and about, walking around, living their lives in the daylight.

194

She looked up to glance at the sun but it instantly blinded her. She lowered her chin, seeing spots. It didn't hurt, but she wasn't ready to do that again anytime soon. She tightened her arms around Glacier.

He released the hand grip and gently cupped her hand over his waist at a red light. "It's going to be fine. How are you doing?"

She realized since she could hear him so well that there must be a speaker inside the helmet. She hadn't noticed when she'd first climbed on the bike. "I'm good."

"Can you see anything?"

"Things are a bit blurry but it's getting better. It's so...bright."

He chuckled. "Get used to it. You're my mate. This is how it will be from now on."

He'd stunned her again.

"Did you hear me?"

"Yes."

"I won't risk losing you. Now let's have this conversation later, in more detail. I don't know if these headsets are secure."

"I had no idea this was possible."

"That's the point. The highway is coming up."

They merged with traffic and Pest drove up beside them, both bikes sharing the lane. Mandy just enjoyed the view. Her vision became clearer, helping her make out every detail around her. She couldn't see as far as usual but it was beautiful and breathtaking to see sunlight glinting off all the vehicles.

She glanced down at the part of her arm that was exposed. Her flesh wasn't blackened, or even red. It still tingled from time to time but the sensation was so faint it wasn't alarming. She adjusted her hold on Glacier, using his body and clothes to help her shield some of her skin from the sun.

"Are you alright?"

"I'm tingling a bit where the sun is on me. Is that normal?"

"I don't know. No pain though?"

"No."

"Slide your hands under my shirt."

She did it, enjoying feeling his bare skin under her palms.

"Better? You tell me if something starts to go wrong. It shouldn't though."

That didn't reassure her. He seemed to read her mind, or guess what she was thinking about, considering his next words.

"I'll tell you why that law was made. I have to put this carefully, remember." He paused. "I know that once, both of them got along. They didn't always hate each other. Then the ones like you wanted what my kind had. They called it a cure. Which is pretty fucking dumb, because it's not like you take it once and it lasts forever."

She nodded against him. "But it will last for the day?"

"It should. That's what the historical accounts we have say. Sometimes a few days with regular, um, doses."

Feedings, she supplemented silently.

"They wanted to use us."

Again, she could translate. Vampires had wanted to enslave Gargoyles, in order to drink their blood. But she'd seen Glacier shell. She'd probably break her fangs if she attempted to bite him when he became dark gray. "I bet that didn't go over well."

"No, it didn't. Anyone who came after us died. And it lasted for a long damn time."

"You said that." *Thousands of years.*

"Eventually, anyone who had known and tried to get what they called the cure just wasn't around anymore. The battles stopped. Laws were made to keep it from restarting."

"But you broke that law today."

"I got permission. We're also here, and nowhere near where those battles took place. It would still be a disaster if anyone found out. Do you understand?"

She could just imagine. If the council found out drinking Gargoyle blood could give them the ability to walk in the sun, to not burn. They'd do *anything* to obtain a Gargoyle. Every nest might join together to start a new war. Rumor had it that there weren't all that many GarLycans and Gargoyles in the United States. The Vampires would attempt it. They might lose thousands of lives in the process, but it would be worth it if they caught anyone with Gargoyle blood to feed from.

"Shit. It would be horrible."

"Yeah, baby."

"They can never find out." She held him a little tighter. Glacier would be in danger.

"They won't."

"What about when the ones we just left enter the shop? They're expecting to find something that isn't there."

"Took care of that. I had Pest burn something."

She closed her eyes and snuggled into his back, hoping the Werewolves bought that the ashes they found used to be her.

"Why'd he tell them that you left me unchained?"

He chuckled. "To stall for time. They're a bunch of pussies. I want us long gone before they work up the nerve to go in and find what we really left behind."

* * * * *

Glacier didn't like how quiet Mandy had become after their talk. He knew she wasn't in pain though, since she occasionally rubbed his stomach with her hand. It was a form of torture, since he'd had a constant hard-on after she'd bitten him.

They had left the Lycan territory hours ago. He drew his brother's attention and motioned at his tank. Pest gave him a hand signal to indicate he understood. They changed lanes, getting off the highway at the next gas station.

"We're pulling off for a bit. I need to refill the tank and eat something."

"Okay."

"How are you doing?"

"I'm great."

"Is your skin hurting at all?"

"No."

"Talk to me. I'm starting to worry."

Mandy hesitated. "I just keep thinking about how much you've risked for me. Why did you do this?"

"Because you're mine."

He pulled into the gas station and parked in front of a pump. Pest took the spot on the other side. Glacier tapped her hand as he put the kickstand down and killed the engine. "You might feel stiff from riding for hours. Stand up and stretch."

"I'll keep the helmet on."

"Is your skin okay? Don't hide anything from me."

She released him and climbed off. He missed the slight weight of her pressed against his back. She did as he asked, lifting her arms above her head. His gaze locked on her breasts, which were pushed out in the process, and he wished she weren't wearing clothes.

"Enough of that shit," Pest chuckled. "I can't see your face but there's nothing wrong with my sense of smell. Think about sex later. Public bathrooms are nasty. No family of mine is going to lower themselves to screw in one. In a few more hours, we'll settle in before dark at some hotel."

"Motel," Glacier corrected.

"*Hotel*. They have cameras and better security. We want to keep short stack completely off the supernatural radar. Motels are buffets to her kind. Plus, while I don't think we're being followed, that was a crowded highway. We also didn't have time to look over our bikes when we left. Which I plan to do now, to see if they're tracking us. I'll fill the tanks. You go inside to grab us grub and something to drink. Short stack will be in my company, since we want to keep her helmet on. It would look weird if she walked inside with it on; someone might think she's about to rob the place. Humans are too uptight."

Glacier removed his helmet. "Be back. Stick with Pest, Mandy."

"Like glue," she promised.

Glacier strode inside the mini-mart part of the gas station, grabbing some premade sandwiches and water for him and his brother. He waited in line and then paid. His continually scanned the area, breathing through his nose. Only humans were inside the store. He liked it better that way. He exited, dropping off the bag on his bike seat.

"I'm going to take a leak."

"I'll go after you get back." Pest had finished filling Glacier's motorcycle and moved around the pump to his own bike.

"Are you doing okay, Mandy?"

She nodded at him. "Yes."

"Be right back."

Glacier entered the bathroom and used it fast, washed his hands, and took a minute to check his phone. He had a few missed calls from that asshole Kevin, one from Neb, and another from Creed. He texted both of his brothers, letting them know they were on the road and he'd speak to them when they settled for the night.

200

He and Pest ate fast, standing near the pumps since the station wasn't busy. Then while Pest inspected the bikes, Glacier checked over Mandy's exposed skin. It had become a little pink but not enough to alarm him. Otherwise, he'd have dragged her into the bathroom to make her feed from him again.

Pest nudged him. His brother frowned and flashed open his palm.

Glacier identified what he was being shown. "Yours or mine?"

"Yours, under the edge of the seat."

"What's going on?" Mandy inched closer.

Pest dumped the device into the trash with the food wrappers. "We were tracked."

Glacier climbed on the bike, putting on his helmet. "Kevin isn't done with us yet, or he wanted to make damn sure we left his territory. The idiot is probably planning something. We're definitely staying in a high-end hotel tonight, something with at least eight floors. Lycans don't fly. We can."

"Penthouse suite it is, and hopefully they have balconies." Pest started his bike.

"But we're out of his territory." Mandy sounded dismayed.

"I think that's the point. He probably believes he can come after me tonight and not get blamed if I die. He doesn't really want a war with GarLycans. Just me. He's too much of a pussy for that."

"Fucking moron," Pest muttered.

"That's Kevin."

Then they were on the road again. They could leave the main highway, but the smaller ones led to out-of-the-way spots, which would make for an attack easier. Every mile they drove without someone seemingly following them had Glacier relaxing a little more. Still, he kept his attention on his mirrors. He had a mate to protect. He'd allow nothing to happen to Mandy.

Chapter Twelve

The suite had two master bedrooms with attached private bathrooms, a large living space, and a balcony. They were on the tenth floor of a well-known hotel chain. Mandy had kept her chin tucked as they'd checked in and taken the elevator to their floor.

Pest dropped his bag inside the door, addressing his brother.

"I'm going to go eat a real meal in the restaurant, have a beer, and maybe get laid. I'll take my time, since you have a promise to keep." He pointed at Glacier. "Make damn certain the bond is strong. We don't need your girl drawing Lycans to us on the road tomorrow like the Pied Piper of pussy."

"Excuse me?" Mandy gaped at Pest.

"It's not a given that she'll react that way. We're in uncharted territory," Glacier responded.

"True enough, but it's best to be prepared in case it does happen. Tell her about the calling." Pest left the suite, closing the door after him.

Mandy turned to Glacier, arching her eyebrows.

"It's a weird Gargoyle thing, because my kind tend to be thickheaded and emotionally remote. It's possible that you may put off 'fuck me' pheromones that any man will respond to. Lycans are especially susceptible, since they have the best sense of smell. Think of a Lycan woman in heat, times ten. It makes Lycan men lose their damn minds and go into a frenzy unless they're already mated. Even close proximity to humans, despite their duller senses, will make them horny."

She felt a little stunned, yet again.

"It's true. It's why it's called the calling. Your body will make sure a Gargoyle wants to fuck you to seal the bond all the way, to make it strong. The good news is, we get to fuck like bunnies tonight to make sure you're properly claimed." He grinned. "I'm not going to complain about that. Are you?"

She grinned back. "I've seen bunnies fuck. So, you plan to furiously hump me and finish in about twenty seconds?"

He put down the pack he held and lunged.

She laughed as he lifted her, tossing her over his shoulder and walking into one of the bedrooms. He used his boot to close the door. "Maybe not like rabbits, but we're not getting much sleep tonight. I know you have to be exhausted."

"I'm doing good, and I suddenly feel very awake."

He bent, easing her onto her feet next to the bed. "Strip, baby. I'll be right back." He left her and entered the bathroom, closing the door.

Mandy kicked off her shoes and removed her clothes, noticing the pinkness had faded already from where the sun had touched her. The toilet flushed in the other room and water ran. She pulled back the covers, climbing into bed. Both excitement and nerves filled her.

She knew Lycans took mates, and it seemed Gargoyles did as well. But she'd never thought she'd become a mate. Companion to a Vampire wasn't nearly as intense. They agreed to live together, set rules to abide by, but could always part ways if it didn't work out. That wasn't the case with mates. It would be a bond forever, only to be broken with death, from what she understood.

It was tempting to shower. The smell of her hair bothered her, along with the makeup. She jumped out of bed just as the door to the bathroom opened.

Glacier's cool blue eyes roamed down her body and he reached for the front of his jeans. "You're so sexy."

"I want a shower first. I smell."

"I don't give a damn. We're bonding first. We'll shower later."

"I reek, Glacier. Even *I* can't stand it. Wearing the helmet didn't exactly air out this hair color stuff."

He opened his pants, bent and tore off his boots, then his socks. He straightened, shoving his pants off. The shirt went last. She stared at his body. He had an amazing one. Muscular and cut. His cock was thick and hard.

He smiled. "Get back on the bed unless you'd like me to take you standing." He strode to her. "We're mating."

"What does that entail? You need to bite me, right? We have to exchange blood?"

"I need to flux and bite you during sex. It will trigger mating in a Gargoyle."

She frowned. "Flux?"

"I need to partially shift. Wings out, my skin very lightly shelled. I'll drink your blood while I'm fucking you. It will trigger me to secrete hormones that I release into you with my sperm. That will mate us. Do you understand?"

205

She really didn't, but she thought she got the gist. "Has someone like you ever mated to a Vampire before?"

"Not that I'm aware of. That's not saying it hasn't happened, but no one wrote about it in our history books we have at the cliffs. You'll be my mate though, regardless of whether your body reacts the way other women's do to mating."

"What happens normally?"

"The calling, if we don't bond strongly. If we do, I'll be able to track you anywhere you go. It's a mate thing. My instincts will lead me to you."

"Like a homing device or something?"

He stopped in front of her but didn't touch. "Yes."

"What about me? Will I be able to sense and track you?"

"That's a Gargoyle thing, so I doubt it. But regardless of our physical responses to this mating, you're mine, Mandy. Make the commitment to me. Say you'll be my other half."

She reached up and pressed her hands to his chest. "I can't have babies. You'll be giving up becoming a father."

He didn't flinch or react in any way. "I'm aware."

"Mating is for life with you, right? You're half Werewolf."

"We like the term Lycan better. Yes, this is for life, Mandy. I'm never going to let you go. I don't give a damn about having kids. One day, if that ever changes, we'll figure it out."

"Can your blood change mine enough to make me fertile?"

"No, baby. There would have been warnings written about it. I'm certain that's impossible. I'm sorry if you were hopeful. Walking in the sun without burning is the best I can give you."

"That's not true. You're offering me the world. I just wish I could feel as though I'm giving you the same. Instead, I'm cursing you to a life without having a family."

He moved, sat on the bed, and hooked her waist. He pulled her onto his lap and held her there. "I already have a family. My father got my mother pregnant four times with his sperm. He was a shit dad. I won't go into all the details, but let's just say when my youngest brother had to kill him, it was warranted and approved by the rest of us. Emphasis on the *had to kill him*. Father left Creed with no choice.

"My mother is dead because she was a Lycan mated to a coldhearted bastard who never loved her. He didn't give a damn that he slowly killed her with his absolute neglect of her emotional needs.

"The point is, they had a family, and look how bad *that* turned out. One day, if we want kids, we can adopt. I've come across plenty of orphans, both human and Lycan, who I helped find homes for after shit hit the fan in their lives. Other guardians have experienced the same tragedies and dealt with the survivors. I can put word out to my clan, and even to the VampLycans, if we're ever ready to raise a child. We won't be able to pick the race or sex, but I don't give a damn. A child in need of love is all that matters. But right now, I just want you. Let's worry about the future later."

He never ceased amazing and stunning her.

"What other roadblocks do you want to throw up? Go ahead. I'll tell you how we get around them. Bottom line, we'll work it out. That's what mates do."

She slid her hands into his hair...and leaned close to kiss him for the first time.

He met her lips with his. A soft growl came from his throat as their mouths merged. She knew her fangs slid out, but he had some too. Bigger, more vicious. It made kissing momentarily difficult, but she tilted her head a little more and he was right...they could work things out.

Her GarLycan could *kiss*.

He turned, flipping her onto her back, and came down on top of her on the bed. She parted her thighs to make room for his hips. He moved into position, rocking his stiff cock against her pussy. Desire and need rose stronger until she moaned and released his hair, clawing at his back. She spread her legs wider, wrapping them around his hips.

He broke the kiss. "Slow down, baby."

She loved the husky, rough edge to his voice. "Rabbits, remember? Just last more than twenty seconds. I want you inside me."

He nudged her face with his and she exposed her throat. The thought of him biting didn't frighten her in the least. It excited her more. She'd heal regardless of what his big fangs did to her. She also trusted him not to hurt her. He needed to drink some of her blood, but he'd probably only nick her.

He reached up and offered his wrist.

"Bite, baby."

She hesitated.

He didn't. He licked her throat, placing hot, wet kisses on her flesh, and then his fangs sank into her skin.

She latched onto his wrist, grabbing hold of it to keep it against her mouth while she drank from him. Glacier's fangs left her skin but he continued to suck from her. She moaned louder, grinding her pussy against his cock.

He adjusted his hips and entered her deep in one thrust. Pain and pleasure blurred but it didn't matter. He fucked her hard and fast. The bed creaked but she barely registered the sound, too lost in bloodlust and ecstasy. Her climax built as he pounded into her harder, and he suddenly yanked his wrist from her mouth. She wanted to protest, until she realized his wrist, still in her hand, didn't feel as it should.

Mandy opened her eyes, staring at his skin, still so close to her mouth. It had turned gray, and his wings were spread out over them, blanketing the bed around them. They were black and beautiful.

She released his wrist and reached out to them, running her fingertips along the velvety surface that hardened as she stroked it.

Glacier snarled and fucked her violently, sending her over the edge. She cried out his name as her climax struck. She forgot about his wings, or that he'd partially shelled while inside her, on top of her. Mandy closed her eyes to ride it through as he extended her pleasure and continued fucking her.

Finally, he tensed, bucked his hips, and groaned her name.

His hips jerked with every stream of semen he shot into her. Their bodies felt fused together. He had her pinned tight to the bed under him, his wings all around them, and she clung to him. He stilled his hips finally, breathing hard.

"Fuck. Was I too rough?"

She smiled. "I loved that."

"I put a new spin on rock hard, don't I?"

She ran her fingers over his skin. It was soft and supple again. No longer that odd texture. "I have no complaints."

"Just for tonight, if I offer you some blood, take it fast. I damn near fluxed while your fangs were still in my skin."

She let that meaning behind that concept sink in. "Shit."

"Yeah. It could have been bad."

"Has that ever, um, happened?"

"Once." He lifted up a bit.

Her gaze met his. "Will you tell me about it?"

"Some bastard surprised me in a club. He dropped down on me like a spider from the ceiling before I ever heard or scented him. He sank his fangs into my shoulder. I shelled instantly and then flung him off me. The fangs stayed put. He didn't."

She flinched.

"Yeah. My skin locked his fangs in place. It tore the fuckers right out. He was still screaming from the pain and shock while I removed his head. He was a bad guy who had to die anyway, since I wasn't sure if he'd managed to drink some of my blood before I reacted. I unshelled and pulled his fangs out. It seems they don't ash if they've been removed from a Vamp first. I gave them as a gift to the Lycan woman he'd kidnapped."

She got past her trauma of the idea of having her fangs ripped out. It would be an agonizingly slow death. She'd be unable to feed without them and starve over time. Fangs didn't grow back. "Why did he kidnap a Werewolf woman?"

"He wanted to breed her. It's against the law for anyone to create a VampLycan without permission."

"Had he succeeded?"

"No. I was called in after he'd attempted to steal a few women from a pack in Georgia. They had managed to fight him off. I was already in town when he actually grabbed one. I tracked her scent to where he had her locked up. She had a strong mind, he hadn't been able to tear into it yet. With time he could have, but I located her too fast."

"Why did he want to do that?"

He shrugged. "Who the fuck knows? I didn't exactly give a shit. He died and the problem was resolved. The Lycan woman returned to her family with his fangs as a souvenir of her ordeal." He adjusted his body over hers, kissing her lips. "No more talking. We're bonding, baby. You ready to go again? Because I am."

He was still inside her, still hard, and began to slowly rock his hips. She kissed him back, closing her eyes. It seemed GarLycans didn't need recovery time the way human men did. She was totally onboard with that.

* * * * *

Glacier ordered room service and met the waiter at the door before he could knock and wake his mate. Mandy slept after the hours they'd spent making love, finally giving in to her exhaustion. Vampires weren't like GarLycans. They needed daily sleep, something she'd been denied while they traveled on his motorcycle. He paid in cash and tipped the human.

He sat at the table, scarfing down food, and texted Pest. His brother responded that he'd return to the room soon. He called Creed next, not worried about the fact that it was the middle of the night. His youngest brother answered immediately.

"Are you safe with your mate?"

"Yes. I take it Kelzeb filled you in?"

"He did. A Vampire." Creed chuckled. "You always were ballsy and not one to follow the norm. I'm putting you on speaker. I'm with Neb."

That surprised him. "What is Neb doing in Alaska?"

"I'm not," Neb responded. "Creed came to me. He grabbed a flight from Anchorage to Seattle yesterday, and then took another flight to meet up with me last night. We're currently driving through Utah toward the borders of Colorado and Wyoming. That's where Kelzeb said you're aiming for, last you spoke to him. We were just waiting for you to call in. Where are you?"

"Arizona. Turn toward us." He gave them the city and hotel. "We put in some hours yesterday and a lot of miles, but we had to stop before the sun went down. That asshole Kevin put a tracker on my bike, but we found it right after we crossed the border out of New Mexico."

"Do you think he's planning on attacking you?" Neb paused. "Get me directions, Creed."

"I'm looking at the map. It's about a six-hour drive from here but with you behind the wheel, we can be there in five or less."

"We could abandon the rental and fly. It's faster."

Creed hesitated. "No, Neb. We wouldn't make it in time before the sun crests. Even at top speed, we'd fall short of reaching them. We're trapped in this car with your lead foot. It's amazing we haven't been pulled over. You're doing a hundred and ten miles an hour."

"There isn't shit out here. Do you see many other cars at this time on the freeway? No, you don't."

"It's called an interstate. So much for you being the older, wiser brother."

Glacier sipped his drink and grinned, listening to his brothers rib each other. A road trip with both of them sealed inside a vehicle together sounded hellish. "We'll stay here until you arrive. As for the question you asked, Kevin hasn't sent someone after us so far. It's looking like he put a tracker on my bike to make certain I left his territory. We're staying on alert just in case." He gave them the room number right as the door opened, admitting Pest into the suite. He motioned him to take a seat since he'd ordered a few meals.

"We're on our way." Creed ended the call.

Pest sat at the table and inhaled. "Smells like you bonded to your mate a lot. Good."

"Keep your voice down. Mandy fell asleep."

"Vampires usually do that during the day."

"She couldn't yesterday. She's wiped out. Creed and Neb are six hours out from us. According to Creed, they can make it in five with the way Neb drives."

Surprise flickered across Pest's features. "Shit. I guess I should have answered when both of them called me, but I just figured they wanted the details on you and short stack. That's *your* situation to explain to them."

"Would it kill you to call her Mandy? She's my mate."

"She's adjusting to my nickname. It's as cute as she is. I'm not picking up the calling. At least, I don't have a boner."

"Don't be an ass."

"I'm being honest. You either sealed the bond or she's not going to suffer the effects of mating you by putting out pheromones. What do you think? Did you do the deed enough to avoid it or is it because she's a Vamp?"

"I don't know. This is the first time I've taken a mate."

"No shit." Pest unwrapped his napkin and dug into the nearest plate. "Spaghetti with meatballs. My favorite."

"I ordered for both of us."

"That's got to be weird."

"What?"

"Having a mate you'll never share dinner with. Or should I say a very early breakfast, considering the time."

Glacier frowned. "It doesn't matter."

Pest shrugged. "Think of all the money you'll save over the years. No date nights at fancy restaurants to impress her. Your food bills won't increase unless you need to eat more to keep your blood levels up after you give her a vein."

Glacier flipped him off. "Where have you been?"

"I hung out at the bar until closing to keep an eye on the lobby. No Lycans have shown. Then I took the hot server to another room I rented on the third floor with a view of the parking lot. I banged her against the damn window. She didn't seem to mind. I got to nail her while keeping guard. I doubt the Lycans would use valet parking the way we did." He winked. "I had just showered and gotten her out of there when you'd texted me. I had planned to stay there in case any of Kevin's pack arrived. I'm disappointed they haven't."

"Why the hell did they put a tracker on my bike if they didn't plan to come after me?"

"To be assholes? Maybe he just wanted to make certain you left his territory by keeping tabs on where you headed. Who knows? He wasn't the brightest bulb on the tree."

Glacier nodded, taking a bite of food. "Maybe."

"Has he called you?"

"Six times. No messages or texts. He hangs up when I don't answer."

"I bet he was pissed when he sent his enforcers into that shop, only to discover ashes in the basement."

"I just hope they bought it was Mandy and don't suspect anything."

"Who the fuck would think the woman who walked out with us was a Vampire? There was direct sunlight streaming overhead as she stood there getting on the bike with you. They watched us drive away. She didn't turn to ashes. He'll believe she was one of ours."

Glacier hoped so. "The council needs to be dealt with."

"I was thinking about that as well. If that master was being protected by someone on their council, they aren't going to be pleased when they learn of his death. It would be stupid of them to send more assassins after the Lycans. It's possible they might though."

"I'm not willing to risk it. I hate Kevin, but his pack shouldn't have to pay with loss of lives because he's an idiot."

"I concur. We'll wait for our brothers to arrive and make a trip tonight."

"Where? We don't know how to get ahold of their council."

"No, but you said there was another assassin in Kevin's town."

Glacier nodded. "Olivia, Mandy's friend. She may have fled if she found Mandy's tracker with the ashes in the alley."

"You said they're friends. Would you just walk away if your friend got killed, or would you stick around trying to find the bastard responsible?"

"Point made. Unless she was ordered to leave."

"We can be hopeful that this Olivia hung around and we find her. She'll have a number for the council."

"I don't want her hurt. It would be painful for Mandy."

"Un-fucking-believable."

Glacier held his brother's gaze. "What?"

"Before now, we'd have killed this Vamp just because she's an assassin for the council. Now you're all kittens and puppy dogs, sweet on your mate, and you want to spare her friend's life. Assassins are *killers*, Glacier."

"So are we. It doesn't mean we do it for kicks. Olivia was left with no choice but to work for the council. Same with Mandy. They're servants led by their masters and refusal means death. Let's see if we can track Olivia and reach out to the council to send them a message. We'll say we kept her alive as a good-faith gesture."

Pest sighed. "Fine. What about short stack? Do we leave her here on her own? Is she safe? I hate the idea of flying hours away, possibly having to spend a whole day away from her, and her being left undefended."

"I'll ask Creed to stay with her. The three of us can handle the damn Vampire Council."

"You chose him because he's mated, didn't you?" Pest grinned. "Instincts are a bitch."

"Fuck you."

"I wouldn't hit on your mate. I can be a dick but not that much of one. You know me better than that."

"I didn't say you would. I know you have honor."

"I do, but I agree. Creed is the best choice to play guard."

Chapter Thirteen

Mandy stretched and blindly reached across the bed for Glacier. She had a mate. It was an odd but wonderful concept.

All she felt were sheets and an empty space next to her.

She snapped her eyes opened and sat up. The soft murmurs of male voices came to her. Two of them belonged to her mate and Pest. The other one wasn't familiar. She slid out of bed and headed into the bathroom since there were no sounds of fighting.

Curiosity had her hurrying her shower. The black dye ran down her wet body. She grimaced as she shampooed and conditioned her hair, wondering if it would all wash out. It didn't take long to find out when she exited the hot shower and wrapped a towel around her waist, staring in the steamed mirror. The color had faded but it wasn't back to blonde just yet. She shuddered, hoping she never had to use that canned stuff again.

She left the bathroom and put on the clothing from the day before. Once dressed, she approached the window and carefully pulled back the drape, standing out of the way of the sunlight that streamed in. She shoved her free hand into the light. It didn't burn. Her skin didn't even tingle.

"Shit."

The voices silenced from the other room and seconds later, the door opened, admitting Glacier. He closed it behind him and smiled. "Are you alright? We heard you moving around, the shower coming on and going off, but then you cursed."

She opened the drapes all the way, standing in front of the window to peer out. The view of the buildings and homes, lots of land in the distance where the population hadn't spread, was beautiful. Her vision wasn't as hazy as it had been the day before. The details were clear and crisp. She just couldn't see as far as she could at night. "I'm fine. Just stunned."

He came up behind her and wrapped his arms around her waist, tugging her back against his front. His chin rested on the top of her head. He inhaled. "You smell better."

She grinned. "Yeah. Shampoo and conditioner are a wonderful thing. That hair color stuff wasn't. The pillow is stained from my head where I slept. I noticed that as I got out of bed."

"It doesn't matter. How are your eyes doing?"

"Much better."

"Daily doses of my blood should help a lot. You'll adjust over time."

"I don't need to feed every night."

"You will while we're traveling. I won't have you susceptible to the sun, baby."

"This is so weird, Glacier. It still freaks me out a bit. Yesterday, I was mostly in shock over the fact that I was outside in the sun and worried we'd be attacked. My focus was on you. Today, it's just kind of hitting me full blast. I'm standing here, not burning, and seeing this view in real life. Not on some television screen."

He turned her in his arms. "Look at me."

She peered up at him, placing her hands on his biceps.

"Get used to it. This is your new normal. I won't have you vulnerable to being burned. We're mated. That makes us a team. My blood is yours. You will take it to keep yourself strong and without weaknesses."

She nodded, not willing to fight with him since she had no urge to do so. "It's a miracle though. That's how I feel. Who's out there? I heard a voice I don't know."

"My two other brothers arrived about twenty minutes ago. They'd like to meet you."

She felt her guts twist.

"It's okay."

"Are they upset? I mean, over what I am?"

"No. They are happy I have a mate. It's what every man hopes to find."

"You never slept with the same woman twice. They must be shocked."

"You're special to me though. They're aware of that."

"How can you say that? You don't know me all that well. I changed a lot after becoming a Vampire. Yesterday was so frantic, and now that we're safe...do you regret it? Feel forced into mating me since it was the only way to save me?"

"Never. No regrets, Mandy. You're mine. You're still a sweetheart, just tougher. I think you're perfect. We're going to make this work. I was always drawn to you in ways no one else made me feel. It was a sign. Now that I've found you again, I'm never letting you go." He paused. "As a matter of fact, I'm grateful that you're not human anymore."

That surprised her. "Why?"

"I feared my life would horrify you if you ever found out I wasn't human. That if I let you in, you'd want to flee the second I told you the truth. Some humans break mentally when they learn that they aren't the only thing walking this Earth or, in my case, sometimes flying over it. I'd have had to call in a favor from a VampLycan friend to wipe your memories to keep you safe before I walked away. Now I never have to let you go."

She blinked back tears. He was the sweet one, not her. "We're in this together for life. It's my vow."

"Good. Now come meet all my brothers. We could use your input."

"On what?"

"How to scare the shit out of your council. We don't want them to go after the Lycan pack since I wiped out that nest."

"I don't think they will."

"I'm not willing to risk it. They need to know what went down wasn't acceptable. Lycan kids died. If you were right, and someone in the council was protecting Marco, they also need to know about it."

She understood. Someone had sent her and Olivia to kill the enforcer they believed was taking out Marco's nest. That never should have happened if someone had investigated what was really going on. Marco had earned a death sentence. No one else. "I have an idea."

"So do we." He hesitated.

"What is it?"

"I have no plans to hurt your friend Olivia, but I'm guessing she's still in New Mexico looking for your killer. I wouldn't let that go if someone took out one of *my* friends. She'll have a number for the council. I want to call a meeting with them. My brothers and I will capture her to take her phone."

She bit her lip. "I can call her."

He cocked his head slightly, frowning.

"I don't remember all the phone numbers on my cell but Olivia is different. We memorized each other's numbers in case of emergency. You don't need to hunt her down. Just give me access to a phone." She needed to say it. "Thank you for not going after her before, when I know you could have."

"You never asked me if I saw her."

"I was afraid of the answer in case you had gone to her hotel. I wanted to pretend she was fine."

"The last thing I ever want to do is hurt you, Mandy. Killing your friend would put a wedge between us."

"I'd have understood though."

He cupped her chin, leaned in, and brushed his lips over hers. "Thank you for that. Now, my brothers are waiting."

He released her, stepped back and offered his hand. She clasped it, feeling a bit nervous. She might be mated to a GarLycan but it was still a frightening concept to be in a room with four of them. Pest seemed to like her though. He'd been kind overall, but she wasn't about to forget how he'd said he'd take her out if he felt the need.

Glacier opened the bedroom door and led her into the living area.

Pest sat at the small table and two big men were seated on the couch. She could see the family resemblance, with their size and black hair. Some of their facial features were the same as well. Both men stood, showing off their impressive heights, just like her mate. The one with the longer hair smiled.

"I'm Creed. You must be Mandy. Welcome to the family."

He didn't offer his hand but then again, he wasn't a human. She just smiled back. "Thank you. It's nice to meet you."

"She's *really* a suckhead."

Glacier tensed at her side and released her hand, stepping forward. "Neb. She is my mate. Be nice, damn it."

Neb's eyes seemed to lighten as she watched. They went from a murky blue with what appeared to be some purple, to a paler shade. He stared at her mate grimly. His gaze met hers next. "My apologies. I mostly take out bad nests. It's my main gig. Welcome to the family."

"Thank you. I'm not a huge fan of Vampires, either. I always say I only like one out of every ten that I meet. I totally get it. Some of them are pure assholes with a God complex."

His eyebrows arched.

"I'm serious," she admitted.

He slowly let his gaze roam down her body before meeting hers again. "I take it that you didn't ask to be turned?"

"No. I didn't. I was grabbed to be some sicko's newest addition to a harem of female sex slaves he kept locked up in his basement. My friend

223

Olivia and I were the newbies. The council, who wiped out that nest, decided we hadn't been tainted yet and put us through their assassin training. Olivia has assured me many times that they did us a favor. She was turned a week before I was. I'll take her word for it, since the master never got his hands on me. She wasn't so lucky."

Glacier put his arm around her. "I'd have gone hunting for you if I'd known a nest had taken you."

She turned her head, staring up at him. "It's okay. Let it go."

"I should have checked on you when you didn't come into work."

"The Vamp who snatched me took my car. I saw it parked outside when the council led us out of the building we were kept in. You would have known something was wrong if he'd left it behind Bucket. It's done and over with."

He didn't look happy but gave a sharp nod.

Neb cleared his throat. "I have some questions for you, Mandy."

She looked at Glacier's brother, tensing. It had been a lot of years since she'd dated, but she remembered meeting the families of a few men. They always wanted to ask about *her* family and upbringing. She'd dreaded it every time. Things hadn't changed. "Alright."

"I want you to tell me everything about assassins. How many. Where they are. What kind of training they have." He paused. "The rules they follow, or if they feel they are above the law."

"Come on, give her a break, bro." Pest stood and walked over to stand on her other side. "She's our brother's *mate*. Not someone for you to interrogate."

224

"It's okay. I understand." She held Neb's gaze. "You said your main gig is killing Vampires. It's important information for you to learn. I'm more than happy to answer your questions."

"Later. First, we need to deal with the council." Glacier let her go and withdrew his cell phone, pressed his thumb to it, and held it out. "Will Olivia answer her phone during the day?"

"Yes."

He hesitated, searching her eyes. "Are you certain you can trust her not to reveal that you're alive to the council?"

"She'd die before doing something like that."

"You can't tell her everything."

"I know."

"It's a death sentence," Neb rumbled. "You tell her drinking our blood can make her withstand sunbathing and she's toast. I'll personally hunt her ass down to take her out."

She glanced at him. "It would put my mate, your brother, in danger. I'd never do that."

Glacier pressed the phone into her hand. "I want a number for the council. Do you mind making the call in here? I trust you. My brothers are going to have to get to know you better. They'll worry like little old ladies."

She grinned, accepting the phone. "No problem."

Mandy felt nervous as she dialed Olivia. It rang three times before it was answered and silence greeted her. Seconds ticked by.

"It's me."

"Oh my fucking God!" Olivia burst out. "You're *alive*?"

"Why didn't you say hello?"

"Unfamiliar number. *Hello*. I can't believe you're alive! How? Why? Where the hell have you been? Shit! I told the council you were dead. I found your tracker in a pile of ashes and your phone a few feet away under a dumpster. What the fuck, Mandy? I've been crying my eyes out and grieving you!"

"It's a long story. I'm sorry. I'm alive, but the council can't find out. You know what will happen."

"They'll have you hunted and kill you in ways that'll be epic horror tales to share for centuries with other assassins. What in the hell were you *thinking*? You can't get away with something like this. Someone will see you eventually. We can fix this! We'll think of something. Like the Werewolves tortured you and faked your death so they could keep you longer. *Something*. I won't let you die! Where are you? How could you plan this without telling me? We never keep secrets." Olivia gasped in a deep breath and then began to cry.

Mandy felt like shit. Glacier stepped behind her, putting his arms around her. She knew he and his brothers could hear the phone conversation clearly, even though it wasn't on speaker. Their hearing was great, and Olivia wasn't exactly yelling, but she wasn't whispering either in her upset state.

"It's okay. It's complicated. I'm so sorry, but none of this was planned. I wouldn't do that to you."

"What happened? Are you sure you're okay?"

226

"I'm fine. Safe. Tracker-free." Mandy leaned back against Glacier's solid, warm body, taking comfort in her mate. "You can't tell anyone I'm alive."

"No shit!" Olivia sniffed, seeming to pull herself together. "They'd have you tracked down to the ends of the Earth! No one escapes the council. I'm not losing you again. I've been a fucking mess since I found those ashes, thinking you were dead. I damn near walked myself up to the roof that morning to meet the sun. We're *partners*. Then I imagined what you'd say if I took the easy way out. I knew you'd have wanted me to hang in for twelve more years to join that nest in Los Angeles."

"I'm *so* sorry."

"What happened? Where are you? Whose ashes were those that I found?"

"The asshole Vamp tracking that kid."

Olivia snorted. "I knew you were going to kill him. So...what? You took out that prick and decided hey, I'll rip out my tracker and fake my own death? Why didn't you tell me first? I would have helped you. I always have your back. Even when you do really stupid shit."

Mandy twisted her head, peering up at Glacier. She didn't know how much she could tell Olivia. He released her waist and cupped the hand holding the phone, lifting it a little.

"Hello, Olivia. My name is Glacier. I'm a GarLycan. I'm the one who removed Mandy's tracker." He paused. "We knew each other when Mandy was still human. I took her from that alley and she's been with me ever since. This was the first time I gave her my phone to call you." He tapped the face of the phone. "You're on speaker. It's safe to talk. I'm not going to allow anything to happen to Mandy. She's my heart."

"Holy shit," Olivia muttered. "For real?"

"It seems GarLycans do leave Alaska after all," Mandy mumbled.

"Wow." Olivia sounded stunned. "Okay. Hello, Glacier. Did my bestie tell you we're owned by the council for another twelve years, and they never let us go early? They'll have everyone and everything tracking her. No way are they just going to let her go. It would encourage more of us to run. They can't have that."

"She did. It's not going to happen. They will believe she's dead. Even if they find out, I'd never allow them to hurt her. She's my mate."

Olivia gasped. She recovered fast though. "Wait—if you knew her when she was human, why didn't you mate her then? I mean, I don't know much about mating but races with mates usually get instincts about that shit, right? Mandy? Why didn't you mention this guy to me?"

"I did."

"Uh, no. I'd remember a name like Glacier."

"He used to go by the name Ice."

"*Shit!*" Olivia muttered. "Bingo. We have a winner. Hot bouncer dude. Man, she talked a *lot* about you. You're the one with the amazing ass, but who was a total manwhore who wouldn't give her the time of day. What the hell is up with *that* if she was your mate?"

"Okay. That's enough reminiscing," Mandy blurted.

Glacier chuckled. "You liked my ass, huh?"

"She said you had buns of steel," Olivia added.

"Shut it," Mandy ordered.

Olivia sighed. "Thank you for letting me know you're alive. Shit has hit the fan here. I needed good news."

Mandy tensed. "What's going on?"

"Someone—your mate, is my guess—took out the nest. The council sent reinforcements to make an example out of the pack. Right before dawn, a team of six showed up. I was given no warning until they called to hold a meeting. Vasquez is in charge. Tonight, we're supposed to do recon on the pack, and the night after, hit them hard. It's all kinds of fucked up, Mandy. The only thing I've accomplished was talking them out of killing any of the kids or civilian pack members. I pointed out to the asshole that it would enrage the VampLycans when they heard. It's one thing to take on an alpha and his enforcers. Something entirely different to kill women and kids. He actually listened for once."

"Who is Vasquez?"

"He's in our group," Mandy explained to Glacier. "Total prick. Ice cold. Talk about a God complex. He's a textbook case. We hate him."

"To put it mildly," Olivia murmured. "He's one cruel bastard. Rumor has it he *asked* to be turned just to become an assassin. It's like it's his goal to be the most brutal killer of all to impress the council. And he's their favorite pet. They assign him to lead missions when a larger team is needed. He seems to get off on it."

"We need a few numbers to reach your council," Glacier informed Olivia. "Not only Corski's, but Mandy mentioned something about having a secondary number in case she wasn't able to get ahold of him. It's got to be another council member, right?"

229

"No. The other number belongs to Robin. That's Corski's second. I had to call it once when he wasn't picking up. Mandy had the same numbers I did. Why do you want to reach out to council members?" Olivia paused. "If you don't mind my asking."

Mandy glanced at Glacier. He nodded, letting her know she could share that detail with her friend. "We were sent to kill a Werewolf enforcer, but the truth was, Marco and his nest had been abducting and killing pups, Olivia. *That's* why Glacier was there."

"Holy shit!" Olivia's shock was obvious. "What the *fuck*? The investigator should have presented that to the council. Our orders..." She went silent.

"You're thinking what I did," Mandy sighed. "Someone lied to the council. They would have ordered us to wipe out Marco and his nest for killing Werewolf kids. Says it all, doesn't it?"

"Corski gave us those orders. Damn. Why would he take a master's side? Were they lovers? Friends? Family?"

"Who knows? His orders might have come from the council and it's possible he wasn't involved. We don't know who lied." Mandy leaned back against Glacier once more. "We were hoping that secondary number was to another member of the council in case it *was* Corski, though."

"Someone was protecting that nest. No way would the council have sent us to take out an enforcer if they knew the truth." Olivia hissed. "What a mess." She was quiet for a moment. "Do you know who *would* have other council numbers, though? Vasquez and the assassins he's leading. Corski didn't send him here. Someone else on the council did."

Mandy was surprised. "Are you sure? I've never heard of that happening before. We always get our orders from Corski."

"Um, yeah. I'm certain," Olivia confirmed. "Corski contacted me this morning to see if I'd found out who'd killed you, and to ask if I'd heard anything from Marco. Let's just say he didn't sound happy when I informed him Vasquez was here—and five assassins from a different house were with him. I also had to inform him Marco was dead."

Mandy was dumbfounded. "I assumed the team was from *our* house."

"Nope. Only Vasquez. I didn't have a chance to chat with the others to see where they're based. When I began to protest about attacking the entire pack, Vasquez grabbed my arm and marched me to another room to listen to what I had to say. When we were done, he ordered me to leave. He and his team aren't staying at this hotel, but one down the street. Which is *also* weird. We usually get rooms grouped together. I even asked if he wanted me to switch hotels, and he said no. I was hoping tonight, when we do recon, that I'd get a chance to find out where the other team members came from and how they ended up under Vasquez for this assignment."

"That *is* weird," Mandy admitted, staring into Glacier's eyes. "We always sleep close together, usually on the same floor, to cover each other's asses if shit hits the fan. Especially if we're dealing with a large group of whatever the hell the threat is."

Glacier scowled. "Olivia, I want you to do me a favor."

"Alright." She sounded a bit hesitant.

"Tonight, when you meet up with this team, tell them you were left a message by the GarLycans at the hotel desk. Act confused as to how we learned who you are and where you're staying. I'm going to send you a location where we want to meet your team. Give it to them while they're together. And I'll word it strongly, so they can't refuse."

"Okay. Um, are you planning to kill us?"

"Not you. Maybe them. We'll see how it goes. You'll be safe though. I give you my word."

Mandy knew her best friend well. She'd be scared and leery. "Glacier means it, Olivia. You can trust him."

"Alright. I trust you, Mandy. I'll be sure to stop at the desk before I leave. We're supposed to meet up at seven."

"The message will be waiting for you," Glacier promised. He nodded at Mandy.

"Get a disposable phone, Olivia. Text this number with it. I'll call you again soon. Love you."

"Love you, too. I'm so glad you're alive."

Glacier ended the call and turned to his brothers, releasing Mandy. "We're traveling back today. Creed, you're staying here to keep Mandy safe."

"Damn." Creed frowned. "I left Alaska to see some action."

"Action would mean my mate is under attack." Glacier shook his head. "You do whatever you must to keep her safe."

"I swear," Creed promised. "Why me though? She'd probably feel safer with Pest."

Pest chuckled. "Our bro here wants her left with a mated GarLycan. He doesn't care that I gave my word not to hit on short stack. He's all protective instincts and irrational thoughts right now."

Glacier flipped him off before turning to face Mandy again. "I'm going to have to leave you. I hope to return by morning. I'm sorry."

"You need to take care of this. I'm going to miss you but I understand." She did. Someone on the council had protected Marco and his nest. It couldn't happen again. Werewolf pups had died as a result. More could have been killed if Glacier hadn't been called in and she didn't have her morals intact. Vasquez, for example, wouldn't have cared about pups. He'd have just followed orders and left town as soon as he'd taken out the threat to the nest. "Just be safe."

"Always. I have you to come home to."

She didn't care that his brothers were watching as she wrapped her arms around him, giving him a hug. "I love you."

He wrapped his arms around her tight. "I love you too, baby."

Pest snorted. "I'm never taking a mate. Ever."

Nebulas chuckled. "That's like begging fate to hand you your ass. Say it again. Hey Creed, want to place a bet that Pest is the next one to be mated?"

"No way. I'm not a sucker. He just fucked himself." Creed laughed.

Mandy smiled against Glacier's chest. She liked his brothers. They were funny.

"Screw you all," Pest muttered. "Neb's going to need a motorcycle since we're day traveling."

233

"Rent me one too." Glacier released her, holding her gaze. "We can drop them off at the rental place once we enter Kevin's territory. I plan to fly back to you tonight as soon as this is finished."

Chapter Fourteen

The six male Vampires looked startled when three GarLycans flew from the sky and landed on the building's roof. The lone female Vampire, Olivia, not so much. Glacier saw fear in all their gazes, though. That didn't come as a surprise. GarLycans tended to have that effect on all races.

The Vamps took up defensive stances, looking tense and ready to attack. Glacier crossed his arms over his chest and allowed his wings to spread outward as he glared at them.

"I see that you got my message." Glacier purposely made his voice deeper than normal. It was meant to intimidate. He slightly shelled his body until his skin turned ashen gray. It might remind the Vamps how easily *they* could be turned gray, too, as they died. "I'm guessing the female is Olivia. Step forward, assassin. I met your partner."

Olivia came forward a few feet and glared at him. "Are you the one who murdered Mandy?"

He smothered a smile. She was a good actress. He gave her a slight nod. "You say murder. I call it self-defense. I wouldn't attack just yet, little Vampire. You'll want to hear what I have to say. That will be difficult if you force me to kill you. I'm not here for that...unless you leave us with no other option. This is to be a friendly discussion. Understand?"

"Bastard," she hissed, and backed up.

Pest snorted. "Are you certain we can't kill her just for the hell of it? I don't like being called names."

Glacier wanted to shoot a warning glare at his brother for that remark. Olivia honestly appeared frightened now. He hoped she realized Pest was bluffing. She would be the only Vampire to survive on the roof if shit went down. He always kept his word, especially to his mate.

Neb withdrew his sword and pointed it downward. "We came to talk—and you *will* listen. That's not up for debate. Don't contemplate jumping off the roof, assassins. There are no balconies on this building and you wouldn't fair well with a sixteen-story drop."

"Splat," Pest muttered. "And forget the roof-access door you came through. You'd lose your head before you even got it open. Just stay where you are and do what you're told."

Glacier drew the Vampires' attention by stepping closer. "I want to speak to your council. I'll assume Vampires have phones. There are seven of you. That means at least one of you can place a call to them." Glacier studied each one. "Who can make that happen?"

None of the Vampires spoke.

"The only reason you get to live is to be useful to us," he added. "Now, I'll ask again—who can contact your council right now? Someone speak."

A dark-haired male Vamp flashed his fangs. "I can."

Glacier had a feeling this one must be Vasquez. He seemed utterly cold and there was a look in his dead eyes that said he had seen a lot of death. He instantly took a disliking to the Vamp, with his leering expression and obvious disdain he didn't bother to hide.

The Vampire removed his phone. "You want me to call the council?"

236

"Yes. I'd like them to see me. I want you to use your camera for a live feed and have them all join in as a conference call."

The male hesitated.

"We don't have to see *them*. You just point the damn camera at me and keep the screen your way. Is that simple enough? Let them know you're surrounded by three GarLycans who are demanding to speak to them. Otherwise, they will be declaring war. Then put it on speakerphone, so I may hear their voices and know they can see me."

The Vamp nodded once and placed a call. Glacier waited while the Vampire connected to someone and whispered quietly. It didn't take more than a few sentences before the Vamp paused, staring at him. "They're conferencing the call and darkening their screens."

"Cowardly," Pest sighed. "But not surprising that they would hide their faces."

"It doesn't matter," Neb reminded him.

A good three to four minutes passed before the Vamp holding the phone lifted it, staring at Glacier. "Where do you want it pointed?"

Glacier strode forward, keeping his wings extended. He stopped ten feet away. "Can they see me?"

The Vamp nodded and touched the screen. "Yes, and now it's on speaker."

Glacier focused on where the camera would be. He gripped his sword in one, fisted the other. "Hello, Vampire Council. You may call me Glacier. I'm with two of my GarLycan brothers. I have a message from Lord Aveoth. He'd have been happy to speak to you himself, but you're difficult

237

to get ahold of. You really should change that policy of yours. I wouldn't be holding seven of your assassins on this roof with the threat of death if we could have contacted you otherwise. Now, assure me I'm actually speaking to the council."

"We're listening, GarLycan," a female voice stated.

"Are you a council of one?" He knew better.

"No," a male denied. "We keep ourselves hidden to protect our identities. Reprisals are something we're wary of. You are speaking to all members of the council. I myself linked this phone to my computer and set up this conference call. You have my assurances."

Glacier wanted to snort but he was willing to give whoever spoke the benefit of the doubt. There were at least two Vampires listening. A female and male. Still...he decided to try something. "Are you Corski?"

Someone gasped.

"No, I am," a third voice answered. "How in the hell do you know my name?" He sounded outraged more than afraid.

"I captured an assassin. You missed that part of the conversation. She tried to kill me. So I felt it was only fair to gain information from her before I ended her life. She said you were the head of her house. But you'll be gratified to know it took quite a lot of pain for her to break. I'm content now that I have your attention."

"Why in the hell did you kill one of our Vamps?" Corski raged.

"You sent two of your assassins to take out the person responsible for killing off members of a nest. Marco was—past tense—the master of that nest. *I'm* the one who put his ass down." He smiled coldly. "I will say the assassin I met in that alley a few nights ago had excellent training, but she really never stood a chance against me. My wings? They become razor-blade sharp when need be. They can slice right through a Vamp body if I want them to. And I did. I'm not sorry to inform you that you're one assassin less now." He hoped they believed he'd killed Mandy.

The wind blew, and no one said a word as Glacier took a deep breath. "Your assassin informed me it wasn't my place to take out the nest, that you police your own." He allowed anger to show in his face and his own fangs dropped. "Yet you didn't. You sent them after *me*, instead. Do you want to explain that decision?"

"You killed off Marco *and* his nest?" Surprise sounded in another unidentified male's voice.

"Yes, I did. Do you want to know why? That sick bastard and his nest were kidnapping Lycan children, forcing them to fight to the death against each other—and for what? To get their dicks hard. You bet your ass I wiped them off this planet. That's some sick shit right there. Cruel. Children are off limits. You fucking know that. So much for policing your own."

The woman spoke next. "That's not true."

"Bullshit. I arrived in this area to investigate after Lycan children began disappearing. It's what we do. I located a building where Lycan kids had been locked in animal cages. Their little bodies were left in trash bags in the basement, tossed there as if they were garbage. The Vampires had left some of their clothing behind, were probably staying there to guard their captives while they still lived. I tracked the fuckers down and killed them. Do you wish me to fly one of your assassins to that building? They

239

can view the same evidence. The local nest stole those Lycan children and killed them. I'm also willing to have them interview the grieving parents."

No one on the council said a word.

"Are you so gullible that you'll believe whatever a nest master tells you without confirmation?"

Still no one spoke.

"That sounds like utter stupidity to me, and something you need to change. You see, we look into *every* situation when we are called for help. We make damn sure the guilty party is at the end of our blades before we start taking heads. We don't pick sides until we're certain who the bad and good guys are. Maybe that makes us and the VampLycans smarter than your council. The point is, you've already lost one assassin who tried to kill me because of your negligence in allowing Marco to go after pack children. You sent her after the wrong guilty party. I was protecting kids from *your* Vamps. That's something *you* should have done."

"We didn't know," the woman stated. "At least, I didn't. We'll get to the bottom of this confusion, GarLycan Glacier. You have my word on that."

"Did you send someone to investigate Marco's lies when I'll assume he claimed an enforcer was killing his nest without cause?"

The woman remained silent a moment, but then spoke. "We had it on good authority that Marco wasn't at fault in any way, and had followed our laws. We originally voted to send two assassins to take out whoever was hunting the nest, clearly based on misinformation. After one of our assassins went missing, we were told by that same authority that the local pack hated all Vampires and wanted them dead. That's why we sent in the

240

team you see before you. Their orders were to make certain no more innocent Vampires were killed because of hatred for our race."

"Well, I'd kill your so-called 'authority,' since they either lied or were incompetent as fuck," he snarled. "*I* took out Marco and his nest. They were child murderers. Kids are off limits. Human ones. Lycan ones. GarLycan and VampLycan. Maybe since Vamps don't have children, you're oblivious to the fallout. Marco risked exposing all of us with those deaths. That's not even touching on the absolute emotional devastation it causes all involved with the loss of those innocent lives. Children of any race never just disappear or die without it drawing attention. Do you understand that?"

"Yes," a few voices on the phone confirmed.

"I believe we all have a common goal in keeping humans in the dark about our existence. Be wiser about who you choose to lead your investigations, and be damn certain before you send out your assassins that they're going after the correct targets.

"There's one more thing you should know. I interrogated a member of that nest. He wasn't very forthcoming before he died, but I did get one thing from him. It didn't make sense to me, but I have a feeling it might to you. They were taking videos of the fighting children...and implied there was money to be made in it."

He picked up the sound of a few gasps and muttered curses.

"Police your own and deal with this shit. It's possible one of you was involved. You'd better clean your fucking houses—or *we* will. This shit won't be tolerated. I was told you didn't think we ever leave Alaska. Clearly we do, and have many times before. You don't want us policing your Vamps? Then fucking make sure we don't have reason to. Lord Aveoth and all four VampLycan clan leaders will put together teams and send them to problem areas if this happens again. We work well together to keep our existence a secret. We're willing to work with you, too. Do you understand?"

It was the woman who answered. "We do."

Glacier walked closer, glaring into the camera. "Nobody wants a war in the States, but we won't shy away from it. We can work together to keep the peace or a lot of blood will be shed. It's your choice. Make it."

He glanced at the Vampires around him then focused on Olivia. "You. Get over here." He pointed at her.

Olivia hesitated but came forward. He hated the fear in her eyes but she approached him bravely. It put her with him in front of the camera when she stopped where he directed.

"I'm making you our contact. Give me your phone." He held out his hand.

She turned, glancing warily at the camera.

"Do it," a male voice ordered. It sounded like Corski.

Olivia removed her phone, handing it to him.

He glanced down, seeing she'd unlocked it. He typed in the number Kelzeb had given him and returned it to her. "You are the *only* one to use that number, Olivia. Congratulations. You've officially become the go-between for your council and Lord Aveoth. Now return to where you were."

Her features softened and her eyes widened. It must have sunk in that he'd just made her too important to kill. The council would need her alive if they really wanted to avoid a war with the GarLycans and VampLycans. She turned from the camera fully and winked before masking her features. She hurried back to her spot on the roof.

Glacier stared at the camera. "We're done for now. Have Olivia contact us with her number so Lord Aveoth can reach you if a need arises."

He strode forward and grabbed the phone the dark-haired Vampire held, crushing it in his hand and effectively ending the meeting. He tossed it aside and backed away.

"You destroyed my phone?" The Vamp hissed, flashing fangs.

"I'm going to reach into my pocket and give each of you a card. It's got a special number on it. Share it with your fellow assassins." He withdrew the cards, approaching the Vamp he suspected was Vasquez. He still appeared furious over his lost phone. Glacier didn't give a damn. "Take one."

The Vamp hesitated but then accepted it. "What's this number to?"

He backed away and let his gaze go from one Vamp to the next. "It's your way to contact us if you're ever given orders you know are wrong. Innocents are *always* off limits. I was informed by the assassin I killed that you aren't given choices on your targets...but decide now who you fear more. Us or your council. And by the way, just because we might receive a tracking kit, doesn't mean we'll come after you. We investigate when we're asked to kill. I'm not saying we'd offer sanctuary with our clans, but I will point out that Alaska is a big damn state, and if someone decided to

243

move there, we wouldn't come after them unless they gave us a good reason. Call that number if you ever feel like relocating, and you'll get some suggestions on where law-abiding Vamps would be safe."

He saw a few of the Vamps grin but their smiles disappeared fast. Glacier walked to each one, giving them a card. Most of them quickly pocketed them. Two stared at the card, as if memorizing the number printed there.

He backed away to the edge of the roof. "You are free to go. I suggest you get out of this city. The Lycan pack here is under our protection. They've suffered enough loss because of Marco and his nest. You will not punish them for the justice I served."

Glacier nodded at his brothers and waited for each of them fly away first. He flapped his wings and tensed, preparing to take flight.

"GarLycan."

He paused, staring at the Vamp who spoke. Again, it was the one he assumed to be Vasquez. "What?"

"We'll never make that call. We're loyal to our council. I will personally burn every card you just passed out. No assassins will *ever* call you."

"Suit yourself."

The Vamp suddenly lunged forward in a blur with a dagger in his hand.

Glacier braced his legs, shelling his skin a little harder, but otherwise didn't move.

The bastard tried to stab him in the throat. The tip of the blade hit his hard skin, sliding off. Glacier reached up as the Vamp lost his balance and shoved him hard. It caused the man to fly back and land on his ass.

"Don't, Vasquez!" Olivia hissed.

Vasquez didn't listen, but instead flipped up, landed on his feet, and dropped the knife. He reached inside a pocket, withdrawing a gun.

Glacier spun, bringing up one wing to protect his eyes without making it obvious, and plowed the other into the bastard before he could pull the trigger. It sent the Vamp flying again, this time into a blond male in head-to-toe black leather. That male caught Vasquez but quickly shoved him forward.

Glacier hadn't planned on killing any of them, but he changed his mind, debating briefly if he should just behead Vasquez or make him suffer first.

He didn't get the chance to do either.

The blond behind Vasquez abruptly surged forward and a steel blade flashed.

Glacier watched in silence as the dark-haired Vampire was swiftly beheaded.

The blond responsible spun on the other Vamps, as if expecting to be attacked. None came at him. They appeared stunned by his actions but no one protested.

The Vampire put away his bloody knife. "Vasquez didn't speak for all of us. His brother is a council member and he volunteered to be an assassin. The rest of us didn't. We can handle our own problems. I just did."

Glacier was impressed.

The blond turned, facing the other Vamps again. "Vasquez boasted about not having a tracker in his body since he was too loyal to ever attempt escape. We'll tell the council he died in a tragic accident on the way home. The fucker loved to live dangerously. Too bad he took too many risks. Agreed?"

Each Vampire nodded, some of them voicing agreement. Another blond male stared at Glacier. "Was that offer to find sanctuary in Alaska sincere?"

"Yes. You have a way out if you ever need it."

The blond who'd killed Vasquez gave him a curt bow. "We'll only share the number with others we know who aren't absolutely blind to the council's flaws. Some of us are still redeemable."

The man came forward a few feet then stopped. "Thank you."

Olivia stood behind all the Vamps. She mouthed the same two words silently when he glanced at her.

Glacier nodded and took flight, soaring away from the building. His brothers waited for him a few miles away on another rooftop. He landed beside them.

"That seemed to go well, bro." Pest patted him on the shoulder. "What do you think?"

"The blond Vamp in the leather killed Vasquez after you two flew off."

246

Neb's eyebrows shot up. "Why?"

"He made it clear he'd take back the cards I passed out, and that no one would be given the number. Blond Vamp disagreed with his plan."

Pest whistled. "Vasquez sounded like an asshole anyway. Good riddance. Are we ready to fly back to your mate now?"

"Yes."

Neb hesitated. "I'm going to stick around for a bit."

Glacier narrowed his gaze at his oldest brother. "Why?"

"Someone needs to deal with Kevin."

"I should do it." Glacier sighed. "He threatened my mate and put those bombs on the building I'd claimed as my territory."

"I already came up with a plan with Kelzeb. Go to your mate, Glacier. This is my pleasure." Neb grinned.

Pest grinned too. "What's the plan? You only look that happy if it's two-for-one hooker night, so it must be good."

Neb shot him a dirty look. "You're confusing me with yourself. I don't do hookers."

"Okay. Maybe. I *do* do hookers sometimes."

Glacier shook his head. "What's the plan, Neb?"

"Kevin isn't fit to lead. I'm going to fly in, kill his ass, and tell his enforcers to work out who becomes alpha. That's a pack issue for them to resolve. Kevin overstepped his authority by pissing off Lord Aveoth when he went after you. I'll make that clear. It shouldn't take me long. I'll see you before dawn. It's early enough that I'll be able to fly to you tonight. Tomorrow, we'll figure out where you and your mate are going to live."

247

Glacier nodded. "Thanks."

"We're family." Neb gave him a hug. "I might not be overjoyed that your mate is a Vamp, but I accept her."

Pest wrapped his arms around both of them, going for a group hug. "In other words, he's nothing like our bastard of a father. I so don't miss him. We really owe Creed another thank you for taking his ass out."

Glacier chuckled. "True."

Neb let them go, backing away. "I'm off now. See you both soon." He turned, ran at the edge of the building and took flight toward the Lycan territory.

Pest grinned. "Let's go. I'll follow you. That is, if your mate instincts have kicked in. Have they? Can you track short stack?"

Glacier closed his eyes and focused on Mandy. Something inside had him turning slightly to the left, and he could almost feel her. "Yes."

"I'm calling you pussy homing pigeon from now on."

"Fuck you." Glacier chuckled as he opened his eyes.

"Hey, it's a bitch to use our phones while flying places to get to the right address. No GPS tonight. You just have to sense your mate. After you, bro."

"Never call me that nickname."

Pest just chuckled.

Glacier ran at the edge of the roof and flew high. Pest followed.

Chapter Fifteen

It was just after four in the morning when Mandy heard a thump on the balcony. She rose from the couch. Creed did too. The slider opened and Glacier walked inside, Pest following behind him. There was no sign of Neb. She scanned Glacier's body, happy to see he didn't look as if he'd been in a fight.

"It's done. We spoke to the council."

Mandy rushed forward and threw her arms around her mate. "How? What happened?"

It was Pest who explained as he grabbed a beer from behind the bar from a mini fridge then took a seat on a barstool. When he finished speaking, Mandy looked at Glacier. "I can't believe the others turned on Vasquez. Not that it shocks me. He was an asshole. I wanted to kill him plenty of times but not enough to die over. It's against the law to kill another assassin. I hope the others don't tell on whoever the blond Vampire was."

He held her by her hips, his hands gentle but firm. "Olivia should be safe. We made her our official go-between."

Her love for him grew. "Thank you."

He shrugged. "You trust her. I'd rather talk to your friend than some stranger."

It was a big deal, despite him making it not seem so. The council would be terrified of angering the GarLycans even more than they already had by killing the Vamp they'd chosen to use as a go-between. The council had already made a huge error by sending two assassins after Glacier. She bet they'd freaked out when they realized that's what they'd done. She didn't feel any pity for whoever had given them false information. "They'll be ruthless to whoever gave them that report to protect Marco and his nest. Someone will die."

"Sounds about right," Pest agreed. "Justice served."

"I'm going to go to my room to call Angel." Creed hugged his brothers and waved at Mandy as he left the suite.

Glacier stared down at her. "Was Creed good to you while I was gone?"

"He was. He told me all about his mate. I'd like to meet Angel one day."

"I'm certain you will."

"We're all one big family now." Pest slid off the barstool. "I'm going to take a walk through the hotel and make certain it's just humans. You two probably need some time alone."

Glacier frowned. "You don't have to go."

"I'm restless after all that flying. I stretched my wings but now my legs feel stiff. I'll be back soon."

Glacier kissed Mandy the moment they were alone. She jumped up, wrapping around his body. "I missed you."

"Bedroom. Now." He cupped her ass, striding toward their room.

His phone dinged and he came to a halt, growling. "I need to get this. Neb was sent to kill Kevin."

She slid down his body as he took the call. It wasn't his brother. "Hello, Kelzeb. Any word from Neb?"

He stayed close, making it possible for her to hear the deep male voice on his cell.

"The alpha is toast. Neb made his death clean and swift. The damn pack offered to accept him as their new alpha. He declined and told them to work it out themselves. Then they asked him to stick around while they hold challenges. The pack is vulnerable. I gave him permission to agree. He won't be returning to where you are."

"Thanks for letting us know."

"Sending you to Wyoming or Colorado is off the table. I trust both family-related alphas, but who knows about the loyalty of their packs. Your mate would be worth a lot of money to betray if any of them figured out what or who she is. We can't risk that."

Glacier's features hardened. "Understood. What's the solution? I know you came up with one."

"I didn't. Lord Aveoth was the one who assigned your next job. Ready for it? I know you hate snow."

"I'll do anything to keep Mandy." He held her gaze and smiled. "Just give me the details."

"Okay. First, head back to Alaska with Creed."

"I'm going to help him be guardian to Angel's pack?"

"No, but you'll only be a few hours from him. Aveoth called in a favor from Velder. You'll be living in his territory. They have a cabin for you and your mate. Ever since Lorn's clan dealt with that Vampire situation, I've been assigning scouts to fly over his territory to help them keep an eye on things. You'll be in charge of those scouts now. They sure as fuck won't care that your mate is with you, or betray her presence."

Glacier smiled. "I like it."

"I thought you would. It helps me out, too. I've got less scouts to assign duties to daily. I'm out."

Mandy stared up at Glacier as he put away his cell. "Who's Velder, and why do you look so happy?"

"We're going to be living with VampLycans."

That wasn't what she'd expected. Everything she'd ever heard about them was the stuff of horror stories. Of course, her mate was a GarLycan. His brothers could be scary but they weren't anything like she'd expected them to be. "The VampLycans will allow me to live with them?" She wanted to add "without killing me" to her question but refrained.

"We have strong alliances with the VampLycan clans now. You'll be safe. Hell, they *are* part Vampire. You should fit right in there."

"What about when they figure out the sun doesn't burn me?"

"Lord Aveoth is more than aware, and he's sending us to live with them. He gave me permission to feed you my blood anytime you need it. I trust his judgement. You'll be safe. That's all that matters."

"We're going to Alaska...and you hate snow. I heard that part, too."

"I hated it because while I lived at the cliffs, harsh snowstorms meant I was trapped inside. We can fly during sub-zero weather but it's not pleasant. Cold doesn't bother us as much as it would a human, but it can be miserable. Being trapped at the cliffs meant dealing with my father.

252

Every time I saw him, he bitched about what disappointments my brothers and I were. He'd track me down to my private quarters constantly to rage about anything he wanted to get off his chest. Mostly, I didn't give a damn. He was an asshole. I couldn't leave Alaska fast enough to escape him."

That made her feel sad for him. "I'm sorry. I know what it's like to have a shitty dad."

"I know you do, baby." He closed them in their room and walked over to the bed, taking a seat. "He mated a Lycan but hated that we weren't completely Gargoyle. Our traits are, but he felt our emotions were our downfall."

She followed and crouched before him, helping him remove his boots. "I like you just the way you are."

He grinned at her while she tugged them off. "I could get used to this."

"I'm your mate. This seemed like a mately thing to do."

He chuckled as she stood, then reached out and hauled her onto his lap. "My father was just an unfeeling prick. I tried to never take it personal. He hated everyone. So it wasn't the snow I hated. It was being there. The weather was a good excuse to use rather than insulting my father. He was on the Gargoyle Council." He caressed her cheek. "Now things are different. I won't be at the cliffs, and my father isn't around any longer to make my life miserable. I'll be living with you. The idea of being snowed in suddenly sounds pretty damn good." He stroked her skin. "We can stay in bed for days or even weeks when storms hit."

"That doesn't sound bad at all." She snuggled against his chest. "I hope this cabin has a fireplace. I love them. It sounds romantic."

"It does, and it will have at least one. Maybe two. The power can go down. Fireplaces are required."

"I've never been to Alaska."

"I think you'll love it. I'll take you scouting with me on good weather nights."

"You can do that?"

"Fly with you? Yes."

"It still amazes me that we found each other again."

"Fate can be cruel, but not this time." He leaned down to press his lips to hers.

Mandy kissed him back, their fangs no longer a problem. He deepened the kiss and let his hands roam her body. It didn't take long before she squirmed on his lap, broke the kiss, and wiggled out of his hold to strip off her clothes. He rose, doing the same.

They both climbed onto the bed naked and tangled together on top of the bedding, kissing again. She moaned against his tongue and broke away, seeking his throat. Glacier bared it and growled as she bit him. He pressed her onto her back, pinning her under him. She was wet and ready when he adjusted his hips, entering her slowly.

Mandy remembered to remove her fangs as he leisurely began to fuck her, rocking his hips. She dug her fingernails into his shoulders, spurring him on. He increased the pace, arched his back, and lunged for her throat, already exposed for him. He used his fangs to nick her skin and drank some of her blood, helping to strengthen their mate bond.

Soon, she was crying out his name, coming hard. He followed her a few thrusts later, her name on his lips.

Both of them panted, clinging to each other.

Glacier knew the moment when his mate drifted to sleep under him, and he chuckled. The sun had risen, and he remembered her comment about having sex and snoozing right after. He gently withdrew from her body and climbed out of bed. He went into the bathroom, wet a warm washcloth, and returned to clean her. Next, he wiped himself off, leaving the hand towel on the bathroom floor. He pulled down the covers on one side of the bed, lifted Mandy and spooned her body in front of his as he lay them both against the sheets.

For him, sleep wouldn't come. His thoughts were on returning to Alaska.

He didn't know Velder's clan all that well. What if they didn't accept his mate easily? He trusted Lord Aveoth's judgement, though. He wouldn't assign Glacier to live with the clan if he felt Mandy would be in danger. The VampLycans he'd worked with in the past had been very likable. He had to hope for the best.

Worst case, he had managed to save a small fortune over the years. He could purchase land and have a cabin built for them near clan territory. It would mean they weren't under anyone's control, but close enough to have backup when needed. Whatever it took, he'd keep Mandy safe.

He held her in his arms, breathing in her scent. The bond between them had already taken hold. The ability to track his mate comforted him. He'd always be able to find her if they were ever separated. His blood made her stronger and the sun couldn't kill her anymore. Profound appreciation came next. Their mating wasn't something that should have been allowed, but his faith in Lord Aveoth wasn't misplaced. The GarLycan had stood by him when it mattered most.

A door closed in the other room and he eased out of bed, put on his jeans, and found Pest in the living room having another beer. His brother nodded at him as he closed the bedroom door.

"You weren't gone for long."

"Is short stack out for the count?"

"Yes. It's going to take her some time to adjust to being able to walk in the sun."

"No shit." Pest removed another beer from the fridge, passing it to him. "Congrats on the mate thing."

"You'll find yours."

"Bite your damn tongue. I'm so not ready for that shit. You'll be settling down in one place." Pest shuddered. "In Alaska. I love traveling around. I'm looking forward to Miami. Warm weather, hot chicks, and working on my tan."

Glacier smiled. "Living in hotels, always carrying your stuff in a backpack, and eating way too much fast food."

"It beats cooking and having to furniture shop. I never have to wash my own sheets or make a bed, either. Maid service is killer."

256

Glacier took a sip of his beer. "You're alone though."

"There is that." Pest took a seat at the bar and motioned to his brother to do the same. "I'm going to miss working with you sometimes."

"Like in Texas?"

Pest chuckled. "Or maybe not. Fuck, it was hell burning all those rogue Lycan pieces."

"None of them got away."

"True that." Pest held his gaze. "I'm happy for you. I can tell you two are in love."

"Has there ever been anyone you were drawn to?"

"Not more than getting them into bed and then getting them to leave without causing a scene. Some women tend to be clingy."

"You'll find someone. Especially since you seem so set *against* finding a mate. But it's understandable. I was afraid I'd never find a mate. It's not as if we had great role models to aspire to. Dad made Mom miserable. I always wanted to deck the son of a bitch for the way he treated her."

"Same. Sometimes her pain was so strong, I swear I could smell it. The worst was when the bastard took Creed from her. What kind of monster gives away his own child?"

"That will never be us."

Pest frowned. "You won't have kids. Did you think about that? Vampire women can't get pregnant. You signed away becoming a father by taking her as a mate."

"We can adopt if we ever want to be parents. How many times have we found orphans after rogue attacks, or after a nest wiped out some small Lycan pack that was able to hide their pups first?"

"I'll be sure to call you the next time it happens to see if you're interested in taking in a kid or two."

They studied each other. Glacier finally nodded. "I'd appreciate it. I think Mandy would make an amazing mother. We just want to be mates for a while but after that, make that call."

"You go it, bro." Pest smiled. "Just don't let her eat them."

Glacier shook his head. "Dick."

"I was joking. Short stack is a sweetheart. She'd no more bite a kid than I would. You were right about her. I like your mate, even though she's a Vamp. Best one I ever met."

"She's amazing." Glacier finished his beer. "I only have one problem."

"What's that?"

"My motorcycle. We'll fly to Alaska, and let's face it, it wouldn't be the best thing to have up there. It's too loud and my new neighbors would complain. I'd like to give it to you."

Pest grinned. "Chicks love bikes. I'll take it."

"Thanks."

"Cool, a free bike. I get the better end of this deal, and I *did* just buy a helmet. Now I get to use it for more than a day."

"I'll get you the keys."

Glacier quickly retrieved them, passing them over.

"Go sleep with your mate. Creed wants to get back to Angel. He hates leaving her alone, even if she's spending time with her parents. He'll want to fly out of here later today."

"You going to be around?"

"I'm driving to Miami. I should be going soon. Tell short stack I said goodbye. I'll make the trip up to Alaska to see you guys once you're settled in." Pest grinned. "In the summer. Fuck the snow."

Glacier gave him a hug. "Be safe."

"Always, bro."

Glacier returned to the bedroom, took off his jeans, and crawled back into bed. He pulled Mandy into his arms. She murmured his name and snuggled into his body. He smiled, drifting off to sleep.

Chapter Sixteen

Mandy got to meet her first VampLycan at the airport. He was tall, muscular, and daunting. Lake had flown from Alaska on a private jet to pick them up. He also got her through the small airport without the use of her ID or her real name.

"We were worried the council might be looking for you," Glacier explained.

"You knew a VampLycan was coming?" He hadn't said anything to her.

"Not until I asked Creed how he wanted to get back to Alaska. Velder sent Lake for us."

"This has to cost a fortune. Private jet. Ouch." She couldn't imagine how much had been spent.

Glacier only shrugged. "The clans have money."

Lake grinned. "This baby used to belong to our enemy. Our clans took possession of it after Decker died, and anyone who needs to fly uses it. The pilots are Lycans from a family pack. They'll mind their own business and not ask any questions. We told them to stay in the cockpit. It's all cool."

Mandy studied him. "You're from Velder's clan, right?"

"Yes."

"You know about me?"

"Of course. Velder informed us." He winked. "You look pretty good for a dead woman. The Vampire council will never find you."

"Is your clan going to be okay with me living with them?"

"Yes. Your secret is safe with us. Not to offend you, but nobody wants a bunch of Vampires invading Alaska to go after our neighbors."

That set her at ease. She also liked the way Lake smiled at her; he didn't seem bothered by what she was.

Glacier hovered close, being protective. He put his hand on the small of her back, helping her onto the jet and into her seat. He even held her hand while they flew.

In Alaska, they landed at a larger airport. That's when they said goodbye to Creed. Mandy, Glacier, and Lake took a smaller plane to a remote area, where the human pilot landed on a dirt road, dropping them off at Lake's vehicle. He drove them into VampLycan territory. The town was small. They parked behind an auto shop.

Mandy felt nervous as she climbed out of the vehicle, but Glacier kept flashing her smiles and whispering assurances. Lake gave them directions to their new home in the woods, before walking away.

Velder met them outside a two-story cabin. He smiled at Mandy and hugged Glacier. "Welcome to my territory, and to your new home. It's a two bedroom with two bathrooms. It was built last year to house visitors. I hope it's to your liking."

"I'm sure it will be. We appreciate this." Glacier hugged her to his side.

"We've always wanted a GarLycan to live with our clan. It will help bond all the clans tighter together. We're honored to have you." Velder grinned. "Everyone can't wait to meet you. I came alone to keep you from feeling overwhelmed. Tomorrow, we're holding a party to welcome you."

261

His gaze cut to Mandy. "It will be held in the evening for your comfort. The sun will still be up when it starts, but I was assured you'd be fine."

"She will be," Glacier agreed. "Aveoth told you?"

"That drinking your blood protects her from burning? Yes. I was pretty surprised. Everyone else in the clan has been told she's the result of a Vampire impregnating a rogue Lycan, but she has few Lycan traits. Aveoth and I thought it would cover all the bases. The rest of the backstory we created is close to the truth—the council found her and trained her to be an assassin. You found Mandy on a mission and faked her death to keep her safe.

"I apologize for making you lie about your history, but it was the only reasonable explanation for someone who smells like a Vampire, but who's also able to withstand the sun. It's rare, but it's happened before with our kind, a child born with predominantly Vamp traits. Aveoth wanted to tell all VampLycans the truth, but decided it's too much of a risk. And I agreed. I understand why Vampires can never find out about GarLycan blood. Also, there could be a danger if anyone in Lorn's clan finds out. Some are still upset about Decker. This would give them an opportunity for revenge. It's better to be safe than sorry."

"I've heard that name before. Who's Decker?" Mandy glanced at Glacier for an answer.

"He used to lead one of the clans. Total prick," Glacier muttered.

Velder chuckled. "What he said. Decker is dead. Lord Aveoth killed him. Some VampLycans in his clan were very loyal to him. The rest of us are forever grateful that he's gone."

"I'll fill you in later," Glacier promised.

262

Velder handed them keys. "We stocked it with food. Everything you need should be here. There's also keys to an SUV on this ring. It's parked behind the cabin, and has a map of the area. We have a convenience store that stocks most food and personal items. Anything they don't have that you need, let us know."

"Thank you," both Mandy and Glacier said at the same time.

Velder left them to explore the inside on their own.

Glacier opened the front door. "Stay here."

She waited on the porch as he entered, turning on lights. It was charming that he wanted to make sure it was safe before she entered. The view she caught of the interior had her loving the place already. It had an open floorplan with a rustic log cabin look. Lots of wood floors, big beams, and a beautiful stone fireplace.

Glacier came back to her quickly and made her gasp as he scooped her into his arms.

"What are you doing?"

He grinned. "Carrying you over the threshold." He entered the cabin, using his foot to close the door behind them. "What do you think?"

She got a better look at the kitchen. It was modern, with an island separating it from the living space. Granite counters, gray and white in color, with stainless steel appliances. "Nice."

"I love it. Did you notice we didn't see any other cabins nearby? We have lots of privacy."

She grinned. "This is going to be way better than living in New York. I bet it's quiet. And look at that fireplace."

"Wait until you see the master." He put her down on her feet. "There's one smaller bedroom downstairs, but the one upstairs is massive, with a walk-in closet and great bathroom. It even has a soaking tub with a separate shower."

"Show me." She took his hand.

Mandy was ecstatic. This would be *their* home. A place where she'd be living with the man she loved.

She liked every room they entered. The whole place was inviting, roomy, and well-furnished in ways she wouldn't change. They ended up in the master last. There was another fireplace in the room, a king-size bed, and a large sitting area with a couch in front of the hearth.

"Well?" Glacier smiled at her. "What do you think?"

"We could be very happy here together. What do *you* think?"

"You're here. It's perfect."

He made it so easy for her to love him. "We should test the bed. You know, to make sure it's not too hard or soft."

He chuckled. "I agree, but there's one more thing I need to do before we go to bed."

"What's that?"

"Get to know the area around our house. How would you like to go flying?"

Excitement hit hard and fast. "Seriously? I'd love that!"

He removed his shirt and led her downstairs, out the front door, and she watched as he grew wings. This time she got to observe from the back. Slits opened near his shoulder blades and the tips grew out, getting larger. Small popping noises accompanied the growth. It stunned and amazed her.

"Does it hurt?"

He turned to face her, meeting her gaze. "Not anymore. Shifters adjust to it. He stretched his wings as he approached. "Come here, baby. You need to hold on tight to me. Later, I'll get a harness from my people sized for you. I can strap you to my chest with you facing forward."

She laughed. "Really?"

"Yes. It will be more comfortable, and you can see a lot more if you aren't wrapped around me in flight. Come here."

Mandy hugged his body and he curled one arm around her back, the other just under her behind. He bent his knees, jumped a little, and his wings flapped as they rose upward.

She glanced around as they reached the same height as the treetops, then they were above them. "Aren't you afraid someone will see us fly?"

"That's the great thing about Alaska, and particularly where we are. There are no human towns nearby and we're in VampLycan territory. It's safe to do this even in the daytime. I just need to avoid the human border areas. One day, when I have permission, I'll fly you near the cliffs so you can see where I was born and raised."

"I'd like that. Are you allowed to go back there now that we're mated?"

He pressed a kiss to her cheek. "I can, but that doesn't matter. I only want to enter the cliffs if you're allowed to be there at my side." He had risen high enough to allow her to spot a bunch of cabins nestled in the woods around them. Most were distanced from each other, giving the occupants privacy. Trees and a few rivers stretched as far as she could see.

"It's beautiful."

"So are you. Hold on to me tighter."

She locked her fingers together behind his neck. He released her back and used that arm to point, turning them a little as he hovered high in the air. "See that? That's Howl. Velder's town."

She squinted. "It looks so tiny."

"It is. A gas station with a few stores. I think they have an auto repair shop, too. Most VampLycan clans have one to be able to get humans back on the road. Not that many travel this far off the main highways. No one is going to ever find you here. You'll be safe."

"Thank you." He'd saved her life and given her an amazing new one. "Let's go home."

He hugged his arm around her back and suddenly swooped downward. She gasped then laughed as they flew fast. She was *flying* with her mate. He kept them just above the trees, the air whipping at her hair. It was a remarkable experience. Mandy knew he wouldn't let her fall.

"I could get used to this!"

He chuckled. "That's good, because you're stuck with me forever."

"I'm never going to complain about that."

He landed in front of their cabin but didn't put her down. Instead, he walked them into the house after retracting his wings. "We have a bed to test out." He kicked the door closed behind him. "And a life to begin."

Epilogue

Two weeks later

Glacier landed, quickly freeing Mandy from the harness. Her feet hit the ground and she shot off to the right fast, dodging trees. He followed closely on her heels.

They were near the border of Velder's land, and he inhaled, picking up the scent of blood. The noise that had alerted them something was wrong still sounded. A bear roared and a faint scream-like cry followed.

Mandy found the animals first. A baby black bear had slid down into a narrow ravine, one of its front legs trapped under a rock that had come down with it. She froze at the top. Glacier stopped next to her. The unhappy mama bear roared at them from twenty feet across the gap in the earth. It looked as if she were trying to find a way down to her baby, but sheer rocks on that side covered any ground she might have used to lower herself.

"What do we do?" His mate peered up at him with a frown. "That poor baby is crying. Or screaming. It kind of sounds like that, doesn't it?"

"I'll distract the mama. You jump down to free her cub. Be careful. It might be young, but they bite and have deadly claws. Ready?"

She nodded. "You be careful, too. Mama looks pissed."

Glacier took flight, making a lot of noise. The enraged mother bear snapped her head up, nearly panicking at the sight of him. He flew to the other side and landed on a boulder, high enough to stay out of swiping range.

Mandy leapt down into the ravine, using a few large rocks to land on before she reached bottom. She crept toward the animal. He was worried, but Mandy had Vampire speed on her side. He expected her to lunge forward, free the cub's leg, and run like hell. They'd practiced him swooping down and grabbing hold of her wrists to get her into the air and swiftly away from danger.

His mate had other plans.

"You poor thing..."

"What the fuck?" He watched her creep forward, hands outstretched toward the cub.

Mandy walked right up to it, her eyes glowing bright. The cub stared at her, holding very still. Its cries ceased. Her voice carried to him, along with the soothing tone she used. "Easy, little guy. It's okay. I'm not going to hurt you."

"What are you doing?"

"I can hypnotize some animals."

"You tell me this *now*?"

"This is my first bear, and I wasn't sure it would work. It seems to. Dogs love me. So do cats. I lived in a city. We don't get creatures like these in New York."

He snorted.

She bent in front of the cub, moving the chest-size rock off its trapped front paw. Glacier grit his teeth as she used her fangs to slice open her hand, rubbing her blood over the bleeding leg of the cub.

"What are you doing now?"

"It will heal him. The leg doesn't look broken."

"That's safe?"

"Exposing him to my blood externally should heal the wound. Having him drink my blood, well, who knows? He'll be vulnerable to attack if he's limping from these nasty gashes."

Glacier crossed his arms, grinning. "I can't believe you were an assassin. You're too softhearted."

His mate straightened, petted the cub's head, and raised her other hand. She flipped him off. "I'm a total badass. I just use my powers for good." She looked up at him with a grin. "How are we going to get him out of his ravine? He's going to have trouble climbing out. Do you think you could lift him and fly him up there?"

He gaped at her.

"Can you?"

"Only if I want him to flip out and tear his claws into me."

"I'll have him sleep for a few minutes. Can you do it?"

"Maybe. I've never tried. I can't believe I'm even considering this."

"What else do you have to do? We've patrolled the area almost every day but never find much except animals in trouble. Well, hello. Here he is. Adorable baby bear. We're helping him."

"The shit I do for you." He jumped, using his wings to slow his fall, and landed near her.

"I love you too."

"I'm so blaming you if he rips me up."

"You're a GarLycan. Shell your body a little. He's just a baby."

"A sixty-pound baby."

She chuckled and stared into the cub's eyes, talking softly to it. The cub didn't fall asleep but it seemed to calm even more. Glacier approached, fully expecting shit to go sideways. He lifted the cub, hardening his skin to battle mode. The cub didn't protest but did keep staring at Mandy.

"Hurry up. Fly him up to his mama. She's really pissed."

He glanced up, seeing the female black bear glaring at him from over the edge of the ravine. Another roar tore from her. He decided speed was best. He backed away from Mandy with the cub and flew up.

The cub freaked, just like he expected, but he managed to keep hold of the wiggling, bucking furball long enough to gently drop it to the ground thirty feet from the adult bear, now barreling full speed at him in a protective rage. He took flight and circled around, landing back near Mandy.

"My hero." She threw herself into his arms.

"I try."

"You love me."

"I do. You should feed. You just donated blood." He took her hand, noticing that she'd already healed.

"I'm good. I'm only biting you when we're naked."

He glanced at his watch. "Two more hours on duty to go."

She released him, turned around, and backed up. "Clip me on. Let's go. We have the south sector to fly over still."

He bent slightly, clipping her harness to his matching chest piece. "Great. Maybe you can talk me into rescuing a big-ass elk next."

"They aren't as cute as baby bears."

"No shit." He hugged her waist as he straightened, lifting her off her feet since he was taller. "Ready?"

"Always."

He took flight. Mandy opened her arms, pretending to fly as they soared over the treetops. He grinned. She amused the hell out of him.

"You like to fly."

"Love it. You're the best mate ever!"

"So are you." He lowered his face, putting his mouth next to her ear. "Are you happy here with me?"

She turned her head and smiled. "There's nowhere else I'd rather be...and I love you with everything I am."

He completely agreed. "I'm glad I found you again."

"You should have listened to me back in nineteen eighty-nine. Don't you know? Women are always right."

He laughed. "I'll remember that."

His cell buzzed and he withdrew it from his back pocket. He read the text on his screen. "Shit."

"What's wrong?" Mandy twisted her head to peer at him. "Watch where you're flying. I don't want to hit a tree."

He put the phone away, turning in the wind to fly them home. "Olivia just contacted us. It seems the council is sending a team to track down a

271

Vampire who fathered one of the first VampLycans. That's all she knows so far."

"That doesn't sound good."

"Velder will want to know about this. The clans actively hunt the Vamps who attacked their mothers. Olivia will send more information when she has it."

"Why would the council send an assassin team after this guy? It happened a couple hundred years ago."

"Olivia will help us figure it out. She's our eyes and ears now with the council. I'll call everyone to let them know what's up." He wrapped his arms around his mate, landing in front of their cabin.

She smiled at him as he unclipped her from the harness, easing her onto her feet.

"Why do you look so happy? We just got potentially bad news."

"I'm with you. That's reason enough."

He chuckled. "Very true. Not to mention, this is one mission we don't have to go on. Whatever happens next, it's someone else's turn to deal with it. I only have to make a few phone calls...and then I get to make love to my mate."

"That sounds like a perfect plan."

He scooped her up into his arms, walking up the porch. Life was pretty damn great.

About the Author

NY Times and USA Today Bestselling Author

I'm a full-time wife, mother, and author. I've been lucky enough to have spent over two decades with the love of my life and look forward to many, many more years with Mr. Laurann. I'm addicted to iced coffee, the occasional candy bar (or two), and trying to get at least five hours of sleep at night.

I love to write all kinds of stories. I think the best part about writing is the fact that real life is always uncertain, always tossing things at us that we have no control over, but when writing you can make sure there's always a happy ending. I love that about being an author. My favorite part is when I sit down at my computer desk, put on my headphones to listen to loud music to block out everything around me, so I can create worlds in front of me.

For the most up to date information, please visit my website. www.LaurannDohner.com